The Backpackers G

CW00738598

Copyright: Sam

Published: 1st Ap... ᴄᴏ ᴉᴴ

ISBN: 978-1-49439-820-0

Publisher: Sam McKenna

CreateSpace Edition

Find out more about the author and upcoming books online at:
http://www.woodforthefire.com
https://www.facebook.com/thebackpackersguidetoaustralia
Twitter: @woodforthefire

For Hilary & Éirinn

Chapter One

I didn't realise until it was almost too late, but it wasn't the first time we had met.

Arriving at the Original Backpackers in Kings Cross, the originality part ultimately, naively, having swung my decision to stay there, had, so far, been anything but uneventful. But, while that is what I had hoped for, it had been eventful for all the wrong reasons.

Jumping from the taxi, throwing my thus far rather new looking, but much travelled, backpack over my shoulder, I stood and watched as it pulled away from the kerb, wondering did I tip him enough then thinking maybe I shouldn't have tipped him at all. If I was going to be a backpacker, it was time I started acting like one. Up the steps to the front door and in I go.

An Asian man holds a guy with dreadlocks against the back wall, his arm placed menacingly across his throat. There's another flipping through what I assume to be a registration book on the counter. A third steps from my right, I hadn't noticed him when I came in, and calmly places his hand on my chest. His look tells me I've come at a bad time. A quick glimpse of a knife hidden inside his jacket tells me he's right. Time slows down as first dreadlock dude, and then the other two men turn to face me. What seems like an eternity passes before the guy casually flips the registration book closed and pushes it across the counter and onto the floor. The tension is broken as his partner releases dreadlock dude from his hold.

'Maybe we see you again', he says, slapping him lightly on the face. It sounds like a warning.

As they walk towards the door to leave, my guy pushes me casually to the side then takes his hand from my chest. They smile as they pass and while I turn to watch the door close, I wonder at the surrealism of it all. I'd wanted excitement and this was as good as it could get.

Dreadlock dude is by my side.

'What was that all about?' I ask.

'No clue man, no clue....,' is the reply.

The three Asian men are already gone, blending seamlessly into the hustle and bustle of the street outside. As we stand there and I wonder 'did that really happen at all', I notice a girl standing on the other side of the street. Nothing out of the ordinary except she looks like she's hiding from someone, slowly peeking from a shop front doorway, looking directly at the hostel, and, it seems, directly at me.

'You still want to stay here?' dreadlocks asks.

'Yeah, sure mate,' I say.

When I look back to the street, the girl is gone.

Chapter Two

As odd as it may seem, I soon forgot about the girl on the other side of the road. After all, I was the hero as dreadlocked dude - his name was Mark - and I recounted the story over and over again over the next two weeks. Instant notoriety and fame at last, though in the smallest possible way. As Mark told it, he had everything under control, but was glad when I arrived to back him up as things were close to getting out of hand. While this couldn't have been further from the truth – we were both bricking it – the embellishments to the story were neither something we had discussed, nor did we see any reason to rectify as the days passed and the drama unfolded again and again. Everybody wanted to hear the story, and we were only too happy to tell it. In truth, I never brought up seeing her at all because some might have construed it as exactly that – embellishing the story. We had already done a good enough job with this as it was. After a few days I had all but convinced myself that I was just trying to see something that wasn't there, my mind working overtime given the circumstances. But I couldn't be sure. All in all however, I couldn't have wished for a better introduction to backpacker life.

Mark and I became good friends in the brief time I spent in the hostel in Kings Cross. Apart from our now infamous heroic encounter together, I found that we had a lot in common. He had travelled to Australia on his own from England only a few months before. The quiet, introverted person he described himself as was long gone, replaced by the cool, energetic person I had now met, and, while I wondered how a person could change so much in such a short space of time, it reflected my own aspirations of the person, the me, I was hoping to become. He was the guy everybody wanted to know. Not necessarily his own choice, but, apart from the few hours spent every day working the desk or cleaning or doing whatever needed to be done, Mark was the chief entertainment manager. Well, the only entertainment manager really. He organised nights out in local bars, almost daily barbeques and quizzes and beer drinking games in the garden out back, and made sure as many people as possible were involved. Much of how the hostel was perceived as a good place to stay was his responsibility. Business was very much by word of mouth and they relied on what people said of the hostel as they moved on further north or south along Australia's coastlines. We talked a lot and when I asked how this had come to be his job, he said that the owner had literally been pinning it to the notice board the day he walked in the door. He had taken it down and, whether he believed it or not at the time himself, had told the owner that he had found his man. He got the job. A decision for which both he and the owner had proven very astute. Mark was brilliant and business was good. As he said himself, life was about taking chances, and this one was paying off.

Inevitably, we talked a lot about the evening I had walked into the hostel. It wasn't my first time there exactly. I had dropped by a few days before to check it out before booking in. Nor was it the first time they had had this kind of visit. Mark's predecessor, an Italian named Allesandro, had been similarly threatened some weeks previously and, having been understandably shaken by the experience, had returned home. The intriguing thing was that nobody knew what this was all about. The police had been called on each occasion but offered little in the way of understanding who these men might be or what they were looking for.

'What do you think it's all about?' I asked, as we mulled over a few schooners and played pool in the Kings Cross Hotel on one of his rare evenings off.

'I don't know,' he replied. 'It's rumoured that it's been happening in a few hostels around Sydney recently. Nothing's been stolen, and while those men didn't actually ask, it seems fairly obvious that they're looking for someone. Who, I suppose, is the mystery. If it were drug or gang related, you'd think you'd be able to spot them.'

'Yeah,' I said, 'if it's anything like home, you'd spot them a mile away. What about this rumour of someone wanted in connection with a couple of murders in Melbourne?'

A story I had first seen on a news channel while waiting in Bangkok airport for my flight to Sydney. It dominated headlines for my first weeks there but had become old news quickly.

'Urban myth I think,' Mark said. 'I've heard those rumours too. There's always some kind of story going around but I don't think there's much truth in it really. Since our own little encounter, I've been told a thousand stories of mysterious men in black cars with tinted windows staking out every hostel from here to Darwin. It adds excitement to everyone's story. Something different to tell when they eventually head back home.'

'But there is something going on,' I ventured.

'Looks like it mate, but I don't think it's anything that we'll have much to do with. I hope not anyway. Between you and me, I was pretty scared that night.'

He hadn't admitted it before, but neither had I.

As I spent those first few weeks as a backpacker in Kings Cross, I reflected on how by pure chance I had arrived there that night and how things could so easily have been different.

On more than one occasion, I had nearly packed it all in and gone home.

Chapter Three

September sixteenth 1994, sitting on an Aer Lingus plane on the runway in Dublin airport, was already a distant memory, and, if it hadn't been for a chance meeting with two fellow Dubs, I'm sure I would never have thought about it again. Not the way I had hoped it would be. After all, this was my great adventure. Heading off into the unknown and leaving everything behind for a while. To find myself as they say, but I didn't believe in all that. The rut I had been in recently was killing me, and worse still, was hurting the people closest to me. There were tears and farewells, but it was a break we all needed. So, when I should have felt exhilaration, I only felt relief.

Minutes after lift-off, the plane was engulfed in cloud. Breaking through on the other side, I watched a sea of white cloud drop beneath us. All thoughts of anything bad that had happened recently were suddenly being left behind. The drone of the engines hummed in my ears, and my last thought as I fell asleep was 'Enough!'

I awoke muttering to myself. Something about being late for work or was it time to get up. As the stewardess offered me an orange juice I quickly realised where I was. I blushed, as I always do, when there's a pretty girl around. The two lads sitting next to me were laughing.

'Nice one buddy,' one of them said, in a real Dublin accent.

'I think I've blown my chances with her,' I replied laughing.

They were on their way to Thailand, and, as it turned out, scheduled to catch the same flight from London to Bangkok as me.

Troy and Alan, as they introduced themselves, were heading to Australia on the year visa, but not before an extended stop in

Thailand to meet up with some friends who were already on their way home. I had planned a much shorter stay, eager to get to Oz as soon as I could. We chatted as the plane descended into Heathrow airport. I was glad we were catching the same connecting flight, always feeling that there's safety in numbers where flights and schedules are concerned. For one, you're less likely to get lost and if you do, at least you won't be on your own. I've never missed a flight, or been remotely late for one, but that feeling is always there. An hour later, we had already made our way to terminal four and checked in on our Thai Airline flight. A full five hours ahead of schedule, just to be on the safe side. With nothing left to do but wait, we made our way to the nearest bar.

Our backgrounds couldn't have been more different, yet, just a few hours after leaving home, who we were and where we came from didn't matter. Suddenly we had everything in common and the only things that mattered were the adventures that lay in front of us.

The flight took off just after lunch and bang on time. After eleven hours of fitful sleep, food which we couldn't pronounce the name of, and admiring the beautiful Thai stewardesses – tall, slim, dark-haired and perfectly featured in their long purple uniforms – we were on our decent into Bangkok. I had laboured through the first chapters of the Lord of the Rings before giving up and putting a Dubliners tape in my Walkman, hoping that before the year was out I would learn some of the songs for which I knew the music, but didn't know the words. The irony of trying to identify with my country the very day I was leaving it was lost on me.

No cloud cover this time as the ground rushed up to meet us, and we had a great view of this enormous city. Having taken turns sitting by the window, I was in the box seat. Hands fixed solidly to the armrests - I hate landing - we touched down. Safely.

Thailand was just at the end of communist rule, but the mistrust of westerners was still evident. Armed soldiers watched suspiciously as we queued to get through immigration. Arranging a visa before travelling hadn't been necessary. You basically showed up, paid a very small fee, and you were in. Any apprehension I had on seeing all those guns and soldiers would disappear over the coming days as I realised what a wonderful and kind people the Thai are.

Things, however, just didn't seem to go my way. The dread as everyone picks up their luggage from the carousel and you find that you are the only one left there. Waiting, in vain, hoping your bag will come sliding down the chute, but it's probably already half way to Venezuela. Then the realisation that everything you have – clothes, toiletries, medicines, everything – are in that bag. My newfound sense of optimism was gone. Just like that.

To their credit, the two lads stayed around as, demoralised, I went through the process of first finding anyone who would listen, then trying to explain to someone with no English, that my bags were lost, my hunch being that some lazy sod in Dublin had pointed them in the opposite direction around the world.

'Ah lads,' I said, as I sat dejected and inconsolable with my head in my hands, 'this can't be real.'

After all that had happened to me lately, I shouldn't have expected anything different. I was trying my best not to think about this.

We eventually got to speak with a Thai girl, who had some English, at an information counter. She was making calls and doing her best to track down my bags but, two and a half hours later, we were still sitting in arrivals.

'Why don't you head on?' I asked, aware that they were only in Bangkok for one night before heading on to Kho Samui. 'There's no need for you to be staying here and waiting for me.'

'Don't worry about it, sure isn't this what friends do?' Troy said, smiling.

'And besides,' said Alan, 'we've been thinking that we might stay on in Bangkok for a few extra days. Well, at least while you're here. I know we've only just met, but I reckon we'd have a pretty good laugh.'

'Guys, you can't,' I said, but I knew that's how they wanted it to be.

And so, minus practically everything I owned, but decidedly less dejected than I would have been had they left me there, we made our way from the terminal to the taxi rank, sweating in a heat I had never experienced before. We hadn't organised any accommodation, but I assured the kind girl trying to track down my luggage that I would contact them as soon as we had.

I wouldn't see my back pack again until I was in Sydney.

I watched from the taxi as Bangkok came slowly to life in the early morning sun. 'This is what it's all about,' I thought. Life. People. An hour later, we had arrived at The Khao San road. Still early as shop doors silently opened and street vendors erected stalls in anticipation of the day to come, the silence occasionally broken by drunken revellers, the last remnants and only clue to the chaos of the night before.

12

We chose The Chada hostel from my Lonely Planet – a present from my sister before I left home and one of my now few possessions – while we waited in the airport. As it wasn't yet open, we sat on the hot plastic patio chairs outside and watched the drama of real life unfold.

The warm air filled with the aroma of charcoal and spices and smells that defied words. The street resonated to the sound of bicycle and motorbike carts selling Pad Thai, Ladna, barbequed duck, pork and chicken, home-made ice creams, and fresh juices like Nam Som. Herbal soups and traditional Thai teas and coffees. Sweets, fruits and sticky rice.

The hostel doors opened, awakening me from my reverie. I had been too tired to contemplate anything other than a black coffee, darker and richer than any I had ever had before, but I promised that I would try many of these new foods during my short stay.

Amid the cacophony of noise from the street outside, we managed to book some dorm beds for just two hundred and ten Thai Baht – the equivalent of about six US dollars and the cheapest place I had ever stayed – sharing with seven other people, most of whom were making their way out for the day as we arrived in. Within seconds I was fast asleep. The oven-like heat, lack of air conditioning, and the unrecognisable six legged lodger I had to remove from my bed were something I would worry about later.

I awoke sometime around eleven o'clock, pushing myself slowly from the bed, my t-shirt – my only t-shirt – soaked with sweat. Disoriented and alone, except for the revving and beeping of a thousand engines, I fumbled my way to the shared bathroom for a shower before making my way downstairs.

Troy and Alan sat at the plastic tables outside, relaxed and sipping some cold beers, already chatting freely to some new friends. Noticing my arrival, they asked if I was ready for one.

'Not before I get myself a new t-shirt,' I replied. I was planning on some new underwear too but it wasn't something I wanted to divulge.

'That won't be hard,' Alan offered, nodding his head towards the street.

Every inch of space was taken by a cart or stall selling everything from food to clothes. Shirts, t-shirts, shorts and jeans. Any kind of trinket, bracelet, scarf or video you could think of.

I wandered aimlessly along the Khao San road. Amazed at what was for sale and by how cheap it was, I laughed at the Levvi and Wangler jeans on offer for only two dollars. I ate Tod Mun Pla, which the old lady assured me 'iss good fish,' and drank refreshing, unrecognisable, fruit juice. I bought a hippy leather bracelet and a pair of Ray Banz, both of which cost less than fifty Baht. When I arrived back at the hostel with my new shoulder bag and shades, fed and re-clothed, I hadn't spent anything more than pocket change.

I grabbed a beer, sat, and eased seamlessly into the conversation. Troy, Alan, and half a dozen people they had never met before talked and exchanged stories like old friends. People regaled us with tales of travels in Australia and New Zealand, Vietnam, Laos and Cambodia, places to which I longed to, and would go.

I watched the two lads, their boundless energy and enthusiasm, as if seeing them for the first time. Alan had dark, tight cut hair and dark eyes set in an oblong face with a slightly rounded chin. Tall and thin, his dark features were in contrast to his pale skin. Wide

14

eyed and inquisitive, he hung on every word of every story he listened to. Troy, in contrast, while also tall, had a more athletic build. Long, fair coloured hair with bright blue eyes, and while he smiled much less, his slightly curved smile suggested a more mischievous, more laid back personality. Distinctive, complimentary personalities, blended seamlessly together by friendship.

Our next few days together would be a haze of temples, buddhas, cheap clothes, cheap beer, and cheap everything. Hot, exhaust fume choked daytimes spent exploring the streets, markets, and temples of this breath-taking city, and nights spent discovering its wonderful social life. The warmth and humility of its people would endear me to them forever. Always smiling, always helpful, always generous, and always gracious.

We became great friends, and when my time came to leave for Australia, it was very hard to say goodbye. As my world had suddenly become a much bigger place, goodbyes were something I would frequently endure as part of my travels, but departing my two new friends was hardest of all. It's such a natural thing to look out for the person on their own and they had taken me under their wing, coaxing me out of myself. Making me realise that I was still allowed, and able, to laugh. That my life wasn't ending, but just starting. I hoped, and deep down felt, that our paths would cross somewhere in the future.

They left for Kho Samui hours before I was due to leave for the airport and, suddenly aware of how lonely I now felt, I wandered the Khao San road one last time, wondering if I would get back there again. My thoughts drifted to home and family, and how I had alienated myself from them and everything good around me, and I wanted, more than anything, to be there.

I caught a taxi to the airport later that evening. I don't know if it was the fact that I was on my own, or the deep longing I had suddenly developed, but had I had all my luggage and belongings, I think I might have turned around and just went home. The excitement I should have felt with pushing on to Sydney, a long harboured dream being realised, was gone. And, if I had turned for home, no-one would have thought any less of me. It was what they all expected.

As I waited for my connecting flight, I resolved not to be that person. Not to be the guy who quits, who blames everything on everyone else, and takes no responsibility for his life anymore. Deep down I knew that wasn't me. I only had to prove it to them, and more importantly, prove it to myself.

With just ten minutes to boarding, I sat staring blankly at a television screen. Channel Seven, one of the Australian stations, had a breaking story. Switching to a reporter in the field, the screen was filled with blue, white and red flashing lights. Police cars, ambulances, cordon and warning tape. There was a shooting in a small town just outside Melbourne. Related, the police believed, to an illegal immigration racket, there had been unconfirmed reports of at least one fatality. They were appealing for witnesses or anyone who may have been in the area to come forward.

I heard the boarding call for my flight. As I took my seat, the story was already forgotten.

Chapter Four

'What kind of questions were they?' Lisa asked.

Lisa was Mark's girlfriend, or, as he preferred to explain their relationship, they 'just liked spending time together.' Though I could guess his motive, he was damn lucky to have her. An attractive, bubbly blond and an English-French speaking Canadian from Quebec, she was a friend to anyone who stayed in the hostel, and probably admired by most of the guys, including myself.

'Not so much about what happened that night,' I said. 'Well they did ask me about it, but it was like they were trying to figure out if I knew anything about something they already knew about. There isn't a whole lot I could tell them anyway.'

The police eventually called to take statements from Mark and I about a week and a half after the incident.

'Then they just asked where I'm from, when I got here, where I stayed before Kings Cross, how long I'm going to stay and what my plans are. Fairly standard stuff.'

'Yeah, it was pretty much the same for me,' Mark replied.

The three of us had met for coffee at a small café just above O'Malley's bar on William Street. Eating croissants and watching the world go by, we mulled over the events of that evening. Everyone had theories of what it may have been about – drugs, gangs, international spy rings, aliens from space – but I found Mark's explanation the most credible.

'It's like I said guys, this is Kings Cross and a lot of bad stuff goes on around here.'

'You're right,' I replied.

As far as I was concerned, that pretty much drew a line under the whole thing.

The hostel, thanks largely to Marks work, had been a great place to stay but Kings Cross had a seedy low undercurrent to it as well. It opened my eyes to things which, during my hitherto sheltered life in Ireland, I had never been exposed.

'Mark,' I said, 'I've decided to move on.'

Regardless of how we had first met, Mark and I had hit it off from the start. I had wanted to tell him before telling anyone else.

'Where are you planning on going?' he asked.

If he was disappointed in any way, he didn't show it. But then again, he just wasn't that kind of guy. Always looking out for everyone else, making sure they were okay. Always interested in the people around him, discovering who they were and why they were here with genuine interest. As he had done with me during those first few days, never pushing me on details of my life, the part of me that I had wanted to leave behind, that I didn't want people to know.

'I've been reading about a hostel down in Glebe,' I said. 'I've talked to a few people and it seems like a pretty relaxed place to stay. The Glebe Village.'

'Yeah I know a guy working there.' He seemed to know a guy everywhere. 'I'll give him a bell and see have they anything available.'

'Brilliant Mark, you're one in a million.'

'He sure is,' Lisa smiled, 'we'll miss not having you around. People like you here you know.'

I didn't know and had never really thought about it.

'Why have you decided to move on?' he enquired, as we strolled back to the hostel.

I had had a great time. I met people every day from all over the world and struck up a particularly good friendship with two Swedes called Kai and Stefan. In an intensely heated debate over a game of pool, and varying interpretations of the rules, I had taken their side, somehow averting the possibility of a mini riot, but gaining two great friends in the process. English, Irish, Dutch, German. There was always someone coming and always someone going. But the undercurrent of drugs, dropouts, and prostitution, though not visible on the surface, never sat easily with me. And what had happened that first evening there had unnerved me more than I had let on. I would miss the people, but not the place.

'I understand,' Mark said, as I explained, 'I'd nearly go with you, but my jobs here, and Lisa, you know how it is.'

'There's something else though Mark,' I said, 'this might seem really weird, but since our little encounter that night, I have the feeling that it really hasn't gone away. That somebody out there is still watching us.'

Chapter Five

Those first weeks had been something of a blur. It felt like only days since I touched down in Australia. The flight from Bangkok had been the longest nine hours of my life. Tired, agitated, and lonely, I hadn't been able to sleep and my feet jumped constantly as I tried to read or listen to music. Anything to take my mind from the question that gnawed away at me. Is this really me? Just a few days into my trip of a lifetime and I already had my doubts.

Finally, the captain announced our decent into Sydney. It was a beautiful clear day, the sun blindingly bright. Within minutes I could see the coastline, the sea a beautiful, sparkling bright blue flecked with white. The plane banked left, affording me a first glimpse of the city, not too far in the distance. We approached the runway, a huge stretch of reclaimed land jutting out into Botany Bay, and touched down softly.

Regardless of how I now felt, with little more than the clothes I stood up in, my passport and a few dollars in my pocket, and regardless of what the following days or weeks would bring, I had made it. I was here.

My lost luggage had still not arrived. A friend had offered to put me up during those first few weeks and I left his as my forwarding address. Matt was expecting me that day but we hadn't really discussed specific times so I caught a bus to Central Station, assuming that this would get me somewhere close to the city centre.

As I walked through the park across from the bus station toward the high rise buildings, I felt the sun penetrate my skin, breathing new life into my tired body, the sadder, harder feelings of recent times beginning to dissolve, the cobwebs of the last few years being blown away in the warm, gentle breeze.

On every corner, streets signs pointed a million tourists from all over the world towards Circular Quay, The Opera House, and the Bridge. Rounding the corner at the bottom of George, I instantly understood why so many made this trip. It is such a beautiful place. Off to my right, the Opera House stoops out over the bright, beautiful blue of Sydney Harbour. To my left the Bridge, vast and monumental.

I spent the rest of the evening strolling around the quay, wandering over to the opera house, and walking further down the 'Rocks' to get a closer look at the bridge. I ate fast food from one of the countless restaurants dotted about and admired many of the colourful characters the area had to offer. Street entertainers, model boat builders and aboriginal didgeridoo players. I watched the ferries coming and going and a million sail boats further out on the harbour, fleeting one way, then another. A warm breeze blew as lights flickered on and dusk settled on my first day in Australia, sooner and quicker than I realised.

That warmth stayed with me as I made my way back to central station for the train to the suburb where Matt lived. I rang to let him know I'd be arriving and while he offered to pick me up, getting there myself would help me get to know my way around in what I had decided would be a very brief stay.

I arrived at his house, the weary traveller, to meet him coming out onto his front lawn. It was some time since we had last met and he didn't look much older, but the difference, the confidence and maturity, were evident. When he spoke, he was still very much the same guy I had known all those years ago. Matt was more of a family friend than a close personal one but welcomed me into his home like a long lost relative, introducing me to his wife and new-born child, like we had always been best mates. We sat and talked about family and friends, what home was like, and how things had changed. He suggested staying with them for as long as I liked.

As I told him how my plans had changed, how my baggage had been lost and how I already missed home, he told me he felt exactly that way when he first arrived. When I asked what changed his mind, he talked about what a wonderful place it could be but that I should find that out for myself. Rather than go home straight away, he said, give it some time.

So I spent the next few days sight-seeing around Sydney. Going to famous places like Bondi, Manly and Central Point, and discovering less visited, but equally beautiful places like Bronte and Coogee. My favourite part of those first few days was the time I spent each evening sitting at Circular Quay watching as people boarded ferries to make their way home for the day.

At night I would sit and talk to Matt and he would tell me how he came to love the place and how it had changed him as a person. A few days later he offered me a job working with his construction company doing fit outs in some of the big bank buildings around the city centre. A few more days, he said, just to see how it goes. Thoughts of longing for home slowly dissipated. Matt's passion had won me over. I wanted to stay.

Still jet lagged, I would sit up late and watch television when they had all gone to bed. The double homicide in a town called Churchill, near Melbourne, dominated the news. I remembered seeing it before I left Bangkok. A witness had been confirmed but could not be located, known to have been at the scene, and a critical part of the police investigation. It was now also confirmed as directly related to a huge illegal immigration racket. No arrests had so far been made, the gang having fled and, as yet, remained unidentified. The people being smuggled into the country were Thai nationals. How, or what route they had taken, was still unknown. Their lack of English and fear for their own safety meant they would give little away. Talk was of deporting them back to Thailand but once they remained witnesses in this major illegal immigration racket and, subsequently, witnesses to a double homicide, this would not happen soon. I was amazed at the extremities a man would go to just to provide more for his family, and ashamed at my own perceived problems. Such risk, and such expense, for the faint glimmer of a better life.

I stayed with Matt for about ten days before moving to Kings Cross. Although he had wanted me to stay longer, I was eager to get out there and start meeting new people.

Chapter Six

Already five weeks since I left home, the move to Glebe couldn't come quickly enough. Everything had happened so fast. Bangkok, staying with Matt, a new job, then two weeks in Kings Cross being a celebrity of sorts, had passed in the blink of an eye. I needed to slow the pace down, to find a more relaxed groove, or it would all be over before I knew it.

I said my goodbyes to Mark and Lisa and left details of the hostel in Glebe with Kai and Stefan, and a promise to let each other know should we plan to travel up the coast in the near future. Then I was ready to go. It was quiet, most people gone to O'Malleys for the night, but I preferred it that way.

I checked out at reception, turned around without really looking, and collided with an Asian girl. Instinctively, I grabbed her hand as she stumbled backwards and fell. Helping her to her feet, embarrassed and apologising, I felt sure we had already met, but considering how many people came and went, I couldn't quite place her.

'Honestly,' she said, 'it's not your fault. I should have been looking where I was going. Are you fed up with the hostel too?'

'Sorry,' I asked, 'how do you mean?'

'I only meant it's not the nicest area to stay,' she said smiling.

'I know,' I agreed wholeheartedly, 'I'm actually moving to the Glebe Village backpackers. I've heard it's a pretty cool place.'

'Excellent,' she said, 'me too.'

If I was surprised by this, I forgot it quickly, still trying to regain some composure having knocked her over, and welcoming the change in subject while she checked out.

'Great,' I said, 'maybe we can keep each other company?'

'Sure,' she replied, smiling again.

As it was such a nice evening, and to save some money – the life of a backpacker – we decided to walk to Glebe rather than pay for a taxi.

She said her name was Anuia, Thai originally, but in Australia for eleven years and living somewhere near Melbourne. She was spending her vacation travelling around Australia for the first time, and in Sydney for a week.

'I have been staying in Kings Cross since I got here,' she said, in a quiet, soft tone, her Thai accent still very much evident, accentuating her words as she spoke.

'Have you?' I asked. I couldn't recall seeing her around.

'I've been keeping pretty much to myself,' she said trailing off, her thoughts suddenly elsewhere.

She nervously brushed her black shoulder length hair – combed from one side across her face – back over her right ear with her left hand. Tanned skin framed almond shaped brown eyes, curving slightly downwards on each side. Her perfectly shaped nose and narrow red lips complemented her soft features. Finding her so warm and friendly, I was surprised at how she had kept so much to herself. I sensed she was glad to be talking to someone. Her relief, having left Kings Cross, was palpable. She was preoccupied with something, but, considering I had known her less than an hour, it would have been intrusive of me to ask. She was happy enough to chat away, and I was more than happy to chat back.

Already, while booking in at the hostel in Glebe, I was convinced that this had been the right move. Everything felt so much more relaxed and laid back. The constant hum of traffic was gone, replaced by ambient Indian music and the sound of water flowing somewhere in the background. Maja, the instantly attractive receptionist, gave us leaflets and advice on places to go and things to do. I felt more comfortable than I had during my previous weeks in Kings Cross.

I was sharing a dorm with a bunch of lads from London and they made me feel right at home. I felt even more welcome when they asked me to join them for a few beers in one of the local bars. It was just what I needed and a second invitation wasn't required. The hostel had organised the night out and, seeing as everyone was going, I thought it would be nice to ask Anuia along too.

We went to the Excelsior, just a ten minute walk away. There were around thirty of us in all and it turned into a brilliant session. An excellent band played as I done the rounds, getting to know lots of these new faces. Some of them had stayed there for some time while working in Sydney, trying to earn enough money to push on to their next destination. Others were nearing the end of their time in Australia. All had good advice on places to go and see and places to stay on my travels. My new English friends were the life and soul of the party, laughing and singing with infectious enthusiasm. On tight budgets and relishing the chance of free beer, they were more than eager to take part in all the pub games. I kept myself in the background during most it. I hadn't yet convinced myself that it didn't matter if you let loose here as much as you wanted. Maybe it's just me, but where I come from, if you're doing something that's way out there, people think you're an idiot. They can't see that you're just trying to enjoy your life the best way you can. As I watched, I realised that they were all here for the same reason. Travel, discovery, and in some cases, anonymity. To get away from the same things as I had, and to do the same things I wanted to do. We all had that in common. I wasn't as loud and boisterous as the rest, but it still felt good. I promised myself this was the way I'd approach the rest of my travels.

When I said everybody was enjoying themselves, I meant everyone with the exception of Anuia. I had looked over at her on a number of occasions during the night to see how she was getting on. The way she would start each time the pub door would open as she anxiously peeled the label from her beer bottle, or watch uneasily as someone she didn't know passed her table, suggested more than simple preoccupation. Was she scared or was this just a feeling I had? She wasn't getting involved as much as everyone else, yet I knew she had the personality to. Everyone made the effort to include her because, like me, she was a new member of the gang. She would laugh at something funny but the smile would disappear from her face as easily as it had come. I asked, more than once, if she was okay but the troubled look she eventually gave me said 'leave it,' so I backed off. Consumed once again by the fun and games, I forgot about it and wouldn't think about it again until the following morning.

I crawled from my bed, thankful it was a Saturday, and made my way to the small pool at the back of the hostel. Even with little of the party atmosphere evident only a few hours earlier and with plenty of hangovers, the mood was good. I landed in a recliner beside Harry, one of my English roommates, to soak up some of the beautiful Sydney morning sun.

'How do you know Anuia?' he asked, as we talked.

'I only met her yesterday,' I replied, my thoughts turning to that distinctly uneasy feeling I had had when I asked her what was wrong. 'We were staying in the same hostel in Kings Cross but I hadn't really came across her at all. She said she didn't like it there. It was just coincidence that we happened to leave at the same time.'

Maybe it was the stale alcohol in my blood or the paranoia that sometimes accompanies my worst hangovers, but I wondered briefly if it had been just a coincidence. I told myself I was watching too many movies, and decided to ask the next time I bumped into her.

I didn't see her until later that evening, after I had checked at reception to convince myself that she hadn't already packed and moved on. When I did, she was in great form, smiling, laughing, and chatting to everyone. She greeted me in much the same way, no evidence at all of the way she had seemed the previous night. As if nothing had happened, or deciding that the best way to avoid any further intrusion was to completely ignore it. Another big night out had been organised and, as she appeared so much happier, I thought it best to let it lie.

The next few weeks passed quickly. I'd work during the day, and enjoy myself almost every night. Some evenings I would just be too tired. I'd find a quiet corner, curl up on a sofa, and read. Anuia would always find me. She'd curl up beside me, sometimes we'd sit in silence, and sometimes we'd talk.

I don't know why, but I had started to feel somehow responsible for her. I knew she hadn't told me anything exactly, but that first night in the pub, that glare, said she had somehow confided in me. I felt sorry for her because the rest of us didn't have a care in the world. It just didn't seem fair. She'd tell me about herself. What it was like to grow up in Melbourne. To go to school and college there and how she worked for a media company in the city.

'Do you remember much about Thailand?' I asked, more than once, but she would clam up, changing the subject, afraid it seemed of where the conversation might lead.

Her mood had improved so much since that first day. She was so much happier and I wondered if I was trying to invent a mystery that just did not exist. Deep down, I knew that wasn't true.

Chapter Seven

I never thought I had a particularly perceptive nature, but I eventually convinced myself that I could tell someone's nationality just by the way they acted. The English seemed English, the German German, the Irish Irish of course, and so on. I loved meeting them, learning about where they came from and their different cultures. I felt that they enjoyed my company too, and, while I didn't consider myself particularly popular, I always tried to get involved in everything. This appeared to gain me some respect among people. A respect I didn't remember having while growing up in Ireland. Starting to grow, feeling stronger as a person, and one of the things that I wanted to be able to take from my travels.

Again, people came and people went. So many new friends and so many farewells as some left on their tour of Oz or as others turned for home or different shores. Always sad to have to say goodbye, making promises to look out for each other along the coast, but wondering would I ever see them again. There were those I just knew in my heart that I wouldn't. My English friends had left a few days earlier and the hostel seemed a much quieter place. They asked me to go with them as they started their trip up the east coast but I declined saying I'd try to catch up with them somewhere along the way. I regretted not going in the few days that followed. I missed their company, but I felt I still had some unfinished business here.

On the twenty first of November I decided that it was time to make my own move. A couple of guys from Galway had decided it was time for them to leave too, and I needed little persuasion to accept their offer of some company along the way. Over the next few days we discussed our best options for travel, agreeing that buying our own transport, while dearer, was best. It would give us more freedom to do things on our own schedules and at our own pace. We talked through finances and decided how much we could spend on a van and some camping gear. While I hadn't brought a lot with me, I had managed to save some of the good wages Matt paid me since I started working with him. The two lads from Galway, Dave from Tuam, and Paul from Galway City, had been working for a few months and weren't doing too bad financially either.

We heard of a car park in Kings Cross where other backpackers tried to sell their motors, already finished touring the country, and made our way there the following Sunday morning. We found it but left soon after, disappointed. Most of what was on offer, some having been used as transport, housing, and beds, had seen better days.

As we walked back across Darlinghurst Road, we bumped into Stefan and Kai, my two friends during my brief stay in the hostel in Kings Cross. We greeted each other in the middle of the street as boisterously as we had when we had been drunk on more than one occasion. It was great to see them again and we decided that a drink was in order. O'Malley's was only two minutes away and, as I hadn't been back there in a while, it was just the place. Introducing them to Paul and Dave, we talked about all that had happened since I last saw them some five weeks before. Getting acquainted over a couple of schooners never takes long, particularly with all the funny stories we had to share. They filled me in on some of the other people I had met before leaving their hostel, many of whom had already left to begin or do some more travelling.

'It's a lot different to staying in Kings Cross,' I said, when they asked about the hostel in Glebe. 'It's a bit more expensive, but it's definitely worth it. Everything is more laid back. It just has a more relaxed feel to it.'

'What brings you down this way?' Stefan asked.

'We've decided to head up the coast,' I answered, 'we were hoping to find a van that we could buy.'

'Us too,' Kai said, his eyes lighting up, 'we were thinking of going in the next few weeks.'

'Maybe you could spend the first leg of your journey with us,' I offered.

After a quick confer with Dave and Paul, we agreed it would be okay but that it would take a few days to organise some wheels. They thought the Paramatta Road was the place to go. I had driven that way every morning when I first started working with Matt. I remembered miles of used car lots and thousands of cars and realised that that should have been our first port of call.

Beer glasses empty, and reminded that it was my round, I made my way to the bar. Kai joined me, offering a hand as I waited to be served.

'Do you remember a Thai girl called Anuia who stayed in your hostel while I was still there?' I asked.

'What did she look like?' he replied, a rather strange expression on his face.

'Small, straight dark hair, tanned, good looking. She moved to Glebe the same evening that I did. I've gotten to know her quite well. She said she had stayed in Kings Cross for about a week before moving but I don't really remember seeing her that much.'

'I'm not sure I remember her either,' he said, 'but perhaps she may be the girl everyone is talking about.'

'What do you mean talking about?' I asked.

My order had arrived and as I waited for my change Kai dropped three of the beers to our table. He left our two on the counter, clear that he wanted a chance to talk to me on my own.

'Well,' I asked, when he came back, sitting on a bar stool and inviting me to join him.

'Those people that were in the hostel that first night you arrived,' he said, 'it seems they have been back again.'

'When?' I asked.

I had called Mark a number of times since I left but hadn't spoken to him in a few days. He hadn't mentioned this the last time we talked.

'Two nights ago.'

'What did they look like? Were they official looking? Police?' I asked.

'I didn't see them myself,' Kai continued, 'but apparently they were all Asian except for one well dressed, well-spoken Australian man.'

'But why is everyone talking about Anuia?' I probed.

'Because they described a girl similar to how you have just described her,' he replied. 'Mark said he remembered a girl staying there, but doesn't remember much more about her. Like everyone else, all he can recall is that she kept very much to herself, never getting involved. No-one even noticed when she had left.'

I knew it. I knew there was something going on with her. I didn't know how serious, but I was starting to think that maybe it was far more sinister than I had imagined. Why were there people looking for her? Then again, maybe it was for some altogether legitimate reason.

'Why were these people looking for her?' Kai asked, reiterating what I had been thinking. 'Has she done something wrong?'

'Kai,' I said, 'I really don't know. I have had the feeling that something has been bothering her, that she may be in some kind of trouble. I tried to find the right opportunity to ask her, but got the feeling that although she needed to talk to someone, that she would in her own time. Can you please keep this to yourself? '

I had to think about what to do. Maybe she was wanted by the police and a funny smile appeared on my face as I wondered briefly what my mum would say if she knew the kind of people I was hanging around with. My smile disappeared.

'Listen Kai,' I said, 'I'm going to head back to the hostel and try to find out what's going on. I'll give you a ring later and let you know what day we're going to leave Sydney and head up the coast. The more the merrier. We'll look to head down to the Paramatta Road tomorrow to buy a van. We'll find something big enough for us all.'

Chapter Eight

By the time I arrived back to the hostel that Sunday evening, I had decided that it was altogether possible that I could be getting involved in something way too heavy. I convinced myself it could be drugs, or worse, and that I would end up in a lot of trouble. Or we I guess. Dave and Paul as well, and guilty by association. If we got into trouble with the law, our visas would be cancelled, we would most likely be deported, and we would never get a visa for Australia again. I couldn't do that to the two guys and I couldn't do it to myself. Inconsiderate maybe, but then Anuia didn't look like she was going to tell me what was going on anyway.

When I met her that evening, I didn't say anything. I took the easy way out, acting like there was nothing wrong. Another night had been organised in the local pub. She asked that I go along. I felt that to decline might have aroused her suspicion so I did. Paul and Dave had arrived back and we talked some more about buying the van.

'Don't mention anything in front of Anuia,' I said.

'Why not?' they asked.

'I'll explain in good time,' I promised.

They were in good form and didn't push the issue. We all went out but I found it hard to get into the swing of things, trying my best but failing. I caught Anuia's eye once or twice and I sensed she knew I was keeping something from her. I was going to run out on her. That's what I was keeping from her. Maybe she needed help, caught up in a situation she couldn't handle on her own, but I convinced myself that I shouldn't feel too guilty. After all, it was her decision not to tell me the truth. If she wanted help she only had to ask. If she was going to ask, she would have to tell me everything.

I wasn't my usual self, drinking more than I normally would, and everyone asked if there was something wrong. The only one who didn't, and the only person I wanted to, was Anuia. Eye contact would have to suffice. She knew I knew something. I wanted her to know. I wanted her to feel guilty for trying to get me involved in this. But it didn't really matter. We were going to leave.

I had the lads out of bed early on Monday morning. Heads banging. They didn't appreciate it too much, but the sooner we got up and started looking for a van the better. We had a quick breakfast and walked to the bus terminal at Central Station. An hour later, we were standing on the Paramatta Road looking around at the car dealerships, heaps of them, and wondering where to start.

'Which way guys?' I asked.

They were as perplexed as me, so we just started walking and looking. With a decent budget, we were optimistic of finding something good. Unfortunately, however, the vans we would have liked most were still more than we could afford. Disappointment settling in, we stopped to have some lunch. It was already one o'clock and we had been walking since about nine thirty. The guys wanted to give up for the day, the booze from the night before taking its toll. I couldn't tell them why, but I wasn't ready to pack it in just yet. I pleaded with them to give it another hour or two, trying not to show too much urgency in my voice, and disguising my anxiety by saying that the sooner we had the van, the sooner we would be ready to leave. They agreed reluctantly as we returned to a restaurant we passed only minutes before.

Half an hour later, our moods had improved. Drinking coffee after a comfort food lunch of burgers and greasy chips, we talked about where we might go, enthusiastically recounting stories we had heard about travelling up the coast. Where best to stop and spend some time, or where to only stay a night or not at all. Agreed that we would give our van hunt a few more hours, I looked aimlessly out the window at a garage on the corner of the junction right across from where we were.

I saw a van that we hadn't really taken any notice of when we passed this way earlier. Standing a couple of rows back on the forecourt of the dealership was a big yellow minibus. I couldn't tell much about it from where I was apart from the high top and a price tag in big fat numbers that looked like nine thousand dollars. Not quite what our budget would stretch too, but a definite possibility.

'Guys,' I said, 'I think I see something.'

I was up out of the restaurant and across the road. A Mitsubishi Starwagon. With a big black stripe down each yellow side, silver bull bar to the front, wide wheels and a sun roof, from the outside it looked perfect. I pulled the handle and slid the rear side door open revealing a clean interior, eight brown leather seats and a stereo. Exactly what we were looking for and perfect for our trip. Easily enough room for five of us and all our gear. It was beyond the top end of our budget but I knew we had to have it.

A salesman asked if we would be interested in a test drive. He had made his way over and stood to one side, smiling and allowing us to discover the electric windows in the front, or the other stereo in the back.

'Definitely,' I said, as he held the keys out.

Piling in and starting the engine, I turned and winked at the two lads as if to say 'leave it with me - just follow my lead.' I edged carefully out onto the Parramatta Road heading away from the city. I hadn't driven an automatic before and chugged a bit before turning right at the next junction for Leichardt. I frowned, though the engine sounded great, trying to give the impression that I knew what I was listening for. None of us did.

'Well guys what do you think?' Tim, as he had introduced himself, asked us.

'Not bad, not bad. What do you think guys?' I asked.

They were sitting in the back and nodded in agreement as, true to a Tuam man's form, Dave was quick on the uptake and added, almost in a whisper but loud enough for Tim to hear, that it was ideal though a good bit more than his budget.

'Look Tim,' I said, 'it's a nice van and exactly what we're looking for but realistically it probably is a bit outside our budget. What can you do for us? Nine thousand for a van this age is off the mark. 'Tell you what, we're three backpackers, obviously on a budget, and we have seven thousand dollars, cash, in our pockets.'

'Ah you gotta be kidding me mate,' he replied.

'That's what we have. There isn't a cent more than we can give you and there's no point wasting your time.'

'Come back to the garage. I'll speak to the boss man and see what we can do.'

He wasn't going to let us go without a fight.

'Seven thousand, cash in your pocket right?'

'That's what we have,' I said.

He disappeared inside to talk to his boss and, while we stood and waited on the verdict, I turned to Dave.

'You big mucka,' I smiled, 'you were bang on. Then again, a Tuam man never misses a trick. It's ours, I know it.'

And sure enough, that's how we came to own the van we affectionately called the 'Yellow Submarine.' The garage did the required pre-sale check, changed the tyres and the brake pads, checked our oil and water, and we were off. Driving (I was driving) back towards Glebe like three kids with their new toy.

Chapter Nine

We had our van. We had all our camping gear and we were ready to hit the road. Anything else we could pick up along the way. I rang Kai and Stefan in Kings Cross and while somewhat taken back by the apparent spontaneity of it all, they said they'd be ready and waiting.

'What do you think Mark?' I said, getting him on the line after Stefan.

He had told me about their last unwelcome visit.

'Do you think it's her they're looking for?' I asked. 'What do you think I should do?'

'I'm not sure,' he replied, 'we still don't know what it's all about. The last thing you need is to be getting into some kind of trouble.'

With the excitement of my first real adventure, out there in the world following my dreams, selfishly, Anuia and her problems were something I was thinking less and less about.

'You'll figure it out,' Mark added, as we said goodbye.

In my mind, I already had.

Everything was quiet, the weekend over and work looming the next day, so, joined by a few of our closest friends, we hit our favourite watering hole for one last quiet drink and to take a bit of time to reflect on where we'd go and how long we had. We decided that the best plan was to get up in the morning, hit the road, and stop when we got there, wherever 'there' might be. Five of us and the perfect remedy for a great adventure.

As we sat chatting, Dave brought up something that had I hoped would go unsaid and slip everyone's attention.

'Are you going to let Anuia know that we're leaving?' he asked.

'Why do you ask?' I replied.

'Well… it's just that you two seem very friendly. Certainly more friendly than she has been with everyone else in the hostel. I suppose I find it strange that you haven't mentioned asking her along.'

'I'm sure she has her own plans,' I said.

'What's up dude? You're the only one who seems to have got through to her over the last few weeks. Don't get me wrong. She's lovely and friendly, but just seems to always hold back. With you it's different. She's always glad to see you.'

'And you mentioned something on Sunday night when we were out,' Paul added.

He was talking about how I had asked them not to tell her.

'Oh,' I said, 'I hoped that would have slipped you both.'

'Well I suppose it has until now but Dave and I talked about it after you left. There's something you're not telling us isn't there? You've been shifting her on the side haven't you?'

They both laughed.

'No! Honestly it's nothing like that. In fact it's nothing important at all,' I said, more abrasively than I had meant, before apologising.

'Look lads,' I said, 'you're going to have to trust me on this. When we get a few miles under our belts I'll tell you what's been going on, though I don't know that much myself. If it's okay with you both, I'd prefer not to talk about it. Like I said, I'm sure she has her own plans. Besides Paul, what about your little crush on Maja.'

Maja worked in reception. She had checked me in my first night there. To be fair we all had a little crush on her, and while I got on particularly well with her, I knew Paul really fancied her. The subject of Anuia was forgotten.

We got back to the hostel at eleven thirty. There were a few of the regulars hanging around, and a few friends that hadn't been in the pub. Hearing that we were leaving, they had stayed up to say their goodbyes. Some had already done the east coast. More advice offered on where to go and the best hostels to stay in. Some scribbled notes and added their addresses at home to the end of them. I was going to miss these guys. I knew I'd never see some of them again as they were at the end of this adventure. Some I would definitely see. They would be heading up the coast as soon as they got some money together. I was glad Anuia was nowhere to be seen.

I got up at six thirty on Tuesday morning. Exactly what I had arranged with the two boys, mainly to get an early start, but privately because I wanted to avoid bumping into Anuia before we went. I was showered and eating breakfast by seven o'clock. No sign of the lads so I ran up and hammered on their door. When I walked in they were still asleep.

'Lazy bastards!' I joked, as I jumped on heads and roared in ears.

'Okay, okay, we're getting up,' they moaned.

There were some disgruntled curses from the others in the dorm but it didn't matter. They were soon down and while they ate I arranged all our gear in the van. At eight o'clock we were ready to hit the road. Just a bit late getting up to Kings Cross but Kai and Stefan wouldn't mind. The last of our food and supplies packed, we sat in the van ready to go. I started the engine.

I hadn't slept at all as thoughts of Anuia swirled around in my head, trying to convince myself that she would be okay. After all, I was doing nothing more than assuming she was in trouble in the first place. Sure, we had become good friends, but had she ever really reached out to me. This thought repeated itself over and over again. Had she ever really reached out to me? I switched off the engine as it finally clicked into place.

'It was her,' I said to myself, 'I did see her.'

'Did see who?' Paul asked, as Dave shrugged his shoulders, a puzzled look on his face.

'Lads,' I said, 'I'm really, really sorry about this, but there's something that I have to do.'

Not sorry for the short delay, but sorry because I knew that I was about to cross a line. I knew that in the next five minutes our adventure together as we had planned it would be over.

Anuia shared a girls four bed dorm on the ground floor. We sat on the veranda outside it talking some evenings. Times, I admitted to myself, that things could be simpler than I believed they were, when I thought we were close, but not as close as we could be. As I stood at her door, I knew that to go without saying goodbye would hurt us both. I had to at least offer the help that I knew she needed. I couldn't spend the rest of my life wondering 'what if?'

Knocking gently but getting no answer, I turned the handle and went in. By the faint light from the hallway, I made my way to Anuias bed and shook her gently awake. She turned and looked at me, startled. In that second she knew I was leaving.

'Meet me on the veranda,' I whispered, not wanting any of the other girls to hear what I was about to say.

'We did meet before,' I said as she sat, duvet wrapped loosely around her shoulders, pulling her feet up onto the seat under her, diminutive and vulnerable.

'You're the girl in the doorway. That first evening in Kings Cross, it was you I saw. Those men, they were looking for you?'

'Yes,' she replied, apologetically.

'Anuia. I'm leaving today. Right now in fact. Paul and Dave are waiting in the van. I can't go without saying goodbye.'

'You think I'm in trouble,' she said.

'Are you?' I asked.

'I'm involved in something and I'm in way over my head. I wanted your help, but as I've come to know you more, I decided I couldn't get you involved. You have been such a good friend to me at a time when I needed a friend most. That was enough.'

'Why not,' I asked, running my hands through my hair, 'how bad can this be? Is it money? Drugs?'

'No, no, nothing like that,' she replied, to my relief. 'It's much bigger. I am so, so sorry, but I just can't tell you what.'

'Anuia,' I said, 'you realise that I have to go. Come with us, we can work this out.'

'I know you have to go. It's your time to be yourself. Just go and do it, I'll be okay.'

'Damn,' I said, remembering these men had been looking for her in Kings Cross again.

'What?' she asked.

'They came back,' I replied, 'only a few nights ago. But it was different this time. Mark said they described someone that looked exactly like you. Like they knew you had definitely stayed there.'

A look of terror came over her face.

'But why didn't you say before now. I'm your friend, you should have.'

'I know,' I said, reaching out and taking her hand. 'I know.'

I felt guilty and selfish but I could never explain why I didn't tell her, too ashamed to admit that I could think of abandoning her.

'Where are you going?' she asked.

'North,' I replied, 'but we don't know where yet.'

'You have to take me with you.'

I had known from the start that she needed my help and now, finally, she was asking for it. I wasn't going to let her down.

'If you want to come with us, you have to tell me what's going on. Paul and Dave have no idea there's anything wrong. They have a right to know too. If we go now, we're in this together.'

'Yes,' she said, 'but not just now. They found out where I was. It's only a matter of time until they find me here too. We've got to go.'

It took five minutes to pack everything she owned and as we bundled into the van, Dave and Paul looked at Anuia, looked at each other, and then looked at me.

'Hi guys,' Anuia said, sheepishly.

'I'll explain later lads,' I said. 'Let's get going. Let's do it.'

They looked at each other again, shrugged, and said 'Yeah!! Let's do it.'

As we pulled away from the curb outside the hostel, I knew this was going to be the adventure of a lifetime. I had no idea why, but we were soon going to find out. Kai and Stefan were waiting outside O'Malleys as arranged, rearing to go. Seeing Anuia as they opened the door, Kai gave me a questioning look.

'Trust me,' I mouthed silently, as he closed the door and I took off.

Explanations would have to wait. For now, I didn't have one and the only person who did, when I checked the rear-view mirror, stared vacantly out the window.

The day was December third, 1996. It was just after nine o'clock as we drove north across Sydney Harbour bridge.

Chapter Ten

I had waited twenty six years for that moment. To leave a town somewhere, not knowing where I was going until I got there, with no timescales, no rules, and no anything. I wanted to drive and asked could I do the first leg. I couldn't explain why exactly, but I needed that small bit, to always have that memory.

We were strangely silent during those first miles, perhaps all having similar feelings, wondering where this adventure would lead us. It had already taken an unexpected turn but for reasons that we did not yet fully comprehend.

North across Sydney Harbour Bridge leaving the city behind. Past Manly heading for the north beaches. Willoughby, Dee Why, one by one they slipped quickly by. I had spent some weekends up around here since my arrival in Oz. I even came as far north as Palm Beach one weekend, lucky enough to arrive on the day they were filming a wedding from Home and Away, the most popular of Australian soaps. Maybe not lucky, but if my mum was in my shoes, I'm sure she would have thought so.

Morning turned to afternoon as I watched the names of towns on signs as the Pacific Highway carried us through the first leg of our journey. Newcastle seemed to be a good direction to be heading. Its letters were bigger than most other towns on our map. Turn offs to Richmond, Gosford and Wyong went by. No one ventured much in the way of conversation. The sight of green fields, then scorched ground, replaced by close ups of breaking waves as the road took us nearer to the coastline spoke volumes on its own. Engraved into the eastern Australian landscape, this road is spectacular, huge walls of rock tower over us on each side, then break every now and again to afford a glimpse of the beautiful landscape, stretching away towards the sea.

We stopped occasionally to refuel or to buy water and junk food as the day passed and the sun shone in the brightest of blue skies. By late afternoon everyone had loosened up, our moods changing to what you would expect of six travellers on their first adventure together. We were laughing and joking. Kai and Stefan just didn't get my Irish sense of humour, expressionless as I delivered the punch-line of one joke after another. They told a few of their own but, once translated into their broken English, they just didn't make enough sense. Anuia was quietest, knowing she would soon have some explaining to do. Was she thinking about how she would tell us? Could she trust us even? We'd know soon enough. By late afternoon we were within touching distance of Newcastle. Dave thumbed through the Lonely Planet.

'There's a place called Forster a bit further on than Newcastle,' he said. 'It seems to have some good camping sites right on the beach. Why don't we go there for the night?'

'Why there?' Paul, who was now driving asked, 'how far is it?'

'But sure why not?' Dave replied.

It was settled. We left the main highway at Buladelah, not too far north of Newcastle, travelling by Myall Lake and on to the southern tip of Wallis Lake. The road to Forster is beautiful, very hilly, and lined with trees. Two kangaroos – my first kangaroos – stood and fought in a field by the side of the road. At about five that evening we arrived at our destination, Sugarloaf Bay. We picked a campsite called Pacific Palms as it was closest to the sea, and slowly made our way there, stopping at a local K-mart to pick up some food and supplies. I was looking forward to our first camp stop. Setting up tents and cooking our evening meal. Kai and Stefan pitched their own five man tent, Dave and Paul the smallest rubber two-man I had ever seen, and I, by virtue of being the majority shareholder, got to sleep in the van. The rear seats reclined horizontally making a decent, comfortable bed. I hadn't even thought of Anuia or where she would sleep.

The sun had started to set by the time we finished our first campsite meal, washing dishes in the last light of a beautiful golden sunset. The smell of cooked sausage, burgers and beans lingered as we got our small campfire going with sticks I had collected on the beach, and all lay around and watched as dusk turned to darkness. I had been in Australia for a while but was still amazed by how quickly the day becomes night. I lay on the ground, hands behind my head, listening to the sounds of other campers coming and going and getting ready for the night. Lights flickered on in campervans and tents while a few lit campfires as we had. We were all very quiet and I wondered why. Maybe it was the heat and the food, or the long days driving. Maybe, like me, they were just lost in their own thoughts.

Anuia hadn't said a lot all day. I wanted to ask her about what was happening in Sydney but I didn't know where to start. I thought the guys might be thinking the same thing. By now most of the noise around the campsite had gone. The flickering lights were down to the last few and campfires, like our own, were nearly out. Finally, without any persuasion, she spoke.

'I think it's time I told you guys what's been going on.'

I looked at her and then at the guys sitting around me, the soft orange glow from the last embers of our fire casting shadows on their faces. Anuia stared into it, deep in thought. She didn't look at any of us. We braced ourselves.

Chapter Eleven

'I came here thirteen years ago. My family live in a very poor village in Thailand about three hundred kilometres from Bangkok. I was very young, just ten years old, but even then I understood how every single day of our lives was one struggle after another. My parents decided to send me to live with my uncle. He and his family had moved here some time before that and had obtained Australian citizenship. They told me I was to come on a holiday and I had no reason to think differently. One day my father and I made our way to the airport in Bangkok. I remember how he held me as we said goodbye.'

She paused, lingering on that thought.

'I arrived in Australia, full of excitement, on the greatest adventure of my life. I had never been anywhere before. Getting to know my uncle and his family was such a fantastic experience. My planned two week stay passed quickly and when they asked would I like to stay a bit longer I jumped at the chance. Days passed, then weeks. Eventually my uncle told me I would not be returning to Thailand. He and my aunt explained that I would have a much better life here. I would have so much that I could never have at home. It broke my heart to think that my family had let me go but as time passed I grew to accept and understand it more. After some time they began to refer to me as their daughter. I looked very much like my cousin anyway. A few years later, they spoke to a lawyer and, after a very lengthy process, I became an Australian. That is how I am here now. I have not seen my own family since. We have always kept in touch but I have struggled to understand why I should have been the lucky one. This is one of the good stories. There are so many young girls smuggled here from Thailand that are not as lucky as me.

'This is where I have grown up, where I have gone to school. This is where my friends are and where I always wish my own family could be. I have a younger brother whom I have only ever seen in photographs. I think about them every single day and feel guilty that I have had a better life. We have tried so many times to get them to Australia but immigration laws are much stricter in recent years. I live in a town called Churchill, not far from Melbourne city.'

Paul had been flicking small pieces of broken sticks into the fire. He stopped and looked towards me, a hint of recognition on his face. We had heard the name before.

'I know you are thinking why I am telling you this,' Anuia continued, 'but it's the only way I can explain and make you understand.

'My uncle and I made many attempts to bring my family to Australia but all have failed. Some months ago I read an article about illegal immigration. A fishing boat was intercepted off our northern coast. Coming from Indonesia I think. I cannot remember exactly. That is when I started to think that perhaps there is another way that my family can come. You hear so many stories about this, but I convinced myself that you only hear about the bad ones. I have met others who came here like me and were allowed to stay. I read about it, talked to people where I could, and found a little information on the Internet.'

I tried to build a picture of what she was telling us, now conscious of where I had heard of Churchill before – the immigration story making headlines during my first few weeks. Could there be a connection?

She stared blankly at the fire, the collar of her wind breaker zipped to her chin, her arms wrapped tightly around her. She looked so small and lost.

'There are many ways people try to gain entry. So many different routes from so many different countries. There are a lot of Thai immigrants living here but it is anyone's guess how many are not legal. Eventually I began to wonder how this could be arranged. How could you make contact with these people? I made some enquiries, spoke to some people who I thought may know, but few were willing to discuss it. At last, desperate, I decided to talk to my uncle. I had considered asking him first but did not know how. Anxious as they were to have my family move here, I could not ask them to jeopardise everything they had worked for.

'I brought up the subject one evening as we ate dinner and I was surprised to hear that they had looked into something similar in the past. My family would have to give up everything and, once started, there was no going back. It could jeopardise so much. The expense, the danger, everything would be at risk. But the hardest part would be to persuade my own father. To convince him that this was the right thing for my family. The only way we could ever be together again. My uncle had a contact that we could approach.'

I thought of the first time I ever heard of illegal immigration, wondering what it was that could drive a family to risk everything, including their lives, to live somewhere completely alien to them. To live somewhere that very often the people around them would not want them there. I guess it's every proud father's wish to be able to provide a better life for his family. Things I had always taken more or less for granted while growing up in Ireland. I thought of my own father.

Now, a long, long way from home, I was starting to realise just how important these things were. Were they thinking about me the same way? 'Wondering if I was okay? I hoped so. Not realising it, the way I thought about everything that was so familiar to me was starting to change. Maybe because I didn't understand all the things I had become so accustomed to or maybe because I was starting, for the first time in my life, to understand myself.

'So,' Stefan asked, 'what is this all about?'

He, along with the rest of us, had been silent up to this point.

'Why are you telling us all of this? The men in Kings Cross, were they looking for you?'

'That's coming Stefan,' I said, 'just give her a minute.'

Anuia was quiet, intent, trying to determine the best way to tell her story. To ensure she kept it as simple as possible while trying not to leave anything out.

'We contacted my father a few days later to put our suggestion to him but, as we expected, he refused unreservedly. I told him how good things would be, pleading that he thinks of the life he could offer his family, but he said their way of life was what they knew. Finally I said that any risk would be better than living the rest of their lives in a slum in Thailand. This hurt him deeply but I had to say anything I could to convince him. He agreed to listen and asked what he had to do.

'So my uncle rang his contact. A man would meet us in a café close to Spencer Street bus station in Melbourne at twelve the following day. They gave no other information so we didn't know what to expect. We arrived, ordered coffee and talked about what might happen or what kind of people we would be dealing with. Forty minutes passed, a half hour later than arranged, before a well-dressed woman who had been sitting at a table by the window approached our table. She asked our names and took a seat next to us. She was not what I expected. Elegant almost, well-spoken and polite. After a cursory exchange about the heat and the weather, she got down to business. How much it would cost. Where, how and when payments should be made. Short, concise and professional. We gave her all my families' details. It would happen quickly she said, and on short notice. Once it began there was no turning back, full payment was expected regardless of the outcome. The last thing she said was that we should not discuss this with anyone. Her broad smile did nothing to veil the intended threat. We had crossed a line. All we could do now was wait.'

'But,' I said, 'surely you must have known that it was too dangerous?'

Not, I imagined what she wanted to hear, but her thoughts were elsewhere. There was a look of apprehension on the lads faces, each fidgeting anxiously, looking at each other inquisitively, wondering where exactly this story was going.

'Take your time Anuia,' I said, as she continued to piece her story together.

'The call came early in August. My uncle paid forty two thousand dollars. They would let us know when the cargo arrived. Once again, left to play the waiting game, we tried to contact my father but they were already gone. On the fifteenth of September we were told that they were here. We could collect them at five-thirty the following morning in a supermarket car-park in Churchill town centre. We were overjoyed, making preparations for their arrival, and all I could think about was what it would be like to be with them again.'

I watched Anuia as she recounted what had happened. Again she paused, her expression turning more intense. For the first time, I really began to see how frightened she was, sensing her vulnerability as she held herself, replaying the story in her mind.

Chapter Twelve

My uncle drove me that morning. We parked a few streets away and I walked from there. I could not believe that I was finally going to see my family again. It was just before five thirty when I arrived and I went to the back of the supermarket. I found a large truck parked in one of the loading bays. As I approached, a man opened the door and got out.

'Can I help you with something?' he asked.

'I'm here to meet my family,' I replied, 'I was told to ask for a man named Ross.'

He looked at me for a moment, then, after checking all around, gestured for me to follow him. As we walked towards the back of the truck, a second man appeared.

'Any sign of him yet?' he asked, 'who's she?'

'No, no sign yet,' Ross replied, 'she's here for some of them.' He pointed to the truck.

'They'd better turn up soon or we'll dump them all here and they'll be someone else's problem,' the second man sniggered. 'You,' he added, 'stand over there.'

His tone was hard, careless and disregarding. I became frightened. I thought of my family and how they had been treated since leaving Thailand. What would they have gone through?

Just then a black car drove into the car park – big, expensive looking, with tinted windows – and parked a small distance away.

'About bloody time,' Ross said, banging the side of the truck.

I heard the rear door unlock from the inside. A third man emerged leaving the door slightly open. My first instinct was to move towards it. I wanted to know if my family were there. I needed to tell them that everything was okay and that they were now safe.

'Stay where you are,' Ross said, as I began to move. 'Nico, you come with me. Keep an eye on her,' he said to the third man, and they walked off towards the black car.

The darkened rear window slid down and he spoke to someone inside. The conversation continued for some time but it was soon apparent that things were not going well. The longer they talked, the more heated their exchange became. I was nervous. Everything was taking too long. I thought it might only take a few minutes. My uncle waited only a few streets away. What if staff began to arrive for work or if the police happened to pass by? How long did we have? We were so close.

The car door opened and a man got out. Dressed in a black suit, he had dark, weather beaten skin, undoubtedly Thai. Very much what I expected my own father would look like. He shook hands with Ross. As if to say, 'look, everything is okay.' They turned and walked towards the truck. The man left watching me pulled the door open as they approached but when the Asian man looked inside, he became very angry, shouting at Ross. He was waving his hands, swearing, his voice growing louder as he pointed at each of the three men. Accusing them, but of what exactly I did not know.

I could hear voices from inside – men, women and children. The Asian man continued to shout and swear, and the three men, becoming agitated themselves, began to shout and swear back as he moved away, returning to the black car. He opened the door and spoke to someone inside, then stood back as a well-dressed man emerged accompanied by two more sitting in front. This man was different. He looked important, wealthy, and maybe official in some way. He had an Australian accent.

A huge disagreement had broken out and I still could not tell if my family was there or not. The argument became more heated and my fear and anxiety began to grow. I could make out what they were fighting about. There were less people in the back of the truck than were expected. My heart sank. My family, had they made it? This was not how it was supposed to be.

'Where are the rest of them?' the Australian yelled at Ross.

'How the hell should I know?' Ross replied, 'we're only delivering the ones that were sent to us.'

I had started moving towards the back of the truck. I had to know if my family was there.

'Stay where you are,' the one watching me shouted.

But I couldn't. I edged closer as the argument intensified, all of the men now becoming involved. He paused, apparently deciding I was less important than what was happening, then moved away to join the fight. I was almost at the truck door when all hell broke loose.

'What about payment?' Ross shouted.

'Payment?' the Australian shouted back, 'I'm not paying anything for what hasn't been delivered.'

They began pushing and shoving each other, but the Australian, regaining his composure, ordered his men to stop and get back in the car. I saw this man Ross reach inside his jacket and take out a gun. One of the Asians, realising what was happening, reached into his own.

I was at the truck door. I looked in and there they were. My mother, my father, and my brother, huddled together, terrified.

I heard a loud crack and turned to see one of the men stumble and fall to his knees. He held his chest, a dark stain spreading down his shirt. He raised his head and looked at me before falling to one side. Everyone in the truck began to scream but I stood there frozen. I heard women and children crying, but I could not take my eyes from the man now lying on the ground.

'Anuia, Anuia,' my father shouted.

There were more loud cracks. I turned towards him and looked straight into his eyes. I couldn't hear him above all the noise but could clearly see as he opened his mouth to say the word, 'run'.

It all happened so fast. I did not want to leave them but I ran. I heard more gunshots and tyres screeched somewhere behind me. Complete panic. When I was a short distance away, I heard police sirens somewhere in the distance. My uncle was waiting.

'What happened? What happened?' he asked, as we sped away, but I couldn't speak.

My family, I left them there.

Chapter Thirteen

Anuia began to cry. Paul, sitting closest to her, reached out and took her hand.

'It's okay,' he said, trying to reassure her, 'you did what you had to do.'

'Anuia is the girl in the news,' he said, turning to me, 'it's her they've all been looking for?'

'Yes,' Anuia replied, answering the question herself. 'I saw everything that happened.'

The other guys looked confused, staring into the fading embers of our fire.

'I don't understand,' Stefan said, 'what is this all about?'

'Have any of you guys been watching TV over the past few months?' I asked.

'No,' they answered in unison – all except Paul.

I told them what I knew going back to the first time I heard it in the airport in Bangkok.

'The witness,' I said, when I finished, 'is Anuia.'

I turned to Paul and Dave.

'Do you remember I told you about seeing the girl in the doorway my first night in Kings Cross?' I asked.

'Yes,' Paul replied, 'but we thought you were just imagining it given the circumstances.'

'Me too,' I said, 'but it was Anuia. It came to me this morning as we were about to leave.'

'Maybe I'm wrong,' I continued, 'but I think the men looking for Anuia in Kings Cross are connected to this gang. The police would never take such a heavy handed approach. How she came to be in Sydney I don't know. We only met the evening I moved to the hostel in Glebe. I've felt for some time that our meeting wasn't necessarily by chance.'

'This is unbelievable,' Kai said, throwing a stick at the fire as he got up.

'Kai…,' I pleaded, but he ignored me and walked away.

'It's ok,' Stefan said, getting up to follow, 'I'll talk to him.'

I looked at Dave. He had sat silently, digesting everything that he had heard.

'What the hell have you gotten us into?' he asked angrily, 'I did not come here for this.'

'I'm so sorry guys,' I said, 'but I didn't know what it was all about. Sure, I knew there was something wrong, but I decided not to get involved. I changed my mind at the last minute, just before we left this morning. Anuia is my friend. I couldn't just walk away. What would you have done?'

'You can still walk away,' Anuia said, 'they have already found me once and it's only a matter of time until they find me again. This is not your fight.'

She got up and walked towards the beach. I followed a few minutes later to make sure she was okay and found her sitting barefoot on the sand. She pulled her knees up under her chin as I sat down beside her. A cool breeze swept in off the sea.

'I'm so sorry,' she said, as I put my arm around her, pulling her close. She was shivering as she rested her head against my shoulder.

'It's okay,' I replied, 'we'll figure this out. Why didn't you tell me?'

'I don't know. I just wanted something normal for a while, someone to be my friend. And you were there at the right time. Everything in my life is going to change now,' she said, 'nothing can ever be the same for me again.'

'Nothing will ever be the same for any of us again,' I said, pulling her closer, kissing the top of her head, 'but I promise you we'll get through this.'

The roar as the waves crashed on the shore was deafening, the moon reflecting on the sea beautiful. I don't know how long we sat there but when we got back, all the guys had gone to bed.

'You sleep in the van tonight Anuia,' I said.

She protested as I unrolled my sleeping bag beside the fire.

'Thank you,' she said, finally.

I threw some more wood on the fire, watched as it lit, then fell asleep.

I woke early the next morning, shivering on the cold ground. I had slept fitfully, awoken by dreams of Anuia, always running from her faceless pursuers. Seeing the first glimpse of light on the horizon, I struggled stiffly from my sleeping bag as quietly as I could, and slipped away towards the beach.

I wanted to see the sunrise. A new day and a new perspective on things. I wanted to think clearly and always find that morning is the best time to do this. I love to watch the sun come up but I hadn't had the chance to do it in a very long time. As I walked on the sand, my mind drifted back to summer holidays as a child in the west of Ireland, to my grandfather's house, and to beautiful summer days getting up at five o'clock in the morning to take the cows home for milking. It was a much simpler time of course. We could disappear for the day and, considering how young we were at the time, my parents could relax knowing that once we were hungry we'd be back, safe and sound, and generally covered in mud. We hadn't a care in the world but we always knew that they were there keeping an eye on us. My grandfather would turn up every now and again as we played at the river that ran through the field at the back of the house. Always watching over us but not letting on.

I stopped as the sun broke the horizon. I stood and watched and felt the first rays of sunshine on my face, the morning chill slowly fading. This is what I didn't do anymore. This was what had been part of me and what made me who I am. And this is why I had come here. To remember the simple things, to rediscover old memories so that I could move on to the next part of my life and rediscover myself.

Standing on that beach on the east coast of Australia I could have been ten years old again, my brother, who was two years younger, standing beside me on the bank of the river on granddads land as we prepared for another great escapade. And here I was today, so many years later, standing on the precipice of another adventure. An adventure I hadn't chosen to be part of, but which, after everything that had happened, after all the decisions that could have taken me elsewhere, appeared to have chosen me, wishing my brother was standing beside me again. Because this was real life and more than I had ever bargained for, and now, somehow, I had to find the answers to the dilemma we had found ourselves in.

Anuia had said last night that there was nothing holding us there. Nothing that should keep us involved. This was true and we could so easily just walk away. Sure, someone could make a connection between us but so what. Backpackers meeting other backpackers. Travelling together, planning together. A small group in a sea of people doing the same thing. But was it that simple? That was the question I needed to ask myself. It wouldn't take inspector Morse to figure out that Dave, Paul and I had all left Sydney together, and that Anuia had left on the same day. Everyone staying in Glebe knew the three of us had planned to travel, sharing in our excitement when we bought the van and made the decision to go. What could be easier? They're the guys in the big yellow van. The problem was that everyone in Glebe also knew how close Anuia and I were. We had spent a lot of time together and more than once people remarked how much more comfortable Anuia appeared to be in my company. Not many could have known she left with us yesterday morning, but it wasn't rocket science. Another problem was that we didn't know Anuias story until last night. We hadn't had a chance to cover our tracks. If we had known, we could have made it look like we were simply parting ways. It wouldn't have taken much – Anuia saying she was going home or us leaving a day before or after and then meeting up.

How easy would it be to find us? I didn't know, but if TV cop dramas were anything to go by, it wouldn't take much and it wouldn't take long. Unlike these dramas however, the hero always had the answers, could always stay one step ahead and always had a plan.

We had two problems. One, we didn't have a plan and two, we sure as hell didn't have a hero.

While Paul, Dave and I could be directly linked to Anuia, Kai and Stefan were different. There was no connection between them and us. No reason to think that we had left Sydney together. They could walk away and I wouldn't blame them. Were it myself in the same position, I'm not so sure I would have been first to stand up either.

We needed a plan. But before we decided on any type of strategy, we first had to figure out who 'we' were.

Chapter Fourteen

When I returned to camp they were all up. The stove was lit, water
boiling, and the smell of frying bacon filled the air. Anuia was busy
taking fresh rolls, butter, marmalade and jam from the eskey and laying
them out on the low fold out camping table we had bought in Sydney.
Paul busied himself with cups, knives and forks. Our first morning on
the road but not, unfortunately, what I had hoped it would be. There
was no sign of Kai and Stefan. Paul said they had got up a while ago,
closed their tent, and went for a walk. Most likely to talk some more
and decide what to do. I was worried. I knew there was nothing
keeping them there. I really hoped they would stick around until we
decided on the best course of action. After a bowl of the cheapest
cereal in the world, the bacon was ready.

Anuia put some more on the pan, saying it was for Kai and
Stefan but there was still no sign of them. While we sat there eating in
silence I asked myself what I really knew about her. What drew me to
her or made me feel responsible for her. I had known her for a while
but these were questions that I now asked myself for the first time. I
watched her, her head bent slightly eating her food, wondering what
could be going through her mind. I admired her strength and courage.

'Good morning.' Kai and Stefan were back.

'Hey guys,' I said, 'how are you doing? Did you have a good
sleep?' I expected this was the last thing they had had, but I smiled
and they knew I was joking.

Stefan spoke. 'We went for a walk to talk about this situation.
This is something we have not expected. And, as you know, we are not
implicated in this in any way. We are unsure what to do. We are angry

that we have become involved, but we do understand that you have done what you think is best.'

He shifted his weight from one foot to the other, nervously looking at the ground, then at Kai who nodded his reassurance.

'I am scared. We are scared. This is to be the best year of our lives. We are to start college in Stockholm when we go home and we may never get the chance to travel again. This is an important decision for us as I'm sure you understand. We would like to help but we don't know if we can. There are many questions we need to ask you Anuia. We do not understand how it has come to this. Why you have not gone to the police for example. Until we know some more, we cannot make a decision to help.'

'Right' I said, getting to my feet, sounding as angry as I possibly could, 'do you know what you can do?'

Everyone stopped, stunned expressions on their faces.

'What?' Kai asked, apologetically.

'Have some breakfast' I said, slapping him on the shoulder. We all laughed.

I had thought about it while walking on the beach, asking myself many of the same questions. Why no police, as Stefan had said. This, to me, would have been the logical thing to do. Why had she come to Sydney? In all the confusion they never actually knew who she was there to pick up, but the gang would have easily figured it out. Wouldn't this have put her uncle and his family in danger? Where were her family now? How would they be, held somewhere in a foreign country, frightened, scared for their daughter.

Or could they have been sent back to Thailand already? I didn't think so considering that mornings events. They were witnesses too, and an important part of any investigation into what had happened. It would have been safe for authorities to assume that if the person seen running from the area that morning had indeed been a witness, and been at the scene, that they could have been there in connection with what was taking place. Some questions Anuia could answer but I'm sure a lot of things she was just assuming too.

'Anuia,' I asked, as we cleaned and packed the gear away after breakfast, 'the most obvious question is the one Stefan asked. Why did you not go to the police? Would this not be the easiest thing to do?'

'Yes,' she replied, 'it would seem the easiest thing to do and maybe I should have but there is something very, very important I need to tell you all. Like I said, my uncle drove me to collect my family that morning. After dropping me off, he returned to a quiet street close to the supermarket. We planned to meet there once my family were with me and safe.'

The look of fear she had had the night before as she recounted her story had returned.

'We did not anticipate that the exchange would take long but, as I told you last night, someone else was expected and the whole thing started to get delayed. My uncle was reluctant that I should go on my own in the first place but we were instructed that there should be one person only. He told me that he couldn't sit and wait for me to come back and decided to leave the car to make his way towards the supermarket. He didn't know what he planned to do when he got there, but I understood that he was so concerned he just had to be doing something.'

68

I could sense some confusion in the story she was telling us. As if she herself didn't understand how events unfolded.

'When he walked to end of the street on which he had parked, a distinctive black car passed with a police car directly behind. He thought it unusual as the police car was so close, not going at speed, almost as if escorting it. His first reaction was that everything was going to go wrong, that the police were going to discover what was happening. I would be arrested. And him. After all, what we had done is not legal even if it was all for the right reasons. He watched from a doorway, hoping that the cars would pass on by, but they didn't. The black car slowed down and turned into the car park. However, what was most strange was that the police car continued a little further on, swung back around to face the direction it had come, and parked. As if they were on lookout. He froze, not knowing what to do. Just then another police car passed. Hoping he hadn't been seen, he chanced another look. The second car slowed to a stop beside the first and the occupants appeared to talk to each other briefly before the second car moved off again. It went to the end of the street and disappeared around a corner. Only minutes later, the exact same thing happened. The second car passed again, slowed near the first and then drove on taking the same turn at the end of the street. They were on watch. He had no doubt. What this meant he did not know but I believe we figured it out.

'Everything happened so quickly after that – the black car, the fight and the shootings. It had all gone so horribly wrong. I had seen a man being shot. Terrified and disoriented, I ran to where my uncle waited and we drove away. We went through what had happened. Step by step, exactly as it had taken place. My uncle told me how he had left his car and saw the same black car arrive at the supermarket. And of course about the police cars.'

'What is it Anuia?' I asked, as she paused, 'what happed?'

'When I was running away, and only seconds before I got into my uncles car, I could hear police sirens in the distance. I can't say how far away, but certainly further away than the supermarket. This is the problem. My uncle saw a police car parked on the street outside and another more or less circling the block as if on patrol. Hearing gunfire, someone somewhere called the police. If these police cars were right there, why did it take so long before I heard the sirens? Why so far in the distance?'

'The police in those two cars were involved. That's unbelievable,' Paul said, speaking for us all. 'The bastards.'

'Man, this just gets worse and worse,' Dave added.

He hadn't said much this morning so far.

'What the hell have we got mixed up in? It's bad enough that this is so big, but to think that the police themselves could be involved makes it far, far worse. I can understand now why you didn't go straight to them,' he said, his tone softening.

'Why did you come to Sydney?' Kai asked.

I'm sure Anuia felt like she was on trial, but we needed to know everything.

'After all that happened, my uncle decided that I should go and stay with some friends of his in Wollongong in New South Wales. We agreed that I should leave immediately, that I should be out of the way while we decided what to do. If the police came, he would say that I had gone to stay with friends the week before. He would speak to his friend in Wollongong, let him know that I was coming and ask them to corroborate what he would say. I packed a bag and prepared to go. I

70

was standing in the bus terminal on Franklin Street, about to buy a ticket on a Greyhound to Wollongong, when I had a different idea. I would go to Sydney instead. I couldn't get anyone else involved. The situation was already disastrous enough. It was better to make it look like I had acted completely independently, that the whole thing had been my idea. My uncle watched helplessly as the bus pulled away. Then I was on my own.'

'What changed,' I asked, 'why did you not go to the police when you got there?'

'We were worried about the police,' she continued, 'how deeply were they implicated? If we went to them, would we be exposing ourselves to those involved? We believed our best chance was to get me to Wollongong and to talk to someone there. Victoria and New South Wales have two different police forces. Maybe our logic doesn't make sense, but at the time it was all we had.'

'No,' I said, 'I think it does make sense.'

We rolled our tents and sleeping bags and packed our gear. Already, everything had its own allocated space in the van.

'It took most of that day for the bus to reach Sydney. It had all gone so wrong. Everything we had, everything my uncle had worked so hard for, was now in jeopardy.

'The first thing I needed was a place to stay. Somewhere to hide. That's when I thought about backpackers. Amongst people my own age that didn't really care who I was or where I came from, people who would just accept me without asking too many questions. What better way to get lost than amongst people from all over the world who were here to do just that.

'I thought about staying in Bondi first. It was the only place I had heard of, lots of surfers and backpackers and plenty of hostels to choose from. More buses were arriving, bringing travellers and backpackers from different parts of Australia. I overheard a small group talk about Coogee. It was quieter than Bondi, more laid back, but an up and coming traveller destination. My mind was made up. It was somewhere less familiar. I rang the Coogee Beach backpackers and booked a bed.

'The minute I arrived I was lost as I had planned among the backpacking fraternity. I was welcomed, asked where I was from, where I had travelled, and how long I planned to stay. A girl from Norway showed me to my dorm. I was sharing with five other girls. When she left, I climbed into bed and slept. I felt safe for the moment.'

We had everything packed and were ready to go as Anuia neared the end of her story.

'When I got the chance, I rang my uncle. The gang had already been to the house looking for me. Even when they threatened him, he told them I had not returned that morning and he had no idea where I was gone. I felt so guilty. He did not deserve this. They warned him not to talk to the police. I told him I loved him and that I would keep in touch as often as I could while I decided what to do. I was still in shock about how badly everything had gone wrong and needed some time to weigh up my options.

'This is why I haven't yet been to the police. I simply cannot decide what to do. I am afraid for myself and for my uncle and his family. If I go to the police, what will happen? I have so far done what I think is best and kept myself hidden as much as possible. What else can I do? And now I know they are on my trail. It seems the longer I wait, the worse the situation has become.'

'What I worry about most,' she finally added, 'is my family. What will happen to them now? At the end of all this, what is left?'

The lads were quiet. They looked at me, waiting for the question they knew I was going to ask.

'Paul and I have talked about this,' Dave said, anticipating it, 'there's no way we're going to let you go this alone and have all the fun. Count us in.'

Exactly what I had hoped.

'Well guys. How about it?' I asked, turning to Kai and Stefan. 'We can't do it without you.'

'I know you can't,' Stefan replied, 'you're Irish. You need someone intelligent for this.'

Kai stared at Stefan, uncertainty in his expression.

'Okay,' he agreed reluctantly, 'let's see what happens.'

I could tell he wasn't happy.

'Thank you all so much,' Anuia said. She had been quiet. 'This means the world to me.'

'By the way,' Stefan asked when we were all sitting in the van, 'what exactly are we doing?'

'How should I know?' I said.

We'd figure something out.

Chapter Fifteen

Our best plan was to have no plan at all. Apart from north along the east coast of Australia, for what it was worth, no-one actually knew specifically where we were going. How far, by what time or where we would stop along the way was anybody's guess. We hadn't even decided ourselves.

We left Pacific Palms, Dave driving and Paul in the passenger seat beside him. Kai, Stefan and Anuia sat in the next two seats chatting amongst themselves. I sat at the back, kicked off my flip flops and stretched out my legs, watching from the back window as we drove. I asked myself if you only really get one chance at this. Would I ever get to travel this road again? We joined the main road and went north towards Forster. Through Booti Booti National Park, Wallis Lake to our left, mile after mile of scorched landscape. Old wire fences lined the road, dead and bare trees, and very often, not too far in the distance, small rock formations covered in dense green vegetation. White cloud drifted in the bright blue sky.

We passed through Forster, on through Tuncurry, and re-joined the Pacific Highway somewhere south of Taree. We had travelled further than planned yesterday originally thinking we would stop somewhere around Newcastle. Port Macquarie was the next big stop, or rather the first big stop on the backpack trail.

We turned off the Pacific Highway in a town called Kew, took the road to the coast towards Laurelton then went north again along the sea until we came to Port Macquarie. It's a beautiful town, trees lining every street, uncluttered. I had read about what a great place it was for its beaches. North Shore, Flynn's Beach and Lighthouse Beach. It was a great place for any tourist to stop, though especially attractive for backpackers. It thrived on tourism, but was just far enough away from Sydney so as not to be too expensive. Plenty of budget accommodation, camp sites and hostels.

By now, an idea had started to form in my head.

'Dave,' I said, as we came to a small park on our left, 'can you pull in somewhere along here. I want to stop and get some water. And I've been thinking about what we can do.'

We opened the side door to let a blast of cool air into the van. The sunroof was open but it still felt like a hundred degrees inside. I hopped out and jogged to a shop across the road. When I got back, a large three-litre bottle of water in one hand and a newspaper in the other, the guys were stretching out on the grass.

'Has anyone got any ideas?' I asked, passing out cups and filling them with water.

'I thought you did,' Paul replied.

'Let's look at the options,' I said. 'We've agreed that Anuia can't go to the police back home. And, we've also agreed that she can't go to the police here because of the threats against her uncle's family. So who do we go to?'

'What about the newspaper?' Stefan asked.

'The press. Exactly,' I said, holding up the paper I had brought back from the shop and dropping it, a little triumphantly, on the grass between them.

'Since Anuia told us what happened in Melbourne that morning, I've thought about who the person in the black car could be. Anuia, you said he was Australian and the car he came in was very official looking? It would make sense that this guy has access to the

75

police. He had an escort after all. Maybe a prominent businessman or perhaps someone within the police force itself.'

'Or a politician or someone in the government?' Dave asked sarcastically, a mock expression of surprise on his face.

But I wasn't losing the plot.

'Why not?' I asked. 'Isn't it possible? Think about it. Who drives around in that kind of car? Wealthy businessmen certainly, but with a police escort? If it was just a few rogue police, why the need for or who owns the black car? If it's a businessman he would have to have access to the police and to someone higher up within the police. Someone would have to sign-off on an escort at that time of the morning. And that's two cars that we know of. Isn't it possible there were more involved? Criminals maybe, but why the need for the police at all? They would have brought their own protection. Risky obviously, but isn't everything crooked in the world? There would have to be someone at that level involved. I'm thinking that a higher ranking police official or political figure of some kind is plausible. No doubt that there's a gang involved, but who better to smooth the way? Someone who might iron out an easy transition for a container arriving on a ship from somewhere or someone with access to customs? If you think about it, do you not think it's possible? I believe this person in the black car is the key. If we can find out who he is it would put us in a better position to go to the police. Dave? Anuia?'

'Okay,' Dave conceded, 'say that you're on to something here, what do we do? Why not go to the police now? Tell them that we think someone higher up may be involved.'

'Because we have no proof and, as it stands, no way of finding out who this person is. We're on our way up the New South Wales coast. This happened in Melbourne. If we talk to the wrong people will they let this person sink into the background or disappear until this all dies down? They'll know that we're on to them and try to eliminate the threat as quickly as possible. It's better that Anuia stays hidden. She's the only one who can identify them.'

'But who do we go to?' I continued, 'how do we find out who this person is? That's the question and that's why I think that talking to the press might give us some hope. A journalist could track this person down. After all, isn't that what they do? If a paper ran this.....'

'But we know there's someone out there looking for Anuia already,' Paul said.

'You're right,' I replied, 'we're going to have to keep moving. We don't know who, but it's a safe bet they're the wrong people. We have to keep moving until we find someone who can help us and who we can trust.'

'This is not going to be easy to do,' Stefan added. I loved his ability to state the sublimely obvious.

'Thank you for pointing that out Stefan,' I said, 'it's a bloody good job we let you come with us. I mean, we may not have found our way out of Sydney without you.'

We all laughed. If we were going to get through this we would need to laugh every now and again.

'You are right though,' I said, 'it won't be easy but I've been thinking of how we might get in touch with a journalist.'

'You've been thinking?' Anuia asked with a hint of a smile on her face, 'my, my, what would we do if you weren't here?'

Touché.

'Seriously though,' I said, 'it was all over the press when I arrived in Sydney. I'm sure it was the same in Melbourne and probably more so as it was local news and a huge story. Anuia, what are the big newspapers there? What would the big daily be?'

She thought for a moment.

'The Melbourne Times, The Age,' she said, 'I don't read the papers much but they're the main ones and I'm sure there's plenty more.'

'They'll do for starters,' I replied. 'We need to get a look at them, get some journalist names, and take it from there. Don't libraries keep newspaper archives? On microfiche or something like that?'

'There's always the Internet,' Paul added.

I didn't know much about the Internet, but I should have. For two years before leaving home I was studying IT by night. Before that I spent a year doing computer programming. In all that time, while I had heard so much about it, I never once used it.

'Where do we go to look at microfiche? Or the Internet?' Stefan asked.

'It's mostly businesses or colleges that have internet access,' Anuia replied, 'but we passed a library a few streets back. It might be a good place to start.'

'First though,' I thought, 'if we're going to stick around for a day or two, we should probably look at finding somewhere to set up camp for the night. Anything in The Book Dave?'

We did call it the Lonely Planet originally, but the more we planned, the more we referred to it as simply 'The Book.' As it if were a mystical guide for the journey we were about to take and held secrets of routes, secret sunsets and sunrises, and secret places to stay. As time wore on we would refer to it less and less, instead relying on word of mouth, and advice whispered by other, fellow travellers, as if guarding secrets that were not to be shared.

'Campsites, campsites, campsites......,' Dave said, flicking through the pages. 'Okay, there's a few all right. Ocean view or river view?'

Port Macquarie is built at the mouth of the Hastings River as it flows into the Pacific.

'We have a place called Sundowner Breakwall Tourist Park. It's near Marine Park on.....Clarence Street. Normal property retail value for this location is about ten million dollars, but tonight we can have that view for just twenty. Or, let me see.....we have Flynn's Beach Resort.'

A minute while he checks the map.

'It's on Ocean Street, just off Pacific Drive, somewhere between Flynn's Beach and Nobbys Beach. Back to that big roundabout we passed, take a left to the beach, then north along the sea. For a site in this location, normally about a gazillion dollars, but we can have it for just twenty two. What's it going to be?' he asked, 'sea view?'

We all raise our hands unanimously. Flynn's Beach resort it was. Forty minutes including a stop at a supermarket for supplies later and we were already setting up camp for the night. I bailed in helping the guys get their tents up. I loved doing it. Helping, organising,

79

annoying. Though I don't think the other guys did mind too much. I grabbed tent poles, hammered pins into the ground, set up the cooking gear and got the food ready, all at the one time. I didn't do it out of sheer enthusiasm, or because I wanted everything done my way. I simply did it because I wanted to help as much as possible. This was always the way I had been. Even at home when I used to work on the building sites, I always seemed to work so hard. But there was always someone willing to take advantage, someone who wasn't just prepared to go that extra yard. Did I mind? I suppose I did. It was just another item on the long list of issues that I was here to fix. And already, in this short space of time, these small, unimportant problems would never be problems again.

The guys loved it too. All pulling and tugging and soon, out of the chaos, we had tents almost ready, fires lighting, fresh rolls ready for eating, and water boiling on the stove. Why we felt the need to have tea when the temperature was in the late twenties is one of human nature's great mysteries. If you camp, and have a stove, you must boil water. And I guess the only thing you can do with boiling water is have tea. So we did.

Paul and I tended to his tent while the other guys worked on theirs and Dave and Anuia worked on getting the food together.

'What do you do anyway Paul?' I asked, 'I mean. Back home, what do you do for a living?'

'I work in IT actually,' he replied, 'I'm a software developer for a company in Dublin. 'Been living there for about four years now. Dave and I. We went to college together in Galway and ended up moving to Dublin together.'

'Yeah my brother works in computers,' I said, 'though what he does, I really couldn't say. He's been at it since he left school. It's funny though isn't it? In all the time I've known you it never crossed my mind to ask what you do.'

'I know what you mean,' he replied. 'But it's a good thing. Dave and I have been living in Dublin. Basically work, sleep, and work for four years now. Add to that about fifty pints every weekend. Copper Face Jacks on Harcourt Street, chasing women and getting none. We kind of hit a wall and didn't seem to be going anywhere fast. We have some friends from Galway in Dublin, but most of the people we hang out with we only know through the job so, every time we go out with them, we find that the most we have in common is work. It's a relief though.'

'How do you mean?' I asked.

'You know,' he said, 'it just doesn't seem that important anymore. Since we've come here I almost forget what we do back home. I mean, it just makes no difference to anyone. It's rare that someone I've met has actually asked what I do.'

He paused.

'It's like...... it's like everyone we meet here is here for a similar reason. To get away from what they do at home. To break the monotony. It's like all we've done since we left school is work. Well, school to college and then college to work. When do we ever take the time to discover who we are or to do something we actually want to do? It's just great to be here, to be thinking about myself for the first time in my life, and to be meeting people in the same boat who are genuinely interested in getting to know me. Without a label. I feel like I'm breaking a spell or something and everyone I meet is helping me to do it because they understand too. Maybe I'm not making much sense.' He smiled and shrugged his shoulders.

'Paul,' I said, 'I know exactly what you mean. That's like totally deep dude.'

We both laughed.

'Seriously though, I really do understand,' I continued, 'isn't it the same reason we're all here after all? What do you think of this idea of trying to talk to the press, or a journalist?'

'It's a good idea. A lot of what you said makes sense and most libraries keep newspaper archives. More and more stuff is going on-line these days too. There seems to be a web site starting up for everything.'

'Where do you go to use the Internet?' I asked.

'Anuia's probably right,' he replied, 'the library might have it. Or a university.'

'Yeah,' I said, 'they had internet access in Trinity.'

'Trinity? I didn't know you went there. I thought you were a carpenter.'

'I am,' I said, 'but it's a long story. Well, it's been a long story for me anyway. I'll fill you in some day.'

He didn't ask any more questions. He didn't feel he had to.

'That's the job for tomorrow so,' I said, 'first thing in the morning, you can educate me in the ways of the World Wide Web or whatever they call it.'

'It's called d'Internet in Galway,' he said, with a big grin.

'It's called the bleedin' Internet in Dublin,' I said, grinning too.

The tent was just about pitched when Anuia called to say that the food was ready. I left Paul to tie down the last guide rope and made my way over to her. She had everything prepared. Food and drink, and the tea. I think she felt she had to try harder than she needed to.

'How are you holding up Anuia?' I asked.

'I'm doing okay,' she replied. 'Certainly a lot better now that I have some friends on my side. For what it's worth, it means an awful lot to me.'

'How did you sleep last night?' I asked.

'Better than I have in a while thanks,' she replied, 'I haven't had many good nights recently. I'll never forget the image on that man's face when he was shot.'

'Hopefully you will in time,' I said. 'Paul and I are going to go to the library first thing in the morning to see if we can get access to these newspaper archives. We'll see who's been writing about this in Melbourne. I'm not sure what we'll find, but we'll see where it leads.'

'Thank you,' she said, 'and I really, really mean that.'

'I know you do, and we'll do everything we can to help you,' I told her.

We sat and talked. We enjoyed the sun and the blue skies. We listened to the sound of the sea. Traffic passed by. Cars, trucks, motorbikes. Almost endlessly, and still, above it all was the sound of the sea. Waves crashing on the shore one after another, soothing and hypnotic.

Everyone had their questions for Anuia, each of which she answered enthusiastically, the burden of the secret she had carried now gone. We were comfortable asking what we each needed to know. No longer people who had just met, with a similar desire to travel, to see new places or to experience new things. We had become more than just friends. Real friends. Building bonds that would last longer than what the next weeks and months would bring. Bonds that would tie us together for life. We didn't know it, but that's what made it all the better.

When the food was finished, we washed our gear and packed it away for use later that night. Kai and Stefan stretched out on the grass, sunglasses on and books at the ready. They were silent as they read but I could see that Kai was finding it difficult to relax.

Paul and Dave spent much of the evening swimming, restless and eager for the day to be over so that we could get cracking the next morning. Most of the campsites were full. Plenty of backpackers like ourselves but a lot of holiday makers too. Ideal for remaining suitably anonymous.

Anuia and I walked on the beach. I told her about where I was from and she told me about what she could remember of her childhood in Thailand. We relished the view and the location, the proximity to the sea, and the moment.

Evening passed, another brilliant sunset as dusk slowly descended into darkness. We had our campfire lit and cooked food on the stove. When we finished, we sat silently staring into the campfire, listening to music on the van radio. I could smell the sea, the sand, and the remnants of food overcooked on barbeques. Sun cream, after sun and sweat. Talk, then laughter and then quiet. Silence except for the chirp of a million crickets, hidden in the grass around us.

We were tired. Not from the days exertions, but tired the way you can get by sitting in the sun drinking a few beers for the day. When you know your body and your mind has relaxed. Eventually, as the last embers of the fire ebbed in the darkness, I decided it was time for bed. We had a lot to do tomorrow.

As I got up and walked to the van to grab my sleeping bag, Anuia followed me.

'Thank you again,' she said, 'for letting me sleep in the van. Can I ask you a question?'

'Of course' I answered, 'anything.'

'We have talked and learned a lot about each other today. I feel like you are all part of......I don't know......a family or something like that. It's hard to explain. But you? You always say the least about yourself. Why is that?'

'You know Anuia,' I said, 'I don't really know. I want to, I really do. I want you all to know me for who I really am. It's like for the first time in so many years I'm starting to figure it out myself. I just seem to have been so lost for so long and until I find out who I am and who I want to be, I'm not sure how to talk about it. I will, I promise.'

'I understand,' she said, giving me a quick peck on the cheek. As she turned to walk back to the camp fire she stopped. 'I think that to figure out who you want to be, you should first try to discover who you are now. Good night.'

'Night,' I said, then called the same to the rest of the gang as I slipped into the tent. Lying there, before drifting off to sleep, I understood what she said and understood it was true.

Chapter Sixteen

We were up early the next morning. Quietly determined that today was the day we would start figuring a way out of this mess. Paul and I were ready to head back into town to see just how our plan would hold up.

'Guys,' I said, 'Can you get the gear packed away and ready to go? We'll get back as soon as we can.'

'Not a problem,' Dave replied. 'Good luck.'

'Can I come with you guys?' Anuia pleaded, 'I can't just sit here doing nothing.'

'Maybe it's best you stay out of sight as much as possible,' I replied, 'we'll be as quick as we can.'

Half an hour later we were parked outside the library.

'Here goes Paul,' I said. 'Things like this always work in the movies.'

It was quiet with only a few school kids hanging around. Through a large double door off the main hallway and into the silence of the main reading room. I waited as the librarian listened to a recorded message on her phone.

'Good morning,' she said. Bright and pleasant with a friendly smile.

'Good morning,' I replied, then told her what we were looking for.

'That's an unusual request. How far back are you thinking about?' she asked.

'Well, only for the last six months to be honest. I know it's a long shot. I'm studying journalism back home and want to write about something I saw on the news when I got here.'

I didn't like lying.

'There was a big story over the past few months,' I said, 'about illegal immigration and an incident where two people were killed in Melbourne.'

'It was bound to happen sooner or later,' she said. 'It's been going on here for a long time. It's a pity it's come to this. I'm afraid though that I can't help you. We're way behind with our back copies.'

We were utterly deflated in a matter of seconds.

'Would it be possible that this information would be available on the Internet,' I asked, 'do you have the Internet here?'

'It probably is,' she answered, 'but unfortunately we don't have access to it yet either. It takes a while for things to happen around here. You would probably need to be looking at the National Library of Australia for newspaper archives, but that's all the way out in Canberra. If you aren't in too much of a hurry, you could always go back to Newcastle. They have a library there but your best bet, especially for internet access, is probably the Newcastle Uni library. The Uni's are pretty well up to date on everything.'

The last thing we had wanted was to be heading backwards. But if that's what we had to do, then that's the way it had to be.

'I'm sorry I couldn't be of more help,' she said, as we turned to go. 'Enjoy the rest of your trip. This is only the start of it. There are some beautiful places further north. The Gold Coast, Byron Bay. You've a lot to see yet.'

We sat on the library steps, our enthusiasm slowly evaporating.

'What do you think Paul?' I asked.

'Look,' he said, 'if we have to go back to Newcastle, let's do it. There's no real point thinking about it. It's the best idea we have. The only idea. It's only a couple of hours back down the road anyway.'

'Is The Book in the van?' I then asked.

'I've been thinking about ringing the hostel back in Sydney. Just to see has anyone come looking for Anuia over the last couple of days.'

Paul agreed that it was a good idea. He'd been thinking the same.

'I'll grab the number and give them a bell now before we go back.'

There was a phone booth back where we had parked the van. I rang the number for Glebe Village.

'Good morning, Glebe Village Backpackers, how can I help you?'

It was a phrase I had heard many times during the weeks I stayed there and I recognised the friendly voice.

'Hi Maja, how are you doing?' I asked.

'Who am I speaking to please?' she asked. Ultra friendly but with the efficiency and politeness I associated with eastern and northern Europeans.

'Guess who? It's only your favourite Irish man in the whole world,' I replied.

A corny line I would never have been comfortable with before I left home but a phrase of the type I now felt much more at ease with as my confidence had started to grow.

Maja had also become a very good friend. A blonde from Sweden, tanned and good looking. Laid back in a way I could only dream of and a personality to suit. She had a welcome smile and greeting for everyone who walked in the door. She loved meeting people and told me this was what had made her travel in the first place. She had been there for about five months when I arrived. She had no particular plan, no itinerary or idea where she would head to next, and she didn't care. I admired this, and as with so many other people I met, saw in her a little bit of what I hoped I could be. It was great to hear her voice.

'No way,' she exclaimed. 'Wow, it's great to hear from you. And so soon? You must have missed us?' she laughed.

'Of course I have,' I said, 'but mostly I've missed you.'

Friendly flirting that had been the norm between us for some time.

'Any news for me?' I asked.

'No, it's been a quiet few days,' she said, 'a few people coming and going as usual.'

'Anything else?' I asked, 'anyone looking for us.'

'You're being very coy,' she said, 'you're looking for information.'

Another thing I admired very much about Maja. She was good at reading people. Intuitive. Qualities which made me like her even more. I didn't answer.

'Anuia left,' she continued, 'she seems to have been gone since you guys went away. How are the two boys by the way?'

'They're great,' I said. 'Paul is here with me now. He says to say hi.'

Paul fancied Maja. He had since the day he met her but no amount of encouragement by me or anyone else would bring him to let her know this.

'He says he misses you terribly,' I laughed, as he thumped my arm.

'Listen Maja,' I said, 'we haven't much time. Anuia left with us. It was a last minute thing that we hadn't really planned. There's the three of us, Anuia, and two guys from Sweden.'

'That sounds like fun,' she said, but then continued in a more serious tone. 'Two men came looking for her last night. They were Asian and said they were having difficulty getting in touch with her. I had a bad feeling about them. As if they were trying too hard to be nice. I told them she had left some time ago.'

'Maja. You're a genius.'

'Thank you, I know that,' she replied.

I could imagine the smile on her face as she said it.

'Are you going to tell your favourite Swedish girl what this is about?' she then asked.

'Maja wants to know what's going on,' I whispered to Paul, 'there have been men looking for Anuia.'

He gave a slight nod of his head to say yes. He trusted her too. And it would be good to be able to contact someone back in Glebe to see if anyone else came looking for her.

'Maja,' I said, 'you know I love you. We're in a spot of bother. Can I trust you?'

'You know you can,' she replied.

And so, I gave her the brief version of what had happened over the months since I came to Oz and how I, and now we, fitted into the equation. The phone beeped and I put the last of my change in the slot.

'Wow,' she said, when I finished.

'Maja, we're going to keep moving until we figure out what to do. It would be good if I could call back every now and again to see if there are any further developments.'

'No problem,' she replied. 'Anuia picked the right guy to help her.'

'What makes you say that?' I asked, somewhat surprised, but the line went dead.

When we got back, they were waiting. Eager to hear how we got on and what we had found out.

'We've nothing to go on,' I said, explaining how things had gone at the library.

'Paul and I have decided that the best thing we can do is to head back to Newcastle to the Uni. Just the two of us.'

Dave glanced at Paul with a questioning look. He nodded as if to say, it's okay, listen to him.

'When we were in town,' I continued, turning to Anuia, 'we rang the Glebe Village. To see if anyone had come looking for you since we left.'

I told her what Maja had said.

'Already?' Kai asked, 'that didn't take long.'

'I know,' I replied, 'they sound like the bad guys to me. We want you to take the van and go on to Coffs Harbour. Paul and I will grab an Oz Experience bus and head back to Newcastle. We should be able to catch up with you again tonight. There's a place called the Park Beach caravan park. If you can get us booked in, we'll be there in time for supper.'

I smiled, trying my best to make light of the situation. We didn't want to split up.

'I don't know,' Anuia said.

'Trust me,' I told her, 'we'll have caught up with you by tonight.'

It was already twelve o'clock. We had to get moving.

'Drop us at the Beachside Backpackers Dave,' I said, giving him directions from the street map. It took about ten minutes to get there and Paul and I hopped out of the van.

'Guys,' Stefan said, 'be careful.'

'Thanks Stefan,' I said, 'you too. We'll see you all later tonight.'

'We've a lot to do if we're going to catch them by tonight,' Paul said, as we stood watching the van drive off. 'I hope there's an Oz bus due to head back that way some time soon.'

'Only one way to find out,' I said, as I turned and walked into the hostel.

Chapter Seventeen

A bus was leaving to head back down the coast at quarter past one and we had our tickets. First in line, we grabbed two seats at the back and watched as one by one, and slowly, the bus filled with weary, hung-over backpackers. A full forty-five minutes had passed before the driver cranked it up, a plume of blue smoke coming from the exhaust that made its way directly in through the window I had opened beside me. I gasped for air as I slid it shut.

'First time on the Oz bus dude?' the guy sitting in front of me asked. He had an American accent.

'Yup, first time,' I replied.

'Rookie mistake,' he said, laughing.

The bus was quiet as it took off, but it wasn't long before everyone came to life again. We stopped off at two more hostels to pick up other passengers before leaving Port Macquarie. There were lots of greetings. So many of them had already met and appeared to know each other quite well. I suppose a lot of these guys were on the last leg of their journey down the east coast, a well-worn route. Most backpackers stopped off at similar points going in either direction, with only the most adventurous, and those with their own transport, looking for new places to explore. It was great to see so many friendships that had been made. So many different nationalities. So many different walks of life.

'Where are you headed for?' the guy in front of me asked.

'Newcastle,' I replied.

'How come you've made it this far and never been on one of these?'

'We've been travelling with other people up to now,' I told him. 'We had our own minibus. They're staying on in Port Macquarie for a few more days. We've run low on money so we're going back to Sydney early to look for work.'

'I know the feeling,' he said, 'I'm Jeff by the way. How long have you been travelling?'

'Not long at all,' I replied, shaking his hand. 'We're not in Oz that long and we're hoping to get some work and then travel the coast properly. This has been a bit of a whistle stop tour for us.'

'Don't worry about it guys,' he said, 'you've got all the time in the world.'

'Where are you staying in Newcastle?'

'We haven't thought about it that much,' I replied. 'Where are you staying yourself?'

'There's a place some guys we met told us about. It's called Backpackers Newcastle. They said it was a pretty good place. Not too dear. Plenty of nightlife and they have surfboards and bikes that you can use for free. We said we'd give it a go and have a bit of a blow out before we get to Sydney. Then it'll be back to looking for some work. You're more than welcome to tag along and give it a try.'

'Thanks Jeff. We haven't decided where to stay yet but that's great to know. We've a few things to take care of when we get there.'

'If we get there,' Paul whispered.

It was already gone three o'clock and we had only just left Port Macquarie. We'd never reach Newcastle by five. This was a slow boat whatever way you looked at it. No chance of reaching the library before it closed. Our best bet now was the university. But this late in the evening? My mind was racing. What if we don't get back on a bus tonight? What would the guys do? Would they wait for us tomorrow? Paul kept glancing at his watch.

Jeff introduced us to some of the people he knew. I think he actually knew them all. Or everyone knew him to be more precise. He seemed like a good guy and up for a laugh. By the time we reached Newcastle we had a lot of new friends and unending advice on places to go further up the coast. More than one suggested that to really get into the backpacker groove, we should stay in the hostels instead.

It was six thirty when we finally arrived. We were way behind schedule. The bus stopped at Jeff's hostel and we jumped out.

'Paul,' I said, 'it's not looking good. The library will be well shut by now and we've no idea where the uni even is let alone what we're going to tell them when we get there.'

I presumed you couldn't just walk in off the street and start using their books and computers.

'Let's book a room here for the night. Even if we don't use it. At least we'll have a place left to stay.'

'Yeah, good idea,' he said, 'but what about the others? They'll think there's something wrong?'

'Let's see how we get on first,' I said. 'Let's organise some beds, check the last bus time heading back north, and take it from there.'

We followed the rest of the gang from the bus and, once they had all checked in, asked about beds for ourselves for the night. We paid our deposit saying that it was possible we might not stay. It earned us a curious look from the guy behind the desk. I asked about bus timetables heading north. I was relieved when he told us that a lot of buses, including the Oz bus, ran overnight in both directions. It suited a lot of people on particularly tight time schedules, allowing them to sleep on the buses and hit their destinations with more time on their hands. There was still a chance we'd be back on one tonight.

'How far is it to the uni?' I asked.

'That's about ten miles outside the city,' he replied.

He had introduced himself as Adam when we came in.

'It's a bit late to be heading out there,' he said, with a raised eyebrow.

Finally I had walked into a lie that I wouldn't be able to talk my way out of so easily. I wouldn't tell him everything but I had a chance to test this backpacker loyalty I had heard so much about.

'Okay Adam,' I said, 'here goes. I could tell you some cock and bull story about how we planned to look at somewhere else to stay tonight. Hedging our bets. But I'm not going to. Paul and I have told a lot of lies today already. We're in a bit of trouble and we're on the run from some pretty bad people. Before you ask, we haven't done anything wrong. We're just helping a friend of ours who needs to stay hidden for a while. We need some help.'

'Hang on a sec,' he said, walking from behind the counter. He asked the other guy to cover for him.

'I was due a break anyway,' he said, 'let's head into the bar.'

'Good idea,' Paul answered, 'I'm starving.'

It was the first time I had thought of food all day. Having not eaten since breakfast, I was starving too. There was a special on Bolognese. Five dollars for spaghetti, garlic bread, and a glass of cold beer. Exactly what we needed.

'Okay,' he said, as we sat down with our food, 'let's hear it.'

The first thing that crossed my mind was that I didn't even know this guy. He had a serious, attentive expression on his face. With an American accent, he looked very much the stereotypical college jock but his tone was quiet and amicable. I liked him, and whether I could trust him or not, we needed all the help we could get.

So I told him about meeting Anuia in Sydney and everything that had happened since. That eyebrow lifted again a few times, but he heard me out.

'This is some kind of situation you're in,' he said, when I finished talking. 'I think I can help you out.'

I knew he would help even before we told him our bizarre story. This was what every traveller looked for. This is what I had looked for. That chance of adventure. The chance of finding something that would be the catalyst to break us free from the life we had known. To be able to carry on knowing that we had achieved something and allow us to stand up and say 'No', we were different.

'Adam,' I said, 'we need all the help we can get.'

Adam was from New York as I had thought. From Queens to be exact and, like many Americans, was of half Irish decent. He had been travelling for just over a year but had been in Australia for only about half of that, stopping in Newcastle for the last two months as a short, four night stay to try a bit of surfing with some of his west coast

American counterparts turned from days to weeks and eventually to months due to a chance meeting with a blonde Australian girl on his second night out on the town. It wasn't really a chance meeting though, as he admitted he had seen her on his first night and made a point of dragging his friends to the same place in the hope that she would be there again. And so, by chance or not, fate had dealt him a card, he had stayed here, and we had someone who could help us.

Adams girlfriend Lily was from Newcastle. A student at the Uni studying IT. He'd been to the campus on a number of occasions to use their library and, more than once, had been able to get access to the Internet. Not that he knew what to do with the internet access, but she had shown him how it worked and how he could find information by typing a subject in a browser.

'Some day you'll be able to find everything you want on the Internet,' she had told him, but he didn't really believe her.

'I'll give Lily a bell and tell her what you have in mind,' he said, 'she'll want to know why, but I trust her.'

That was good enough for me. My main concern now was the rest of the gang. I had to get in touch. Between a couple of beers and chatting to Adam, I slipped back out to reception and rang the number of the park where we agreed they would stay. I got no answer, their reception most likely closed for the night, so I went back to the bar.

'Lads,' I said, 'I tried ringing the caravan park in Coffs but there's no answer. The guys will be going crazy if we don't show up tonight.'

If our plan was going to work, we had little choice other than to stay, spend some time at the uni in the morning and follow them to Coffs as soon as we could.

'Right,' Adam said, 'I'll go and ring her now.'

When he left I asked Paul what he thought of him.

'I think he's a pretty cool guy,' he said, 'I really do. I had a decent chat with him there while you were away. But it's another person that knows us and who we are. I'm not sure if that's a good thing. And now Maja knows too.'

Paul was right. It was another person that knew who we were. Another person who could potentially, unwittingly, expose us when they came looking. But it could also be another person who would help cover our tracks and buy us some time. As long as we stuck to our plan, relying on the help of people, travellers and searchers, like ourselves, I believed we would be okay.

'Lily will be glad to help,' Adam said, when he got back. 'I didn't tell her what this was about. I just explained that I had a few friends who needed access to press archives and the Internet. She thought we could go to the uni tonight but it would be real difficult to get in without answering a lot of questions. She thinks it's better to wait until morning when there are a lot of students around. She'll be here at eight thirty.'

'Thanks Adam,' I said, 'another drink anyone?'

When I was at the bar, Jeff and some of his buddies walked in, ready for another night on the beer. He made his way over.

'Hey man, you decided to stay for the night?'

'We did Jeff,' I replied, 'thanks for letting us know about this place, it's pretty cool. Do you want to join us.'

'Sure,' he said, 'I'll be right over.'

Jeff and his friends joined us at our table. He squeezed in beside me while his friends pulled up chairs and stools. It didn't take long for everyone to get acquainted. Adam had finished work and we convinced him to stay for a while. Jeff had lots of questions to ask about what to do around Newcastle during their stay.

All I could think about was the guys. Sitting by a fire in a campsite, waiting, not knowing, minutes then hours passing until they knew we wouldn't arrive. What would Anuia think? Would she believe something had gone wrong? Suddenly, as if my thoughts had somehow made her materialise, there she was on the television. Her picture was right there in front of me.

'Paul,' I said, tapping his shoulder, 'look.'

'Holy shit,' he said, almost involuntarily, 'I don't believe it.'

Seeing our reaction, Adam stopped talking to Jeff mid-sentence and turned towards the TV. He didn't recognise the face, but he understood what he saw.

'Yes,' I said, before he asked, 'that's her.'

'No way,' he replied.

'No way what?' Jeff asked.

'Paul, Adam,' I said, 'can I have a word?'

I nodded my head towards reception but they were already on their feet. As I got up to follow, Jeff put his hand on my arm.

'Seriously dude, what's up?' he asked, 'you look like you've seen a ghost.'

After all that had happened, the news, the media speculation, finally there was a face. The witness that everyone had heard about came suddenly to life. Anuia's greatest weapon, her anonymity, was gone.

'Not quite Jeff,' I said, 'come with me.'

'That's her?' Adam asked again, after I checked to make sure there was no-one else about.

'That's her all right,' Paul answered, 'though she looks a good bit younger in that photograph.'

'Damn,' I said, 'this is not good. Not good at all.'

TV reports said that the police had identified this girl as a witness to the double murder in Melbourne some months earlier. Connected to the illegal immigration racket. Somehow, someone somewhere had decided to put her face on TV. They would have known who she was for some time and having had no success in finding her or with the investigation this far, decided that they had a better shot at locating her if they splashed her identity all over the news. Or maybe the authorities had held it back, believing there may be a threat from within and hoping to gain their own advantage by finding her first. Either way, we were still no better off than we had been. We still couldn't go to the police. Who could we trust?

'Guys,' I said, 'we're going to have to get moving with this as soon as we can. We need to get someone involved that can help us and give us some kind of coverage. Anuia's face is out there now.'

I wondered then if it was possible that Anuia, Dave, Kai or Stefan could have seen this. In a campsite, this didn't seem plausible.

They didn't have a TV. What if they were there waiting for us, sitting in plain view, exposed where anyone could recognise her.

'Look,' Adam said, 'it's nearly eleven o'clock now anyway. Let's get some sleep and be ready to go first thing in the morning.'

'Yeah,' Paul agreed, 'let's stick to the plan. We'll head for the uni tomorrow, hopefully get something we can use, and be heading for Coffs before lunch.'

'You're right, both of you,' I replied. 'I'm just worried about the guys. They probably have no idea of what we just saw. By this time tomorrow this could all be over. You do realise that outside that gang, Anuia is the only person who can identify the man in the black car. If this goes as high up as we think is possible, if they get to her first........'

Jeff stood listening, wide eyed and open mouthed. He had no idea what was going on but it wouldn't take a genius to figure out that it wasn't something good.

'Guys,' he said, 'can someone tell me what the hell is going on here?'

'Okay Jeff,' I said, 'just remember, we're the good guys.'

As I lay in bed, sleep didn't come easily. Now Jeff knew and said he'd be waiting for us in the morning. Thinking of Anuia and the three lads, I hoped that they had somehow seen what we had. Hope though, was all I had and somewhere between these thoughts, I eventually drifted off.

Chapter Eighteen

Adam woke us in our dorm at half seven. Almost more eager than we were. We got up quickly and showered. True to his word, Jeff was there and ready to go. We talked while we made coffee and buttered toast. Jeff was from Boston and he teased Adam about being from New York.

It was just after eight when Lily arrived. A tall, good looking, blonde Australian. Easy to see why Adam had fallen for her. Not, as it would seem at first, for her good looks, but because of her open friendliness. After she kissed Adam on the cheek, she turned and introduced herself to us one at a time with a big broad friendly smile.

'So guys,' she asked, 'what exactly are we looking for here?'

I didn't know how much Adam had told her the night before so I turned to him as if to say 'do you want to answer this one.'

Adam, taking his cue, sat and asked Lily to sit next to him. We were the only ones in the kitchen but Adam gave Lily the background on what was going on in a hushed tone. She listened intently, digesting everything. When he finished, she thought for a moment before she spoke.

'I know exactly what you're looking for. We certainly have access to written media archives at the Uni, and I'm sure a lot of what you're looking for is already online.'

'When you're ready, we'll get going,' she added.

A simple, direct, pragmatic approach.

She had brought her car. A battered, weather beaten Oldsmobile Custom Cruiser station wagon. A big monster seven litre engine that must have cost a fortune to run. Which I said of course. But that was me, always focusing on the important things. She laughed saying she never had to drive that far in it anyway. It was ideal for stowing surfboards and surf gear and, when required, was great for sleeping in when long days at the beach with friends turned into warm nights sitting around a fire drinking a few beers. Adam twisted uncomfortably in the front seat, a smile on his face. I could tell he had been present on just such occasions and that the sleeping arrangements were just fine.

'It must be great to live around here,' I said, 'you know....long summers, good weather, beside the sea.'

It wasn't really a question, more a statement or a wishful thought, but Lily was quick to answer.

'It sure is,' she said. 'I love it here.'

We arrived at the uni and Lily pulled into the car park, found a spot, and killed the engine.

'Right guys,' she said, 'there'll be a lot of people knocking around at this time of the morning. Anyone can come onto the campus so I wouldn't expect to be asked any questions. Just in case you are, say you forgot your ID and that you're in IS 101. That's what I'm in myself. Oh, and guys. Try not to look too suspicious.'

We didn't but she got a kick out of saying it anyway.

The campus was huge and, as Lily expected, very busy. Hundreds, or probably thousands of students hanging out and chilling in the morning sun. After a walk through modern halls filled with the murmur of students, we came to the Ourimbah library. One of a few in the university but the one, Lily told us, which homed the audio visual, journal and reference databases. This is where we could hope to find what we needed.

She led us upstairs to a section on the first floor. We were surrounded by computers, cameras, video recorders, and a lot of stuff I didn't recognise. We sat at a desk and she switched on a terminal saying she'd need to log on to access the journal and reference databases. It occurred to me how screwed we would have been had we came out here on our own. She had logged in so quickly and started a search that I could barely register what she had done. When the result page came back with a list of headings she turned to us.

'Guys,' she said, 'we're in luck. We can get access to The Melbourne Times, The Age, and The Sydney Morning Herald. I'll just check the reference database and see what format they're in.'

Formats, reference databases? I had no clue what she was on about.

'Back in a minute guys,' she said, and she hurried off.

'She knows her stuff all right,' Paul said.

She returned a few minutes later setting two boxes on a table close to what looked like a portable television with some unusual controls.

'This guys,' she said 'is a microfiche reader and this is microfiche. These two boxes contain archives of both the Melbourne Times and The Age, two of Melbourne's larger broadsheets, for the last six months. Jeff, Adam, could you guys grab a seat I'll show you how to use them.'

'No problem,' they said, 'but what exactly are we looking for?'

'We're looking for the paper that gave this story the most exposure over the last six months,' I replied, 'particularly around the time of the killings back in Melbourne. Who covered it, who were the prominent journalists, and who protracted the story.'

Adam listened while Lily showed Jeff how to mount the microfiche in the reader and how to use it, referencing the index on the bottom right of each card. The boxes themselves were organised by date every fortnight which would help.

'Any name at all that you think we could use,' I continued. 'A political correspondent or someone who has written about a similar subject. Even if it's not on the same story. We're looking for someone who knows about it. Someone who could recognise the potential and look to crack open a big, big story.'

'No worries,' he said, turning back towards Jeff who had already started to scan the first frames.

Lily went back to the computer terminal. Dave and I followed.

'Right guys,' she said, 'let's see what we can find out online. I'll check for newspapers first. It'll be interesting to see how far they have progressed. Everyone is moving towards the Internet now.'

While Jeff and Adam busied themselves going over archived newspapers, Paul and I were given a first class lesson on how the World Wide Web worked. Lily explained how the Internet was starting to become more and more popular in Australia. People everywhere were starting to get online. Companies were starting to use it for sharing information, buying, selling and communication. Paul already knew much of this stuff but to me, experiencing real use of the Internet for the first time, it was fascinating. She said that this was just the start, alluding to what I had already heard on my courses. The world was going to become a much smaller place.

Some of the newspapers were there but access to archived papers was not extensive. We focused instead on political correspondents who reported on illegal immigration, discussing each and wondering if they would be the right person to talk to. We also focused on the Melbourne broadsheets. This was where it all happened. We scribbled names on a notepad with pros and cons, trying to see who would have covered it first, how much and what their view on it was. Australia was still very much divided on the illegal immigration question. Or immigration of any kind. They, like a lot of countries worldwide had been in a recession until recent years and a lot of Australians believed jobs and opportunities should be given to their own people first. We were looking for a reporter who would have an objective view on the subject, but also someone just waiting to crack open one of the biggest stories in Melbourne for a long time. The first was easy to spot. We just read over article after article taking the names of the journalists. The majority of stories were written by the same few people. The problem was picking one that might help. Selecting one that expressed an open mind on the subject and then who gave it the most analysis. After about two hours we kept coming back to the same name.

At last, satisfied, I turned to the other guys.

'What've you got?' I asked, wheeling my chair over to them.

'Well, not too much in the way of names,' Jeff replied. 'Both the papers covered the story extensively at the time and have been continually running with it since. It's gone off the front pages, but not gone off the radar. There is still some tension down there due to what happened.'

'We do keep coming back to the same guy though,' Adam added. 'He works for the Melbourne Times. A political writer who seems to have an interesting opinion on it. He's written extensively on the killings, but we've gone through a number of his articles since and he seems to be asking all the important question. Like, if this problem is as big as it's supposed to be, why has no-one been caught? Or why have more people not been injured or killed. It's hard to say if he's for it or against it but he could be the guy.'

'Lee Taylor?' I asked.

'Bingo,' they said, holding up their pad.

Lily turned back to the computer again and was busily typing away. She scribbled down two numbers then started another search using Lee Taylor, Melbourne Times as the subject.

'Might as well see what this guys all about,' she said.

We crowded around, peering over her shoulder as she clicked into one page after another.

'There isn't a whole lot up there about him,' she said. 'He's worked at the Times for about four years. A twenty-nine year old political correspondent. This could be the guy all right. Just waiting for his big chance.'

I was thinking the same as she picked up the note with the numbers and handed it to me. It was time to make some very important calls. She showed me to some payphones in the main hall then left me alone. I rang the first number. As the recorded message asked me to wait for an operator, I realised that I didn't quite know what I was going to say.

'The Melbourne Times. How can I help you?' a woman asked.

'Can you put me thorough to Lee Taylor please?' I replied. 'My name is Paul Hewson.'

I would have to make it up as I went along.

'One moment please,' she said, and put me on hold.

I had no intention of giving him my real name just yet.

'Mr. Hewson,' he asked, 'what can I do for you?'

He sounded young and confident. I could tell he had no idea who I was, but he wasn't prepared to admit that he may have forgotten an important call.

'Mr. Taylor,' I replied. 'My name is Paul Hewson. You don't actually know me and we have never met. My apologies for that.'

'That's okay,' he said, 'what can I do for you or what is this call in relation to.'

'Mr. Taylor,' I continued, getting straight to the point. 'I may have some information about a story you have written extensively about over the last four or five months. It involves a double murder in Melbourne early last September. Two people were killed when some deal in an immigration racket went wrong.'

'Go on,' he said.

'There was a girl identified as a witness to the shootings. How or why is irrelevant, but I know where she is. She has been travelling with my friends and me. She told us her story and we have reason to believe that there are people following us. We also believe that these people don't have her best interest at heart so we're going to do whatever we can to protect her.'

There was silence, so I continued.

'We saw her face on TV last night. A lot more people will know who she is by now, so our situation has changed. We need help.'

'You're not the first person to call with information about this story,' he said, 'and you won't be the last. That said, I have no reason not to believe you just yet. Can I ask? Why has she not gone to the police? Surely that would have been the wise thing to do? The police will protect her.'

'Unfortunately Mr. Taylor, she can't,' I replied. 'It's the first question I asked and she has her reasons. I have no reason to believe that she's lying.'

'Still,' he said. 'How do I know this is even true?'

I thought for a moment. It was a fair point, but what could I tell him that would convince him that this wasn't just some crank call. I thought back to the story on the news last night. I tried to think of something or some information that had not been given out but that a journalist in his position would surely know.

'Mr. Taylor, I can tell you something that wasn't on the news that I watched last night and that I can only assume is being withheld. I've seen your coverage of the story and would expect that this is something you may already know.'

'Call me Lee,' he said.

'The family of the girl who witnessed the two shootings were in that truck. They had just arrived from Thailand. The girl's first name is Anuia. It seems important that the police have held this back so far.'

'What can I do to help?' he asked. 'Where are you now? How many of you? Why can't you just go to the police?'

I sensed his change in attitude, an excited tone to his voice. Young, eager, this was the phone call that he had been waiting for. The phone call that could change his life.

'Because we think the police are involved. Anuia saw someone there that morning and some things that didn't make sense. It's too much to get into right now. We believe that with the right kind of exposure that should Anuia finally give herself up to the police, this story will have a high enough profile to ensure that she gets the best coverage and help to keep her safe. She needs some kind of assurances from the police that should she go to them, her family will be protected and that they will not be sent back to Thailand. This could be the biggest story you've ever had.'

'You'd better believe it,' he said, 'where are you now?'

'We're on the New South Wales coast heading towards Coffs Harbour. That's all I can say. If you think you can help, give me a number, and I'll contact you as soon as I can.'

'Well?' they asked, when I got back.

I found them sitting on some steps outside.

'I spoke to him,' I said. 'This could be our guy. He believes us anyway. That's a start. Paul, we'd better get going.'

'Adam has offered to drive us to Coffs,' he replied, 'we'll drop the guys off at the backpackers before we go.'

'Brilliant,' I thought. It would save some valuable time.

Before leaving the hostel, Paul and I hugged Lily and Jeff. They wished us luck and we thanked them again for their help.

'Jeff,' I said, as Adam was about to take off, 'when you get to Sydney there's a hostel called the Glebe Village. It's a great place to stay. Ask for Maja. She'll look after you. I'll be ringing her every now and again, so if you hear anything before you get there, let her know.'

'Thanks dude, much appreciated. I sure will.'

We waved as Adam pulled off and we drove away. The window was down and before we got too far away I stuck my head out.

'Jeff,' I shouted, 'tell Maja that Paul loves her.'

I laughed as he dragged me back into the car.

'They're good guys,' I said to Adam. 'I can see why you fell for Lily. Do you think you'll ever move here? I mean, if you ended up staying with her?'

'It'd be tough,' he replied, 'I'd sure miss back home. But to be with someone that you honestly think could be your soul-mate, isn't that worth any price?'

'It sure is,' I thought, 'it sure is.....'

Chapter Nineteen

On the move again, heading north on a now familiar road. Past the turns for Forster and Taree then on through Port Macquarie and Kempsey. I was lost in thought, watching the road go by, seeing signs for turns that I wondered if I would ever get to take. I had originally planned that I would make all the stops that few other travellers got to. I wanted to be just that bit different. Turns for national parks and nature reserves, coastal towns and beaches. Through Macksville and past a turn to Nambucca Heads. I met someone in Sydney who had told me it was a beautiful place to stop if I wasn't in a hurry. Never imagining that I would be, or how events might unfold, my thoughts turned again to Anuia and the boys.

I knew they wouldn't be happy that we didn't make it back to them last night. I could picture how worried they might be, imagining what could have held us up and fearing the worst. I was concerned that I hadn't been able to get in touch when I saw Anuias face on the television. I hoped they had somehow saw the news and managed to keep her out sight.

The sign for Coffs Harbour had my heart racing. I turned to look at Paul. He shrugged and said he was sure they'd be here. I hoped he was right.

'We're looking for a place called the Park Beach caravan park Adam,' I said.

'I know it,' he replied, 'Lily and I spent a couple of days up here a while back. We passed it a couple of times along the main beach.'

He knew where he was going and it wasn't long before we were driving up Ocean Drive, the huge expanse of the Park Beach campsite on our right. Passing tent sites, then caravans and RVs, and

115

finally coming to cabins as we neared the huge sign marking the entrance.

'No sign of the yellow bus,' Paul said.

I had been straining to see it since the park came into view. Hoping to see the van parked amongst the sites and our tents pitched beside it. It would have made sense to stay in the one place while they waited for us. We parked in the car park.

'I'm going to take a walk down by the campsites guys and see if there's any sign of them. Paul, can you check in reception and see if there's anything you can find out?'

'What kind of van?' Adam asked.

'A yellow Starwagon,' I replied, and he went to search in a different direction.

I walked to the end of the campsite, retracing my steps once I had reached the end. But they were definitely gone. Assuming they had been here in the first place. I hurried back to the main office.

'Anything guys?' I asked. They were already back and waiting for me to return.

'Nothing,' Paul answered. 'The girl on reception wasn't working yesterday. Do you know what the registration of the van is? She said they keep numbers of anything that stays.'

I had no idea what it was. In all the time we had had the van it had never occurred to me to remember it. I had written it on a form for insurance and local parking back in Sydney but I had never remembered what is was.

'Was it FRE of GRE something?' I asked.

'I'm sorry dude, I don't know,' Paul said, shrugging his shoulders.

I turned and looked at Adam. He raised his eyebrows and smiled.

'Not me dude,' he shrugged.

'Damn,' I said, heading for the office, 'she must be able to tell us something.'

'Hi,' I said, 'I'm with the guys outside. They were asking about some friends of ours. We thought they'd be here but there's no sign of them. Is there anything you can do to help us? It's really important.'

'Do you have the rego?' she asked.

'I honestly can't remember,' I replied. 'I think it might have been FRE or GRE or something.'

She ran her finger down through a list of numbers, flicked over the page, and done the same again.

'I'm really sorry,' she said apologetically, 'there's nothing here. Give me a minute . I'll ring Chris. He was working the afternoon shift yesterday and might be able to tell me if they were in. A yellow van, right?'

While she was on the phone, I leafed through a few pamphlets of things to do in the area. Sailing, scuba diving, snorkelling. I heard her explain our situation and ask about the yellow van. My eyes drifted over a large notice board on the wall. Not looking at anything in particular. Notes offering a lift further up the coast, some looking for

117

one. Some selling camping gear, tents and stoves. A small notice on the bottom of the board caught my eye.

It said:

- The Yellow Submarine. Need a lift. Wait for us here. –

There was only one yellow submarine that I knew of.

'Chris thinks a yellow van came through yesterday,' she said, finishing her call. 'It didn't stay. Maybe that was them?'

I took the note from the board and held it up to her smiling.

'Any luck?' they asked, as I came out.

'What do you make of this?' I said, showing it to them.

'That's gotta be them,' Paul replied. 'But why didn't they stay here like we planned? Something must have happened? What'll we do now?'

'We'll just have to wait,' I replied.

I turned to Adam.

'I'll hang around for a while and see what happens. I'd like to meet the other guys too,' he said.

We took our packs and some sandwiches we had bought earlier and sat on the grass to wait. I wondered how long it would be before they showed. Time passed and just when I began to wonder, we heard a loud car horn coming up the road. I looked up, relieved to see the van pulling in, the window rolled down. Dave and Kai jumped out and ran across to us. They didn't look happy.

'What the hell happened?' Dave asked.

'I'm sorry guys,' I replied, 'we got held up. I'll fill you in later. Where's Anuia? Why didn't you stay here last night?'

'Anuia's fine,' Kai shouted angrily, 'have you seen the news? Who's this?'

'Take it easy Kai,' I replied calmly. 'This is Adam. He's been helping us out. Are you all okay? Where did you stay?'

'We camped on a beach just north of town,' he said, calming himself. 'We thought it would be better to stay out of view for the night.'

'Tell him the rest Stefan,' Dave interjected, 'tell him what we know.'

'What?' I asked, 'what is it?'

'When you didn't show last night we rang the hostel in Glebe,' Kai now told us, almost apologetically. 'They know Anuia has been there and gone. A man was snooping around asking questions. Maja overheard a conversation in the common area. Before she could intervene, one of the girls who had shared with Anuia had already told him that she may have left with you.'

I realised that keeping our perspective and staying calm was everything now. We had to support each other.

'You did the right thing guys. Let's push on further north this evening and see how far we can get. We have the name of a journalist from The Melbourne Times. I spoke to him, explained our situation and told him we'd be in touch. He reckons he can help.'

While it is what we had expected, the game had now definitely changed. The chase was on.

'Thanks for the lift Adam,' I said, as I shook his hand, 'we appreciate what you and Lily have done for us. We'd better get going.'

'No worries mate,' he replied, 'stay safe.'

'I plan to,' I thought to myself.

It was time to put some distance between ourselves and our pursuers.

Chapter Twenty

We drove north to the beach where they had spent the night. It was just far enough out of town to be quiet. Anuia and Stefan were there waiting. When we got out of the van Anuia hugged Paul then turned and hugged me.

'It's so good to see you,' she said quietly, 'we didn't know what to think when you did not arrive last night. We thought.... I thought you were gone.'

'I'm sorry,' I replied, and I told her what had happened. 'But we're here now.'

'Did the guys tell you?' she asked.

'Yes,' I said.

We had to get going. It was already late evening but I still thought we could make Byron Bay, even if it meant driving on through the night. I had to ring Lee Taylor. Whatever help he was planning to give us, we needed it now.

'Lads,' I said, 'it's a couple of hundred kilometres to Byron. Let's get the stuff together.'

We were on the road again. I wondered how far we could make it. I had hoped Byron Bay but was it safe to drive so late into the night to get there. We were all pretty tired. I checked the road map. At least three hundred kilometres and way more than I had thought. I was far more anxious since seeing Anuia's face on TV. It would only take one person to recognise her and to go to the police. I'm sure she knew this herself. We had to keep moving and somehow keep her out of sight as much as possible.

'Guys,' I said, 'I want to make a quick stop in Grafton. It's about an hour away. I'm going to call Lee Taylor.'

'Can we trust him?' Stefan asked.

'That's what we have to decide Stefan,' I replied. 'He's our only option. Let's meet him and see what he has to say. We'll see how he can help and how he can use a story like this to help Anuia.'

'I've been thinking,' I continued, 'maybe we would be better staying in hostels for a while. The camp sites are too open, too many holiday makers. There are too many people out there who could recognise us.'

'But isn't it the same in the hostels?' Kai asked.

'No,' I replied, 'the hostels are full of people like us. Travellers, adventurers. People like Adam, Lily, Jeff and Maja. People like you, and me. None of them hesitated to help even when we told them the truth.'

'I agree,' Dave said, 'I think he's right.'

'What about the rest of you? What about you?' I asked, turning to Anuia.

She nodded. They all did. Dave looked at the book as we drove and I asked had he any ideas on where to stay in Byron.

'There's a place called the Arts Factory,' he said. 'It looks a bit alternative. More of a back to nature place about ten minutes walk outside town. It might be a good bet?'

We were coming into Grafton, everyone silent, wondering how Lee might help. We found a telephone box and I rang his number as the others huddled around.

'Lee Taylor speaking.' He answered in seconds.

'Hi Lee,' I said, 'this is Paul Hewson. I spoke to you this morning.'

'Paul, I've been waiting for your call. Where are you? We need to talk. I've spoken to my editor and he wants to run something on it right away. This could be huge.'

'Hang on Lee,' I said 'you don't have anything to run on it yet. I want to know how you can help Anuia first.'

'I know, I know,' he replied, 'but we've got a great story here.'

I repeated that I would only talk to him.

'Lee,' I said, 'if I see that anything has been written on this without our consent, the story's gone. You'll never hear from us again.'

'I understand Paul. When can we meet? I can be on a flight from Melbourne tonight.'

I told him where we were, and our plans to get to the Arts Factory in Byron Bay.

'Can you get there by morning?' I asked. 'We'll be waiting for you.'

'I'll do whatever it takes,' he replied.

'Anuia's my main concern Lee. If I see anyone else, we'll disappear.'

'How do you know her?' he asked. 'Why are you helping her?'

'She's my friend,' I replied.

'Would you trust a journalist?' I asked them, as I hung up.

'No,' Dave replied, 'I'd never trust a journalist looking for a big break.'

'Me neither,' I thought.

I made two more calls. One to the Arts Factory Lodge in Byron Bay to book a campsite for the night, and the second to the Glebe village in Sydney. Maja answered.

'Hi Maja,' I said, 'how are things going back there?'

'Hey,' she said, sounding delighted to hear my voice but then turning grave. 'I should be asking how you are. Stefan rang last night. He told me everything.'

'I know,' I replied. 'So they know where she's gone?'

'I think so. There was a man hanging around yesterday. One of the girls from Anuia's dorm spoke to him. She wasn't to know, but she said she left with you. Luckily, that's just about all she knew.'

But with what she told me next, any thought of respite was short lived.

'They came again last night,' she continued. 'I told them I didn't know who they were asking about but then things got nasty. They held me on the floor and went through our register. They know you all left on the same day. They said things, threatened me.....'

She went quiet.

124

'Maja, Maja,' I asked, alarmed. 'Are you okay?'

'Just some bruising,' she said quietly. 'I've never been so frightened. I didn't tell them anything.'

'Oh Maja,' I said, 'I'm so, so sorry. Look, we have to get going. I'll ring you again as soon as I can.'

'Please do,' she replied, 'let me know how you're getting on and when you get it sorted out, come back and see us. We miss you. I miss you…,' she added, almost as an afterthought.

'Thanks,' I said, wondering if I had heard right.

'What is it?' Paul asked, as I angrily slammed the phone back in the receiver.

'They were back. Maja was hurt. She's sure they've put us all together.'

As we drove on into the night I told the guys what we had learned back in Newcastle. We talked about Lee Taylor and how he might help. Then we became quieter, everyone exhausted by the events of the last two days. Paul had dozed off in the passenger seat beside me. I checked the rear-view mirror and the others slept silently. Anuia's head rested on Dave's shoulder, eyes closed, her worries momentarily forgotten. I leaned over and switched off the radio. 'Let them sleep,' I thought, glad to have some time to myself. I listened instead to the soothing, rhythmic hum of the engine. I rolled down the window for some fresh air and drove on, revitalized.

My eyes flew open. I had heard a loud thud. The van veered towards the wrong side of the road. Instinctively, I grabbed the wheel and spun it in the opposite direction. It was way too much. I slammed on the breaks. The van locked sideways, spinning out of control. I heard Anuia scream as I fought to bring the van to a halt, but it continued to spin. When we hit the ditch it stopped facing the wrong way, two long black tyre marks, illuminated by the headlights, measuring the distance we had travelled. There was something in the middle of the road.

'Are you all alright?' I yelled. 'Is everyone ok?'

'What happened?' Paul shouted.

'I hit something,' I replied, jumping from the van.

They followed as I ran back down the road. I stopped.

'It's a kangaroo,' I shouted, 'just a kangaroo. I thought I had hit someone.'

I dropped to my knees and put my head in my hands.

'It's okay,' Paul said. He put his arm around my shoulders. 'It's okay.'

I had killed it instantly. Blood gushed from a wound, one of its arms almost completely severed. Its head lay at an unnatural angle, its neck broken. Anuia was crying.

'Take her back to the van,' I said, as I got to my feet. 'We'd better get it off the road.'

'Do you remember what happened?' Paul asked, while we checked the van for damage.

The bull bar had taken most of the impact but our right indicator and parking lights were smashed.

'I fell asleep,' I replied. 'We'll have to stop.'

126

We took the next right hand turn for Evan's head and parked at a point jutting out into the sea. We set up the tents by the light of the headlights though, in reality, the night was as bright as I had ever seen. Struck by the beauty of the moment - the moonlight, the tranquillity, the sea - I stopped and stared, realising our crash could have ended so much worse. As I climbed into my sleeping bag, my last thought was of what tomorrow would bring, thankful that there would be a tomorrow.

Chapter Twenty-One

We were up early the next morning. Byron Bay was just up the road. I had heard so much about it in the hostels in Sydney. Pure white sandy beaches, blue skies, and a mecca for surfers and back packers from all over the world. The first really big party place on the map. Our less than auspicious arrival there meant partying was the last thing on our minds.

As we cooked and prepared what was ultimately going to be our last camping meal, or that was the plan, I wondered did it bother any of the other guys. Did they think they were missing out on something because of the circumstances we found ourselves in? Then again, we all had had the choice right from the beginning. We had accepted that this was the card fate had dealt us. This was the adventure we had chosen to have.

We joked light heartedly as we shared breakfast, trying to diffuse the gravity of the situation. Our mood was lifted as we contemplated what the day would bring, what help Lee Taylor would be able to give to us, and mostly the fact that there just might be a way out of this.

As we ate, I considered Lee. Could we trust him? I suppose the answer was why not. Could Anuia have known to trust me? Could I have known to trust all the people who had got involved and helped so far? Sure, he had a whole lot more to gain from this than I did. But his ambition might just prove to be Anuia's, and her family's escape from this nightmare. One of the first things I was going to ask him to do was to try and find out how her family were. Nothing was more important than this. It was the question Anuia asked herself over and over again. Every time we talked she wondered hopelessly how they might be.

And every time I told her not to worry, believing that they had to be in safe hands. Or wanting to believe it.

With breakfast finished we set about taking down the tents. It was only five o'clock in the morning, the sun still not up, the dusky blue on the distant horizon the only clue to the impending blue skies of another day in paradise. As waves crashed on the shoreline, we were greeted by a thunderous roar which slowly faded as each broke perfectly down the beach, only to be followed by another.

Leaving Evans Head, back to the Pacific highway again then turning north towards Ballina, we'd be in Byron Bay within the hour. We had lost valuable time, but we couldn't risk driving any further last night. I had hoped to see the lie of the land as it were, before Lee Taylor arrived. The worst thing was that we knew there were people on our trail but we didn't know how far they might have travelled by now.

What were they going to do? Go to every hostel between here and Sydney. It didn't seem possible but it did cross my mind that if our guess was correct and it did go as high as we thought, how far-reaching could it be? Was it, as they said, 'just like in the movies'? Criminals knew criminals and information could be got. If Anuia didn't exist, then their problem didn't exist. Anuias family would be sent back to Thailand. To nothing, in the knowledge that they would never see their daughter again and that everything had been in vain. This was what I couldn't allow myself to contemplate.

We had taken the coast road from Ballina, mile after mile of beautiful coastline, arriving In Byron around six thirty in the morning. Through the town towards Clarks Beach, then turning right onto Lighthouse Road towards Cape Byron. It was early but we had made the decision last night. To make up some lost ground and to get to Cape Byron before the sun rose.

As we neared the lighthouse the dusky grey sky exploded with a million golden rays of sunshine. The perfect time to be here. We weren't surprised that we weren't the first. People sat and huddled against the cool morning breeze coming off the sea. We joined them, each taking our place, huddling close together. For warmth, for friendship.

'There,' someone whispered, pointing just off the head. But we had all already seen. A school of dolphins broke the water not far out to sea. One, then two, then more surfacing in turn as they rounded the cape, speeding on their way, black shadows against the blue grey of the sea.

As we watched in silence I looked at my friends. Kai and Stefan, blonde woolly heads and ruffled beards. Dave, broad chinned and broad shouldered. And Paul, my confidant and my closest friend. It was him I spoke most to about what best to do. I would talk and suggest and he would guide me gently in the right direction. I looked at Anuia, her face lit up in the morning light, tears escaping down her cheeks. I put my arm around her and pulled her close and we sat like that until the dolphins were just a speck in the distance.

'Thank you,' she whispered, when it was time to go.

I was going to go back into town to find the Arts Factory. The rest of the guys were going to park up and wait. It didn't make sense for us all to turn up. We didn't know who might be waiting and we didn't want to give everything away to Lee Taylor. I would meet him first. Alone.

We drove back into town along Lawson Street. Kai pulled the van over into a parking spot facing the beach. I had the book with me opened to the page showing the small map of Byron Bay. I could walk from here to the town centre and back along Jonson Street to the train station. If I crossed the tracks there I would be heading straight for the Arts Factory.

'Guys,' I said as I turned to leave, 'I'll be back as soon as I can. Can you leave the van here even if you wander off? At least I'll know you're close by.'

'We'll be here,' Paul said, pointing to the van, or we'll be just down there.' He was looking at the beach.

'Dave,' I said, as I turned to walk away.

He looked at me, waiting on instructions or some words of wisdom.

'Try to look even a little bit inconspicuous, you big farmer. Go and buy a pair of board shorts or something.'

We all laughed. He had been wearing the same pair of Gealic shorts since I first met him. The Galway colours of course. Short like the stubbies worn by the Aussie rules players. He stared at me wide eyed and stuck his middle finger up as he started to laugh. I smiled to myself as I walked down the street.

Another beautiful day and a clear blue, cloudless sky overhead. The place was starting to come to life, shops and restaurants beginning to open. A few cars and vans passed heading back in the direction from which I had just came, loaded with surfboards and surfers looking for the first perfect waves of the day. I came to the roundabout in the centre of town. A sign pointed towards the railway station.

I passed a park on my right. A group of aboriginals sat drinking at the base of a big tree. Down and outs. Something I had seen before in Sydney and I wondered why it always seemed to be them. They looked at me and I looked back, one of them eventually raising his hand in salute.

'It's a smashing morning,' I shouted, returning the gesture.

'It sure is brother,' he replied, and I walked on.

I passed the railway station, crossing the dirt ground and the unfenced track to a street on the other side. There were already less houses and, after walking five minutes, only sparse properties with tin roof bungalows and wire fences. I could tell I was going in the right direction when I met a number of people walking back towards town. All dressed in colourful baggie sand pants, baja hoodies, tie-dyed tees, hemp bracelets, beads and the occasional CND necklace. I hoped I didn't stand out too much in my Kmart's best basketball shorts and Quiksilver tee. I did have my black and white stripped Guatemalan drawstring pouch slung over my shoulder, something I picked up on one of my Sunday morning trips to the Paddies market back in Sydney, but hippy I was not. Some spoke in hushed, apprehensive tones as they passed. I wondered was it because they could tell I wasn't 'one of them.' The thought passed when I saw the Arts Factory with its big bright multi-coloured sign in the distance. There were two police cars parked outside. I had a bad feeling.

My first thought was to stop and turn the other way but then I figured it's probably nothing. A minor disturbance like the bongos being played too loudly into the night. But what if it wasn't something small. What if it was something to do with Anuia. I steeled myself and walked on telling myself to stay confident and don't look suspicious. I needn't have bothered. The two policemen out front gave me nothing more than a cursory glance as I passed.

The reception area was bright and colourful. I smelt incense burning, and heard the sound of Buddhist music playing somewhere in the background. The book had said it was alternative, but it was more alternative than I expected. The door to the office behind the counter was open. I could see two more police officers inside, talking to some people.

An attractive, friendly dark haired girl behind the counter looked up and asked if she could help.

'Hi,' I said, unintentionally looking past her and through the open door to the office, 'what's going on? Why all the police?'

'Things are not good today,' she replied. 'We had some very unwelcome visitors late last night.'

'What happened?' I asked, thoughts already forming in my head. She told me a familiar story.

'Some Asian men arrived just after midnight and said they were looking for someone. A girl. Sky was working and told them that we don't give out any information on anyone who stays here. One of them pushed her into the office and held her there while the others went through our registration book. Not finding what they wanted, or expected, they proceeded to search all around the lodge.

'That's not good,' I said, 'what's it all about?'

'We're not sure,' she whispered. 'They went through all the dorms, switching on lights waking people and checking faces. It was very frightening. Sky called the police but as no-one was hurt or there was no serious damage, they said they'd come back this morning to go over what had happened.'

'That's kind of strange isn't it,' I ventured, seeing if there was any more information to be had. 'Is Sky ok? What's your name by the way,' I asked. 'I'm Paul, Paul Hewson.'

'Hi Paul, I'm Wildwind. What can I do for you?'

'I've just arrived on an overnight from Brisbane and hoping to stay in Byron for a few days. I'm meeting a friend here. I read about you in the Lonely Planet and thought it might be a fun place to stay. Can I be honest with you Wildwind?' I asked.

'Of course,' she said, 'I wouldn't have it any other way.'

'I'm not sure if this place isn't just a bit too alternative for me. I mean, I've never been into the hippy culture. I like Neil Young's music but I've never been into the sand pants and beads.'

I felt stupid as I said it, hoping I hadn't insulted her.

'That's quite a pouch you have over your shoulder,' she said, grinning. 'Maybe you're more 'one of us' than you think? You have to start somewhere.'

She wasn't offended, and as I watched her laugh, I didn't think there was anything that could. None of that self-righteousness I associated with some of the people I had met before. The type who just wanted to be hippy so they could run back home and tell their friends how alternative they had been while they were away.

'Why don't you have a look around?' she asked. 'You might actually like it here. There hasn't been anyone in this morning that I don't know, so I'd say your friend hasn't arrived yet. Where are they travelling from?'

'From Sydney,' I replied.

They weren't of course. It was Lee Taylor and he was travelling from Melbourne. I thought he'd be here by now.

'Have a look around anyway,' she offered, 'if you like it, I promise, it's a great place to stay. We have some interesting activities and pretty cool parties most nights. You might discover something about yourself that you don't know.'

'Wildwind is a beautiful name. Where does it come from?' I asked.

'I don't really know,' she replied, 'it's just a name I remember from my childhood but I don't know why exactly. I love how it sounds and because I've been here a while I got to choose one. I don't take it too seriously though. My name is Silvie, I'm from Germany.'

As I walked among the trees and bushes of the Arts factory, I thought about how these men could have caught up so fast. How did they even know we were here? Could they know we were here? I'd ask Wildwind if she had heard of any other disturbances in hostels in Byron overnight. I thought about Lee. He seemed like an okay guy – from what I could tell from speaking to him on the phone anyway. Could he have told? It didn't seem possible. He wanted this story.

I continued to explore, realising that not everyone here was as far out as I had thought. Some guys lounged by the pool in their board shorts and I passed a couple of girls in denim miniskirts heading out to the beach for the day. This mightn't be a bad place to lay low for a while should the need arise. They had already been here looking and I reasoned that it wouldn't make sense for them to return as the police were now involved.

I got back to reception just as the two cops were leaving and overheard the end of their conversation.

'If you hear anything, let us know. It's important that we find this person as soon as possible....'

Wildwind and two others who had been with the police in the office – I assumed one of them was Sky – nodded in agreement. Wildwind turned. She hadn't noticed when I came back in.

'Oh, I didn't see you there. Sky,' she said, introducing her friend, 'this is Paul. He's just arrived from Brisbane. Paul, this is Sky and this is Ziggy.'

My facial expression asked the question. Ziggy?

'Don't worry about it,' he laughed. 'We don't take it too seriously here but we invite everyone to come and share our home with us whenever they want. Have you had a look around?'

'Yes,' I said, 'I have. It's a pretty cool place. I don't know if I'll stay though. I'm supposed to be meeting someone here this morning so will see what happens after that. Is it okay if I hang out for a bit?'

It wasn't a problem of course and we talked for a while before Ziggy and Sky went off about their work. I liked them. They seemed pretty far out but didn't for a minute try to impose themselves on me, accepting me for whatever they thought I was.

'How long have you been here Wildwind?' I asked.

I couldn't help repeating her name over and over. It had such a lovely ring to it.

'About eight months,' she said. 'I love it here. It's so...peaceful.'

She stared out the window to the gardens, lost in a thought. The momentary pause before she said 'peaceful' suggested that thought was a million miles away from here. I wondered what her story was. Was it so different from my own? That part of me I had been so reluctant to talk about but which I knew I would eventually, when I was ready. She was beautiful in an unconventional way that I couldn't really describe. Very pretty as opposed to very beautiful, which I liked much more. Long dark hair tied back in a coloured band. Bright green eyes and smooth, sallow skin. She wore a black waistcoat over a white t-shirt and a long flowing skirt. I had learned to observe people much more since I came to Oz. In a way I had forgotten how to do back home. I saw people every day but how often did I actually look at them, to see them as more than just someone I worked with, or socialised with. Or grew up with.

It was quiet except for the hypnotic sound of the music, the sweet smell of incense lending itself to the peaceful, friendly ambiance. She was right. Something told me that I could learn something here, maybe even something about myself.

'Were there disturbances like this in any of the other hostels?' I asked.

'Yes,' she replied, 'the police said there was similar trouble at two other hostels in town overnight.'

'Do they have any idea of what it's about? Or who?'

She looked at me, weighing me up. Was I pushing too far? I think she decided I was someone she could trust.

'I'm not really supposed to say,' she began. 'The police are looking for someone. Possibly the same person that these men were searching for. They believe she may be travelling with some companions and that she is connected to some serious crimes in Melbourne.'

'But that could be anyone who comes through your door,' I said. 'Did they say what it was about?'

'No...,' she paused, 'no they didn't.'

'But?' I asked. There was something she wasn't telling me.

'Okay,' she said, 'this might sound a little bit silly, but a rumour has begun amongst backpackers that there is a girl travelling the east coast who may be connected with two murders. A couple of guys arrived two days ago going north and they had heard it in Port Macquarie.'

'That's interesting,' I said, 'but there is always some story going around the back pack community about one thing or another.'

'I know,' she said, 'but, not that I have a lot of interest in what's happening in the news, the big story at the moment is about a girl who is wanted for questioning about a double murder in Melbourne. So maybe there's some truth in it.'

'I guess,' I said. 'I mean, if the police are looking for someone there must be something in it. But who were these guys who showed up here last night?'

'That's the million dollar question,' she replied with a smile.

I heard a car pull up outside and looked to see a Honda Civic in the car park. New enough to be a hire car I thought. Wildwind and I watched a tall dark haired man get out. He wore a bright grey suit and a white shirt opened at the collar. The dark tie hanging loosely around his neck gave the impression of someone who had travelled overnight. Putting his sun glasses on, he turned and opened the back door of his car. He leaned in, retrieving a notepad and laptop case.

'That's my guy,' I said, turning to Wildwind. 'His name's Lee and I've been trying to meet him for a while.'

To tell a lie, even a small lie, to someone you know and who has placed their trust in you is a hard thing to do. We had only just met but I thought we had made some kind of connection. I knew she had a story to tell and she in turn, knew I had one too. She had confided in me without revealing anything at all. But none of what she had learned about me was true and it hurt.

'Wildwind,' she turned to face me, 'thanks for your help. I hope that I can see you sometime again soon. I like it here. I have some other friends arriving and depending on them, maybe we can come back and stay for a few nights?'

I held out my hand but she moved closer and hugged me.

'Come back and see us soon Paul Hewson,' she said, as I turned to leave. 'We have a lot to talk about.'

'Thanks,' I replied, as I walked out the door.

'One thing,' she said.

I stopped and turned.

'Paul Hewson is a singer isn't he?'

'Yes,' I replied.

'Paul, friends are always welcome here. I hope I see you again.'

I hurried towards the man in the grey suit, hoping to keep him as far away from Wildwind as possible. I didn't want her to hear anything.

'Lee?' I asked.

'Paul? Paul Hewson?' he replied.

'It's good to meet you Lee,' I said, holding out my hand.

He shook it vigorously.

'It's good to meet you mate,' he said. 'You're on your own?' He looked around, not expecting that I would be. 'Where's Anuia? I'd like to talk to her.'

There was no doubting his priorities.

'Look Lee, we thought it better that I should meet you alone first. I'm sure you can understand that?'

'Yeah sure Paul,' he replied. 'What's your real name by the way?'

'Does it matter Lee?' I asked, 'I'm not really going to be your story at the end of the day. Paul is fine for now.'

'Not a problem mate,' he said. 'I stopped off in the town to grab a coffee. I was on a red eye from Melbourne and left Brisbane as soon as I hired a car. I hear there were some disturbances in some of the hostels?'

'There were,' I replied, 'if you had been here about an hour ago there were a couple of police cars knocking about. Some men came through last night and ransacked the place. They were looking for someone and I'm sure it's safe to assume that someone is Anuia. I didn't expect them to catch up so soon. We had hoped to stay here for a day or two but it seems that plan is gone out the window.'

'Paul,' he said, suddenly serious, 'we need to talk. Let's go back into town and find a restaurant. I'm starving.'

As we walked towards his car, I noticed Wildwind, still standing in the doorway watching. She raised a hand to say goodbye, then went back inside.

We drove to the first café we could find and I ordered cereal, toast, juice and a cup of tea. When the waiter had gone, Lee got straight down to business. I had some important questions I needed to ask first.

'Lee,' I said, 'before we go anywhere with this there's a few things I need to ask you. Questions Anuia needs answered. You should also know that Anuia and the other people travelling with us are not in Byron Bay. They left as soon as we heard what had happened here overnight.'

I was lying of course.

'Oh,' he replied, unable to hide his disappointment. 'I had been hoping to talk to her, to get her side of the story and to start building a profile. If I'm going to write this, I need to know about her and how all this came about. We know we're onto something big here. We've a whole team waiting.'

'I understand that,' I said, 'and that's exactly why we've asked you to be involved. We need to get this story out there. Make it impossible for her to be touched, particularly by the police or whoever is behind all this.'

'That doesn't help with the bad guys though,' he said, 'assuming there are bad guys, and assuming that there are people chasing you.'

'We'll get to that,' I said, annoyed at the suggestion. 'First I want to know about Anuias family. Her real family who were smuggled into Australia. Where are they now? Are they safe? I'm assuming you've already looked into this?'

We were playing a small game of cat and mouse. I wasn't his story and he knew it, but he had to humour me. I on the other hand, still didn't know if I could trust him or not.

'They're being kept at the Maribyrnong immigration detention centre in Melbourne,' he said, without hesitation.

He had done his homework.

'They're being well looked after,' he continued. 'A colleague of mine has been out there and I spoke to him this morning. Officials at the detention centre say they are frightened and won't speak to anyone. They'll stay there for as long as this goes on. They're probably in the safest place they can be right now.'

Anuia and I had spoken about this at length and had expected as much. But it was good to hear. The safety of her family was her greatest concern.

'What about her uncle and his family?' I asked.

'From what I can gather they are okay,' he said. 'This story has been getting some high exposure over the past few months. It's picked up momentum again over the last few days. Since the police have gone public in trying to trace her. Her uncle is refusing to say anything. I spoke to a contact after we talked yesterday morning. They've no doubt that they have been threatened. Many believed Anuia to be his daughter. There's a lot of public support to be had here but, it's fair to say, there are a lot who wouldn't be on their side. We're fairly divided on the immigration thing at the moment.'

'I know,' I said, thinking back to the brief conversation I had with the librarian in Port Macquarie.

'I've been writing about it for a couple of years now,' he continued.

'I know that,' I answered, 'I've done a bit of homework too. It's the main reason we chose you. Have you any ideas on who might be involved in this? I mean, someone has to be running this on the Australian side. It's big business and would need a big business behind it, someone with a lot of clout. It would make sense to have the police involved. Have them on your side, as opposed to against you.'

'That's a fairly big accusation you're making,' he said. 'If I write about this, I'll need some pretty substantial evidence. It'll be hard to build public belief if I just start throwing stuff out there. You mentioned it briefly when we talked first. Why do you think this involves the police? Where's the proof?'

I went over all that Anuia had told me. Every little detail that I could remember, the meetings, the arrangements, everything right up to the shootings. Then I told him where I came into the story.

'Why you?' Lee asked.

But I guess I didn't really know. I just happened to be the right person in the right place at the right time, or the right person in the wrong place. Anuia had picked me. Why she had was a question I still pondered and hoped to ask her soon.

'I don't know,' I said, and it was true. 'What's your interest in this story? You seem to have covered it a lot over the last few years.'

143

'It's a hot topic among Australians and something that we are very divided on, but the bottom line is that it sells newspapers.'

He was honest, and for that reason alone, I decided to trust him.

'Do you have any ideas on who's involved?' I asked.

'There are a lot of ideas on who might be involved in these people trafficking gangs,' he replied. 'Some are known by the police, the majority aren't. It's like every crime. We hear about arrests made in connection with drugs for example, but it's the tip of the iceberg. For every one that gets caught, a hundred don't. It's the same here. Immigration is big business. There are just too many bad guys out there willing to exploit poorer people from their own countries. It's interesting that Anuia believes this person is Australian though. Who it could be? I don't know yet, but I'm working on it. I'll be based in Brisbane while this story unfolds. I have resources available to me in Melbourne who are going to work on the story on that side. I need to meet Anuia as soon as possible.'

'Like I said, they're already gone further north. To Brisbane in fact. I'm going to follow and meet up with them. If not today, then tomorrow. I'll contact you when I get there.'

He looked sceptical, handing me a business card with his office number.

'What kind of story are you going to write on this?' I asked.

'Good question,' he replied. 'Anuia's face has hit the front pages. The perception will be that Anuia is involved in this on the wrong side. We need to get a story out there that says Anuia is innocent, her only crime being the welfare of her own family and wanting what's best for them. Let people know that they are the victims. That all immigrants entering the country illegally are only trying to do what's best for their families and are being exploited by these gangs. We need to get public opinion on our side. Let them know that Anuias family has nothing to go back to. This will help when this whole thing unravels. But I need to talk to her. Learn more about her. Get some pictures of her. I want to run this as a story until we can figure out a way to make her safe.'

'Why have the police only released her photograph now?' I asked.

'I think that they held back on it because whoever is involved in this was trying to get this mess cleared up before they had to,' he replied. 'With Anuia out of the way, they could send her family back to Thailand. Who would ever make the connection? But it hasn't worked out for them. If there's a bad police element involved, they could only keep it under wraps for so long. It would have to go public eventually and in a way, this would suit the bad guys. They haven't been able to trace her. As long as she's out there, she's a threat. They're hoping that someone somewhere will see her. Once they bring her in, they can work on getting to her. They'll just pick their time.'

'Until she knows who she can trust,' I said, 'it's better she stays on the run. For her own safety and the safety of her family.'

'Yes,' he agreed. 'It's my job to find out who these people are. How high up it goes, and what we need to do to bring them down. It's your job to keep Anuia safe until I do.'

'I can organise to have Anuia stay somewhere in Brisbane,' he continued, 'put you up in a hotel while we work this out. No-one except us need know. Surely it's better than running all the time?'

'I don't think so,' I replied, 'we've been finding help in the most unexpected places. With people like us. People we can trust.'

'What is your name anyway?' he asked again. 'Paul Hewson is a compatriot of yours. I checked but I should have known.'

'Do you know what?' I replied, 'it's not really important right now. I'm only starting to figure out who I am myself.'

I'm not sure if he understood though it didn't matter to me if he did or not. I'd tell him when I was ready. When, I believed, I had the answer myself.

'I'll ring you tomorrow,' I said, 'as soon as I get to Brisbane. Anuia will be anxious to meet you too.'

'Do,' he replied. 'We'll want to run this as an exclusive as soon as we can. I'll be quoting you on some of what we've discussed.'

I assured him I would and he shook my hand as we parted ways. I watched as he walked back down the street to his car, and then as he pulled out into the traffic and disappeared into the distance. When I was sure he was gone, I turned back towards the beach. I crossed the road, passing Beach Hotel on my right. I heard someone say that it belonged to Paul Hogan. Or Crocodile Dundee as he was better known. Flicking off my sandals, I walked barefoot towards the lighthouse end of the main beach. The sand, already hot from the morning sun, felt soft and clean underfoot. I made slow progress. I had so much to think about. Not just about Anuia, or our predicament. I had a lot of questions I was starting to ask about myself and I wasn't sure what the answers would be. I'm not even sure I needed answers. I was just somehow glad that I had started to ask the questions. I wanted to figure out what had gone so wrong in my life. Instead of looking for someone else or something else to blame I was starting to realise that

146

the only person I had to blame was me. The only thing that had been wrong was inside my head. And that the only person who could make it right was myself.

Chapter Twenty-Two

I found them sitting on the beach. I had seen the van, still parked up where I had left them.

'Hey dude. Good to see you back. How did you get on? Did you meet him?' Stefan asked.

'I got a free breakfast anyway,' I said smiling, as the others turned towards me.

'Can he help us?' Anuia asked.

It wasn't the question I knew she wanted to ask. She needed answers to the things we had talked about before.

'Firstly,' I said, 'your family are safe and being well looked after. Your uncle's family are safe too. Lee Taylor has had people look into both back in Melbourne. Your own family are being kept at the immigration detention centre there and he believes that's the safest place they can be for the moment. It's like we had talked about. They'll be staying there for as long as this goes on. They're witness to everything that happened although they are not saying anything. But they are frightened.'

Anuia started to cry and, even though I knew they were tears of happiness, my heart was breaking for her. I wanted to hold her and tell her everything was okay, but Dave, sitting closest to her, put his arm around her and held her until she stopped.

'He wants to meet you Anuia,' I said.

'What's he like?' she asked, 'do you think he can help? What do you think of him yourself?'

It was a funny question but indicative of the trust we had built up between us. What I thought of him was important to her and she trusted my judgement.

'Well,' I began, 'he seems okay. I think he can help us and we've talked about how he can do this. Can we trust him? I believe so. Do I like him? To be honest, no. He knows what he wants and he knows how to get it. He's ambitious and interested in his career above all else. This could be the biggest story he's ever likely to get close to and he knows it. He seems to have good backing from his bosses which is important. Do I believe he can help us out of this? Yes. Yes I do, and that's what matters.'

'He thinks you guys are half way to Brisbane now though,' I said smiling.

'Why's that then?' Paul asked.

He'd been quiet so far. But that was Paul. He listened and digested everything that I had to say.

'I have some not so good news,' I said, my smile disappearing.

I told them what had happened in the Arts Factory overnight.

'Wow,' he replied. 'I didn't think they'd be catching up with us so soon. How could they have known we've even come this far?'

'I'm not really sure Paul though I may have an idea. I met a girl called Wildwind. She works there and I got talking to her while I was waiting on Lee to show up.'

'Wildwind?' Dave asked.

'I know how it sounds. Look, it's a pretty far out place. Lots of incense and bongos. But Wildwind and her friends are pretty cool. Sky and Ziggy. They don't take the hippy names too seriously but they believe in who they are. You'd like them.'

'I look forward to meeting them so,' Dave replied, 'I think.'

'What about Wildwind though,' Stefan asked, 'you were saying?'

'Oh yeah,' here's the thing. 'There's a rumour going around the back pack route on the east coast about someone that's wanted by the police in connection with a double murder in Melbourne. They say they are travelling with some companions as backpackers. Wildwind said that a couple of other hostels here in Byron got the same treatment last night. It seems to me that they're asking questions and making their way north.

'I think we can use this. Maybe we could get in touch with Adam in Newcastle or Maja back in Sydney. Let them know how things are developing and ask them to start using this rumour, hopefully to our advantage. Put the word out that we've been there and are heading south or north or whatever the case may be. You know how rumours spread. We can confuse the situation as much as possible. In the meantime we can work with Lee and get Anuia's story out there. This could give us time to figure out who's involved in this and who the enemy are.'

It was more of a question that I posed, guessing all the time but wanting to believe what I was saying, trying to make the others believe it to.

'Paul. What do you think?' I asked, as I valued his opinion the most.

'Sure isn't it something we Irish are good at,' he answered, smiling. 'I mean, we all know a friend of a friend who has heard something or other.'

'I think we should stay here for a day or two,' I said. 'The bad guys are working their way north. I don't think they'll be worried about here for the moment. They've checked and didn't find anything and the local police are now involved. We can start working on our rumour. If we stay in a hostel here tonight we can see who leaves, going north or south, and start dropping the story into conversation. Give it a week and we'll be spotted all the way from Melbourne to Darwin.'

'Where will we stay tonight?' Paul asked, smirking.

We agreed we'd stay at the Arts Factory, again reasoning that these men wouldn't be back. It was our original plan anyway. I can't say I wasn't pleased and I had a slightly ulterior motive. I wanted to see Wildwind again. Our first meeting had been brief but I felt there was some small connection I needed to explore.

We stayed at the beach for a few hours. We swam, we talked, and we laughed when we could. Later in the afternoon Dave and Kai walked back into town to buy food which we ate as the heat of the day started to cool, the beach started to slowly empty, and another day moved towards its end. A day with true friends, soon to be just another memory. These were the days we should have been spending together but I wondered if, under different circumstances, we could ever have met. I liked to believe we would. I wanted to believe that life sometimes did have a design for us, that not everything was purely by chance. Was our path chosen for us or did we choose our own. Did it matter?

We drove back to the Arts Factory later that evening. Sky was working reception and I introduced her to everyone. Seeing her warm, friendly smile, Dave's scepticism soon disappeared. While we had planned not to camp anymore, the Factory had tent sites strategically placed in the shade of tall trees so we decided to pitch the tents one more time.

When they were up, everyone taking their place around the camp light, I slipped away to make some calls. It was just after nine at night and I guessed it would be somewhere around lunchtime at home in Dublin. I had a strange feeling, as if I was going to talk to my folks for the first time in years. And I suppose in some way, it was the truth. I was nervous as I picked up the phone and dialled their number. While I waited for it to connect and ring, I worried about what exactly I should say. Hearing the familiar, reassuring voice of my mother, I knew I needn't have.

'Hi Mum, it's me,' I said, somewhat apprehensively. 'I've missed you.'

She knew what I meant. She understood I wasn't just talking about the time I had been away, but talking about the last few years and how we had grown gradually apart.

'It's so good to hear from you,' she replied, 'we've missed you too. How are you getting on over there?'

I talked to her for a while. And then to Dad. I told them where I was, the places we were getting to see, and for some reason, the trouble we had found ourselves in. Why, I wasn't really sure. The last thing I wanted to do was worry them but it seemed, somehow, right.

'I'll ring again soon,' I promised, as I hung up.

Then I rang Lee. He was waiting impatiently for my call and wasn't too pleased when I told him about another change in our plans.

152

It was for reasons outside our control, I assured him, but Anuia was looking forward to talking to him. I told him how pleased she had been to hear of her family and how grateful she was. He finished pleading that I would ring him again the next day.

I rang the backpackers in Newcastle and then I rang Maja in Glebe. It was good to hear her voice. While we exchanged the usual chitchat, she sensed something different in my voice.

'Are you ok?' she asked, 'is there something wrong?'

'No, nothing's wrong,' I answered, 'it's just..... it's just good to hear a friendly voice.'

It wasn't really what I had planned to say to her but I hoped in some way she might understand.

With all my calls made, I wandered aimlessly about the hostel gardens, hoping that I would bump into Wildwind. I found her sitting on a lounger beside the pool, reading a book under the dim light of a post lantern.

'Hi,' I said, and she looked up.

'Hi Paul Hewson,' she replied, but without surprise in her voice. 'I had hoped to see you again.'

'My name's not Paul,' I said, then I told her what it really was.

Did I ever have romantic feelings for Wildwind? Although romantic is probably not the right word. Did I fancy her, have a crush on her? I was attracted to her. There's no doubt about that. She had so many qualities that made her appealing. Her eyes, her hair, her beautiful smile. How she was with people around her and how she was with me.

'Have a seat,' she offered, so I pulled up a lounger, aware of how comfortable I was in her company, and we talked.

She told me about herself. How she had grown up in Hamburg but had never really come to terms with the life her parents had planned for her.

'I had everything I ever wanted,' she said, 'but there was just so much more I needed to do with my life.'

'How long have you been travelling?' I asked.

'Eighteen months altogether,' she said. 'I spent a lot of time in Thailand, Vietnam, Camobodia and Laos. I worked in Sydney for a while when I arrived in Australia first and I've been here for six months.'

As we talked, I couldn't help admire her independence. I longed to visit the places she had been as she described the likes of Hoi An in central Vietnam. I wanted to experience these places, their beauty, and their people. She appeared so strong, so complete. So at peace with herself.

'Have you found the answers you were looking for?' I asked, but she didn't answer.

'Tell me about you,' she said instead.

The hostel had come to life. There was a bonfire organised on the beach and everyone prepared to go. The rest of the guys had found us, still sitting at the pool talking. When I introduced Anuia, Wildwind turned to me with an inquisitive look. Or a realisation.

Once we were all ready, the crowd started towards the beach. It was dark and warm. There was laughter and excitement. Groups

154

walked and talked together but Wildwind and I, walking slower than everyone else, lagged behind.

'So, are you going to tell me about yourself?' she asked when we were alone. 'I can't help thinking that you've come here looking for something too.'

I thought about it again. I was afraid that she wouldn't find my story very interesting. After all, what had I achieved that would rival her own experience? She prodded me with her elbow and smiled.

'Where do I start?' I asked.

In many ways our stories were very similar. I had a great family life, never wanting for anything. Education and opportunity presented themselves but I just wasn't willing to make the effort. I had a job, worked hard, and had great friends. What I didn't have was direction. I didn't know where I was going or what I wanted to be. That's when I started searching. For what though, I wasn't sure. The more I searched, the more I receded into myself. I was angry, moody, introverted. I alienated myself from the people closest to me, relying instead on people I didn't know, who would never understand, or care, about who I was.

'What happened?' Wildwind asked.

I thought back to my last birthday. Mum and Dad had organised a surprise party in the local pub and invited all the people they thought I would like to be there.

'I saw my best friend standing inside the door,' I said, 'but he opened it and left. I followed him outside to ask where he was going.'

'I don't belong here,' he replied, 'I don't know these people.'

'But you're my best friend,' I told him.

'I just don't know you anymore,' he replied, and walked away.

It summed up everything my life had become.

'That's when I knew I had to go,' I said, 'if I was ever going to find my place in the world, I had to find out who I was myself.'

'It's not wrong to look for something different,' she offered. 'To look for something in life means that we haven't given up, that we understand that life has endless possibilities waiting to be explored. It shows spirit and belief that so few people discover. On the other hand,' she said, 'to really achieve something you have to accept who you are. Not try to be someone else.'

'So, are you going to tell me the rest?' she asked, 'I have a feeling that there's more to this story.'

'Have you ever been in love?' I stuttered.

'Yes,' she answered, taking my hand, 'yes, I do think that I have been in love. But that was some time ago.'

I was moving into territory that I wasn't comfortable with, painful territory. I was never good at talking about my innermost feelings even at the best of times. Does a person talk when they are eventually ready I thought? Do they talk when the time and place are right? Or do they talk when they meet the right person to talk to? Maybe it's all of these things. So I stumbled on.

'Is that why you're here?' I asked.

'Yes and no,' she replied. 'To be honest I think I would have made my way here anyway. It's a path I chose. I met someone while I lived in Stuttgart. For the briefest moment in time I believed that I had met my soul mate but, for one reason or another, it wasn't to be.'

The funny thing about her answer was that I didn't detect any profound sense of loss on her part. Nothing like what I had felt myself.

'What about you?' she asked.

'I'm not so sure,' I said. 'I met someone I thought I could share my life with. I thought that I had found all the answers I was looking for. For the briefest moment in time, I wasn't searching, everything in my life felt complete. I tried with all my heart but it really isn't possible to make someone love you the same way. The harder I struggled, the more I pushed her away, and in the end I lost her and felt that I lost everything good left in life. Then I started searching again. And I guess that's why I'm here.'

'I think you would have made it here anyway. Maybe not right now, but certainly sometime. Life, and how it turns out, directs you. Sometimes we just can't avoid it. Tell me about Anuia,' she then said, 'I think I know who she is.'

The night was warm and calm and, as we walked on the beach, I told the story again. The sound of the small waves breaking on the shore was hypnotic. In the distance we could see the light of the small bonfire and hear the muffled sounds of talk and laughter. I told her everything, right from the start. She didn't speak until I had finished.

'What if you had never started searching for answers?' she asked. 'What story would Anuia be telling now? What if you had never came along? I don't believe she chose you purely by chance. She must have seen something in you. Something good. I can see it too.'

'You didn't answer when I asked you earlier, have you found the answers you were looking for?' I asked.

'I think I have,' she replied, 'I have found so many answers, but, more importantly, I have found so many more questions. I was just looking in the wrong places. When I realised this, I realised that for some people this is what life is all about. Always searching, always looking.'

We passed back and forth along the beach, sometimes talking and sometimes in silence. She would stop and pick shells from the sand. I threw pebbles into the water. When it cooled, I put my arm around her shoulders, pulling her close, wishing it was another time and another place.

'I'm happy now,' she said after a while, but I could tell. 'I'll go home soon. Back to the places I love, back to the people I love. I'm ready to face the next part of my life, the next part of the journey.'

For the briefest moment I wondered what it would be like to be part of that journey. To be part of this beautiful person's life. To see how it unfolded. The happiness, the sadness, as sadness is inevitably part of everyone's life. But I knew that could never happen. I had my own journey to go on, my own answers to find. And I had something new. She had given me the optimism and belief that I could find what I was looking for.

She stopped, turning to face me. A loose strand of hair blew over her face and I brushed it away, the back of my hand gliding over her soft, smooth skin. I lifted her chin and stared down into those beautiful, bright green eyes, filled with the happiness I longed for. I felt the warmth of her breath as our lips touched.

Suddenly her eyes opened wide and she looked at me, alarmed. I heard shouts in the distance.

'Wildwind, Wildwind,' Ziggy yelled, running down the beach. Paul was with him.

'What is it?' Wildwind asked, 'what's happened?'

'They're back,' he cried, 'the men who wrecked the place are back. One of the guys noticed a car parked down the road from the Factory. Sky and I went to check it out. She's certain it's them. They're definitely watching.'

'Does Ziggy know?' I asked Paul.

'Yes,' he replied, 'I've told him everything.'

'Wildwind knows too,' I said, as her hand slipped from mine.

The moment was gone forever.

The music stopped when we ran back up the beach, everyone sensing there was something wrong. People gathered around Wildwind as she told them what was happening. We found Anuia, Dave, Kai and Stefan.

'Paul and I are going to go back to the hostel, grab everything we can and load it into the van,' I said, 'can one of you come with us?'

'I will,' Stefan offered.

'Good,' I replied. 'Dave, Kai, you stay with Anuia. Make your way to the Beach House and we'll pick you up there as soon as we can. Stay out of sight.'

'Not a problem,' Dave answered. 'Be careful.'

159

We ran to the railway station, slowing as we crossed the tracks. Ziggy lead us to a different, less used entrance. I could see the car parked near the main entrance. They were waiting, watching, as if they expected us to be there.

'Leave the tents,' I said, as we packed sleeping bags and cooking gear into whatever bag we put our hands on first. 'Just take what we need.'

'Wait for a minute,' Ziggy suggested, when we were ready to go. 'The crowd from the beach will be back soon. Wait and go as they arrive. It might just confuse things a bit.'

'Good thinking Ziggy,' I replied.

It was one o'clock in the morning. I told him about spreading the rumour, to let everyone know that we had been there and were going south. I wasn't sure how much it could help. They seemed to be a step ahead of us. I had thought that, considering what had happened the night before, we had some time on our hands but I was wrong. Soon the group started returning. I looked for Wildwind among them. I had to see her one last time before I left. To thank her. To say goodbye.

'We've got go,' I said, when I found her.

'I know,' she replied smiling, 'we've all got to go sometime. It's been an interesting experience. I'm glad we met.'

'Do you think we'll ever meet again?' I asked, as Paul called from the van.

Before she could answer, I leaned in and kissed her.

'Wildwind,' I said, 'I love that name. It seems somehow that we were meant to meet. I hope things work out for you when you go home. I know they will.'

She put her arms around me. I put mine around her, held her close and we hugged.

'Goodbye,' she whispered.

As I walked away, I knew I hadn't lost out on anything. I had gained so much from our brief encounter. I got in the van and we drove away.

Chapter Twenty-Three

There were four of them, silhouetted by the light of a street lamppost. My heart raced, willing the van forward, time decelerating as we inched past. Every part of me screamed 'don't look, don't look' but as we came level with them, my head turned.

They sat, nerveless, staring straight ahead, eyes fixed on the hostel, seemingly unconcerned with the sudden burst of activity. Grim, determined, professional. They had done this before.

Another second I thought, and we'll be in the clear, but before that thought had subsided, instinctively, inexplicably, the one closest to me turned. He stared as I stared back.

Paul drove slowly until we turned back onto Butler Street, then hit the gas. Anuia and the two lads were waiting for us. They jumped in and we raced out of Byron Bay, north towards the Pacific Highway, knowing that this time the bad guys wouldn't be too far behind.

I watched through the back window, my pulse racing, for any sign of a car following. There wasn't when we turned back onto the highway, but soon headlights appeared in the distance.

'Damn,' I cried, 'they're after us.'

'I'm going as fast as I can,' Paul shouted, but bit by bit, it was gaining ground.

After a long stretch of road, we would lose sight of it but then, hitting a long straight part again, we would see the car coming back into view, still some way back, but closing.

'What will we do,' Anuia cried repeatedly, her eyes wide with terror, hands fixed solidly to the seat in front.

162

'Paul,' I yelled, 'the next chance you get, kill the lights and make a turn. Wait until we take a good bend so that they don't see us.'

'Gotcha,' he replied, 'bloody cops and robbers. I used to love that when I was a kid.'

We came to a long bend that dipped on the other side, the headlights behind disappearing from view.

'There,' Dave gasped, pointing to a right turn just ahead.

Paul slammed on the brakes, killing the lights as he made the turn, tyres screeching. We drove about two hundred meters by the light of the moon and stopped. The highway was barely visible, lined with old, dried trees that gave some cover. Less than a minute later it sped past, lighting the motorway momentarily, much closer than I had thought. We sat in silence, afraid to move, until we were sure they had gone.

'Do you think that was them?' I whispered, my heart still pounding.

'I think so,' Kai replied, 'it looked like the same car.'

'What now?' Dave asked, 'we can't go back on the highway.'

'Let's figure out where we are,' I said, looking for the roadmap on the floor. 'Let's see where this road goes. Are you okay Anuia?'

She held her head in her hands, rocking slowly back and forth, crying. Dave put his arms around her.

'It's okay,' he repeated over and over, as we sat motionless. 'It'll be ok.'

I checked the road map, trying to figure out just how far we had come. We passed the turn for Brunswick Heads a while back. That much I did know. How long since then before we had stopped? Fifteen or twenty minutes, though it seemed longer while the car was chasing. I guessed we were about twenty kilometres past the Brunswick turn. Heading towards Tweed Heads.

'Guys,' I said, 'according to the map, if we continue on down this road it will take us back to the coast somewhere around Pottsville or Hastings Point. We'd come back to the highway just south of Tweed Heads. What do you think?'

We sat and waited a while longer, still in shock, before Paul started the engine and drove off, as slowly and carefully as he could. We turned left at the ocean. Only then did he put the headlights back on. We passed through Kingscliff and re-joined the highway, constantly checking for cars in front or behind. Not knowing if they could be lying in wait. They'd know by now that they had been tricked. We had fifteen kilometres to go before we could get off the main road again. If we made it to the turn for the coast road it would give us some breathing space. Unless the bad guys had gone that way, but I figured they might have realised they missed us before now and doubled back.

We arrived in Surfers Paradise at half four. I had a call to make. Though it was the middle of the night, I didn't think Lee would care too much. We had to meet, and we had to meet now. We stopped at the first phone box we saw. Our stay in Surfers would be brief.

The phone rang and Lee answered drowsily.

'Lee,' I said, 'it's me. We've had some trouble. Can we meet?'

'Absolutely,' he replied, as he found his bearings. 'Where, when?'

164

'We'll be in Brisbane first thing in the morning. Where are you staying?'

He gave me a name.

'We should be there early,' I said. 'I'll ring you as soon as we arrive.'

When I hung up, I thought for a minute then rang home.

We had to get to Brisbane, take our chances, and there was only one way. Follow the Gold Coast highway for as long as possible and rejoin the Pacific. It was a risk but once we got into the greater Brisbane area we would have a choice of routes other than the main road. The first chance I got, and when Anuia was on her own, Dave having taken the passenger seat since Surfers, I moved over beside her.

'How are you doing?' I asked.

'I'm okay,' she replied, '…I think. It's all a bit unexpected. I mean, I knew it would come down to this, but I wasn't prepared for it. Dave has been great.'

I had noticed, but I hadn't really twigged it until now. They seemed to have spent a lot of time in each other's company over the last few days. I thought back to yesterday at the beach. How Dave had comforted her and been so close to her, helping, encouraging. I smiled.

'What?' she asked shyly.

'You like Dave, don't you?' I replied.

'Yes,' she answered, 'I do. We've become close over the last few days. I hope you don't mind.'

'Mind?' I asked. 'Of course not. Why would I possibly mind?'

I knew what she was getting at.

'Well,' she said, 'I always thought that when it came down to it, it would be you and I who would be closest among the group. I thought that when you chose the time to talk, it would be to me that you told your story. I hoped it would. But I saw the connection you made with Wildwind. I think in another life you would have suited each other, that you could have been something special. But, while you're off trying to save my life, Dave has been so much help to me.'

'Anuia,' I said, 'thank you. I'm sorry I haven't been here enough for you. What you said about Wildwind - I think we were destined to meet though destiny is not something I would choose to believe in, but I think maybe I do now. Would we have been something? I'm not so sure. Talking to her has helped me so much. I'm starting to understand myself more, bit by bit.'

'I'm glad,' she said, hugging me and smiling.

As we continued towards Brisbane we talked. More than we ever really had before. She told me about herself, her dreams and ambitions. I told her about me, the happiness and the sadness in my life. All the things I couldn't explain up until now. And it seemed so easy to talk to her, something that had been so difficult to do before.

'Anuia,' I asked, 'In Sydney, in Kings Cross, why did you pick me? Why did you think I could help you?'

She paused.

'I think I just saw something in you that I thought I could trust,' she replied.

Those simple words meant the world to me. I had lost the ability to see this in myself, no longer believing or understanding who I was.

'I heard you talking about moving to the hostel in Glebe,' she continued shyly, 'so I just kind of waited around until you were going. Not really coincidence. I hope you don't mind. I should have given you the choice before mixing you up in all this. Perhaps if I had told you about it from the start you might not have helped me. I think you would have all the same. I think you see other people as more important than yourself. It's a beautiful part of you, but I think you should realise how important you are to yourself sometimes.'

I thought about how to reply to what she had said but didn't get a chance.

'Welcome to Brisbane guys,' Paul said from the front. 'Where to boss?' he asked, mimicking the Irish traveller accent.

'The city centre boss,' I replied, in a vain attempt to copy him.

Chapter Twenty-Four

We were all nervous, thinking of the chase overnight, thinking that maybe these guys were just waiting for us, guessing that we would continue on to the cover that only a big city could provide.

The Pacific Highway runs all the way into Brisbane city centre, becoming the South East Freeway at some point crossing the Brisbane River via the Captain Cook Bridge. After that it becomes the Riverside Expressway with exits to the Brisbane CBD on our right.

We left the expressway at Turbot Street and, taking a right on Edward Street, we circled the CBD back as far as a right turn on to Alice Street. At the bottom of Alice, we could take a right on to William Street or continue straight back on to the expressway. That would be our way out.

On the third circuit, once we were happy with the route, we took a left off Turbot at Upper Edward Street, taking a right on to Leichardt and down past Lee's hotel on the corner of Henry Street. Not for any other reason than to waste some time. It was still early and we wanted to arrange to meet Lee when there was a lot more people around. Before we made our way back onto Edward, we stopped at a seven eleven to pick up a breakfast of coffee, croissants, and doughnuts, then drove back around to Alice Street, pulling in about half way down, the Botanical Gardens to our left. It was seven o'clock, already bright and sunny, the city just coming to life. Joggers made their way to or from the gardens as a slow trickle of workers passed.

'What about Queen Street Mall?' I asked. 'It's the main shopping street in Brisbane, pedestrian only and there's sure to be a lot of people knocking about.'

I had picked up a free Brisbane city guide when we stopped.

168

'It runs from William Quay to Edward Street. If there is any problem,' and I honestly didn't think there would be, 'we have an escape route either way.'

I couldn't see how the bad guys could have been waiting for us, or where. And if they were, surely we would have seen them by now.

'Makes sense,' Paul replied, 'who's going to go and meet him?'

'I think it best that Anuia and I do. He already knows me, and it's Anuia he really wants to talk to. What do you think?'

'Makes sense too,' Paul added.

'Kai, Stefan,' I asked, 'maybe you could follow us and hang around at a discreet distance?'

'Yes, for sure,' Stefan replied, 'why?'

'Because that's what they do in the movies,' we all answered.

'Keep up Stefan,' I said, smiling. 'So that you can keep an eye on what's going on around us. If you see anything out of the ordinary you can let us know that we need to get out of there. Paul, Dave, keep circling in the van. If anything happens we'll head for William or Edward. We'll move in the direction we've been going all morning. If we're in trouble you'll catch up with us eventually and we can get out of there.'

Dave didn't look altogether comfortable with the master plan. I think he would have preferred to stay closer to Anuia but he didn't say.

'What do you think Anuia?' I asked.

I needed her to be happy with it more than any of us.

'Let's do it,' she replied.

If she was frightened, she didn't hesitate for a second. She knew what had to be done and why. I admired her courage. She wasn't doing it for herself. She was doing it for her family, her uncle's family. I loved her for it.

'Paul,' I asked, 'can you get me to a phone booth? I'll ring Lee. It's time to get this sorted out once and for all.'

'There's one,' he answered, pointing at a phone booth about ten yards behind the van, 'do you want me to drive you there?'

'Balls,' I said, as I got out, 'it's been a long night.'

'Lee,' I said, when he answered. 'We're in Brisbane. Can we meet?'

'Yes,' he said, 'where are you? Is Anuia with you?'

'Can you meet us at the Queens Street precinct in twenty minutes?' I asked, 'she'll be with me.'

'Yes,' he replied. 'There's a coffee shop half way down the mall. I'll have a photographer with me.'

'Yeah, that's not a problem, but it's up to Anuia if she's comfortable with photographs being taken. I don't want any of me. Is that understood?'

'That's a deal, but it'll help to get photos and personalise the story. I'll see you there in twenty minutes.'

'See you then,' I said, and hung up.

I stopped as I walked back to the van. I wanted to call home again.

'What's the plan?' Paul asked.

'He'll be there in twenty minutes,' I replied. 'I might have some news from home but we'd better get going. I'll fill you in later.'

Paul took the right onto George. Traffic was heavier than I had expected. If we wanted to get out of there fast, it was the last thing we needed. We drove back along George to the Mall. I was reading the book.

'Guys,' I said, turning to face them. 'There's a hostel called 'The Somewhere to Stay.' If anything happens and we all get split up, make your way there any way you can. It's in the West End.'

I scribbled the address on a couple of bits of paper, handing one to Kai and putting the other in my pocket.

'Paul,' I said, as we pulled in at the Mall, 'keep the van moving and keep an eye out for us. We'll follow the flow of traffic. If everything goes okay you'll catch up with us walking. If it doesn't, well...'

Anuia and I watched as the van pulled away. Paul would drop the two boys off at the other end of the mall as they circled. I was worried. I looked for signs of anyone watching, even though I didn't know who to be looking for or what to expect. It must have been obvious.

'It'll be okay,' Anuia said, trying to calm me. 'Let's just see what happens.'

'Shouldn't it be me calming you down?' I asked nervously.

171

I took her hand as we walked along Queen Street Mall searching for the coffee shop. Half way down we found it, Lee and the photographer sitting at a table outside. He stood when he saw us. Barely acknowledging me, he took Anuia's hand and shook it, introducing himself.

'It's great to meet you. Can I get you anything?' he asked.

His colleague waited, camera at the ready.

'Just coffee,' Anuia replied.

'Anuia,' Lee said, after ordering fresh coffee for us all, 'I spoke to a colleague back in Melbourne last night. The latest on your family is that they are doing well. They're still frightened and not talking to anyone. He spoke to your uncle too. He's on his own. The rest of his family are staying with friends. We've no idea where.'

He was good. Talking about her family and letting her know they were safe.

'I'd like to get a bit of background on you,' he continued. 'I'd also like to get a few photos if that's okay. But only if you're happy that we use them.'

She shrugged and the photographer took it as his queue. I kept an eye on him to make sure he wasn't pointing it in my direction. I didn't want my photo plastered all over the newspaper.

He started by asking her some general questions about herself. How she came to live in Australia, her family here, friends and what she did, essentially building a profile as he had put it. Then he got down to business.

'Why illegal immigration?' he asked, 'surely you must have looked at the legal route?'

It was a fair enough question I thought.

'You must understand how I came here in the first place,' she answered, with more composure that I could have mustered. 'It wasn't exactly by the book either. It took a long time and a lot of my uncle's money to get my citizenship. Believe me, if there was any other option, we wouldn't be sitting here now.'

'I understand,' Lee replied. 'When you decided to do this, how did you go about it? Where did you hear about it? Names and places. Who were these people? Do you have anything that would help in identifying them?'

'Unfortunately no,' she answered. 'All contact was by telephone apart from the single meeting in a cafe which lasted no more than ten minutes. I was so nervous, I'm not sure I could even remember what she looked like.'

'What about your uncle?' he asked.

'I'm not sure. I don't think so either.'

'Okay. Tell me about the events leading up to the morning when the truck arrived.'

Anuia went through the story while he recorded the interview. A lot of it I had already told him but he wanted to hear it first-hand. When she finished, he asked some more questions. I had already spotted Kai and Stefan sitting on a shaded bench further up to my left. They watched, heads turning nervously.

'What about the Australian man in the car?' Lee asked, 'he seems to be the big player in all of this. Did you get a good look at him? Would you recognise him again? It's worrying that you believe the police were there that morning and are involved.'

'Yes,' Anuia replied, 'I would recognise him again. I don't believe I'll ever forget.'

'Good,' he said, 'that will be important.'

'This man is the key Lee,' I said. 'I believe Anuia, and I believe everything she has told you. If we can find out who this is, we may be able to get this mess sorted out. We don't have any way of identifying him so we need your help. We need you to tell the story.'

'I get it,' he replied.

I was annoyed with him. We were wasting time. Going over the same ground and it was taking too long.

'I understand,' he said, 'but I need to ensure that all the details are correct. I don't want to go out there with a story not knowing all the facts. Here's what I have in mind.'

Lee gave us his angle on the story. A girl who had come forward to the press to present her version of events. To claim her innocence, afraid to go to the authorities because of who she believes may be involved. Frightened for her family and what might happen to them should she turn herself in. If they are deported to Thailand what would happen to them. She wants to come forward and tell her side of the story but she doesn't know who she can trust anymore.

I stayed vigilant, suspecting everyone, keeping an eye on Kai and Stefan. I listened to them talk, willing them to hurry as I grew increasingly nervous.

'Let us put you up somewhere safe,' he finally said, 'we can look after you.'

Kai and Stefan had sat up, suddenly alert, their eyes trained on the opposite side of the mall. I tried to follow their gaze but Lee's photographer, still snapping away, blocked my view.

'What?' I mouthed soundlessly, as Kai stood and pointed.

I looked again, pushing the photographer to one side, and it was then that I saw them. Two Asian men dressed in black, watching us as we sat. I recognised one of them instantly. It was the same man I had stared at in the car parked in Byron last night. Everything happened in an instant.

'Anuia,' I shouted, 'we have to go.'

'What?' she cried, as she stopped talking mid-sentence.

The look on my face told her everything.

'We have to move. Now!'

As I stood, the two men reacted. They knew I had seen them and that we were going to run. They looked for who or what had alerted me to their presence. Kai stood motionless, Stefan pulling at his arm, moving him away to blend in with the surrounding crowd. But they had already been seen.

'This way,' I yelled, taking Anuia by the hand. 'Run.'

Anuia didn't hesitate. I could hear Lee calling, but we ignored his pleas to stop.

I turned briefly and saw that the two men had already covered the distance to where we had just sat drinking coffee. I looked all around, now sprinting, trying to see if there was anyone else on our tail. They had just spoken to someone on their mobile. We could be running straight towards them.

As we ran I kept telling myself, stick to the plan, stick to the plan, but I couldn't help wonder where the other men were or how many of them there might be. They could easily have decided to cover each end of the mall, knowing we were there. But how did they know? I pulled Anuia towards the next right turn where there were more people. Albert Street. We crossed though traffic, car horns beeping, tyres screeching, and turned left down Elizabeth Street. Moments later I could hear car horns again. They had seen us turn and were after us. We crossed again towards the next right. I noticed the Queensland Irish Association on the corner and remember wondering what it was, before wondering why it should even concern me in the circumstances. Down a side street, coming out at full tilt on Charlotte Street, turning left before crossing through traffic again. We were heading towards Edward Street as planned but taking the more scenic route.

'Are you okay Anuia?' I asked, through clenched teeth.

I was tiring myself. Too many beers and not enough exercise over the previous months. Then again, I hadn't planned to be running too much either.

'Keep going,' she gasped, 'I'm not sure how much further I can run.'

I prayed the van was close by. We were just coming towards the bottom of Elizabeth Street and somehow, unbelievably, I saw it drive past. We couldn't be this unlucky. It would take them ten or fifteen minutes to go around again. Turning right onto Edward Street, I glanced back over my shoulder. They were still there and gaining. All I

176

kept thinking was they're going to catch us. We can't have come all this way to be caught like this. I saw the van in the distance, moving further away. There were people everywhere slowing our pace. The van could never get back around before we were caught. I stole another glance over my shoulder. Three men this time. One must have joined the chase coming straight down Edward Street from the Mall. We had made the right choice not to go straight to the end. But did it matter now. Anuia was tired. I was tired and I knew I couldn't run much more.

'Get off the path,' I yelled, seeing a lull in the traffic. 'We'll be faster.'

We moved out onto the road, gaining pace because we weren't trying to move through a crowd. I could still see the top of the van way in front. Any second now it would turn onto Alice Street and we'd be lost.

But, by some miracle, that's not what happened. Brake lights flashed and the van stopped suddenly. Cars behind blew their horns. The passenger door opened and Dave stood out on the step, waving at us. They had seen us. I looked back again. They were on the road now, running at us. We had to keep going. Just a little bit more. We ran with every single last ounce of breath that we had and reached the van. The side door was opened and we bundled in. 'Go, go, go,' I thought, but Paul didn't need to be told. As we turned onto Alice Street I looked back to see the three Asian men slowing to a stop. They had missed us. For the first time since we left Sydney, the gravity of this whole situation finally hit home. The man I had recognised from Byron had a gun in his hand. I retched involuntarily, vomiting on the floor. From shock or exhaustion I'm not really sure. As we drove down Alice

Street, the only sound was Anuia and me, panting and gasping for breath.

'Guys, guys, are you ok?' I could hear Dave shouting, but it barely registered. I was close to passing out, struggling to breath.

'What the hell happened back there?' he asked, 'where are Kai and Stefan?'

'They were there,' I panted. 'They were either waiting for us or have been following us, but they were there. Kai and Stefan tipped us off.'

'Were they seen?' he asked.

'Yes,' I replied. 'Kai froze but I think Stefan got him away in time. They should be at the top of the mall when we get back around.'

But they weren't. And we couldn't take a chance on waiting. We passed on down George Street and came back across the river at the William Jolly Bridge.

'Head for the hostel as planned guys,' I said, 'they'll know where we are.'

'Did you see?' I asked, 'they were pointing a gun at us, a bloody gun.'

Whether they intended to use it or not there on that busy street was immaterial.

'I know,' Anuia answered, 'I've seen them with guns before.'

And, after all this time, I understood what she must have been going through since Melbourne. For me, for us, it had all just been a big game up until now, that big adventure that we had longed for, just silly games. But now it had become very real.

'Anuia,' I said, 'I'm sorry. I'm really sorry. I guess I finally understand what's going on here. Seeing those guys with guns..... I don't know what I've been thinking up to now. Are we in over our depth?'

'Don't be sorry,' she replied, 'it's hard for you to understand until you see it. But now you know, and now you need to decide what's best for you.'

Chapter Twenty-Five

The Somewhere to Stay hostel is on Brighton Road in the West End. I thought it would be just far enough out of town for us to be out of the way. Even so, when we got there, I dropped the guys outside and drove the van about six blocks away to park in a residential area. If this gang were keeping up with us by monitoring the hostels, I didn't want to make it any easier for them. Paul came with me while Dave and Anuia went to book some beds. He was his usual pensive self but only spoke as we walked back after parking the van.

'What happened there this morning?' he asked.

'I'm not sure,' I answered, 'everything was going okay until these guys showed up again. We were lucky that Kai and Stefan were there. I never saw them.'

'How did they know where you were?' he then asked.

'I just don't know. I can only think that they picked us up on the way into Brisbane.'

'But why didn't they try to pull us before now?'

It was a question I hadn't thought about, but then, the way things panned out, I hadn't really had time to digest everything and how it had gone down.

'Yeah,' I said, 'I don't know. It would have made more sense. Unless they know we've been talking to someone. Maybe they're trying to figure out who.'

'Do you trust Lee Taylor?' Paul asked.

This was something I had gone over again and again but I couldn't see a reason not to. He had a lot to gain with this story. It was in his best interest to help Anuia any way he could and keep her sweet as long as possible.

'Yeah Paul, I think I do.'

Not altogether convincing, but as convinced as I was myself. Something else was bothering him.

'Are you ok?' I asked, 'is there something up?'

'Not really,' he replied, but I knew him.

'Come on Paul, what is it?'

'You've made a couple of extra phone calls over the last few days,' he said. 'Last night and again this morning. Is there anything you want to tell me?'

'Yes,' I replied, 'I've been ringing home talking to my folks.'

'Do you want to talk about it?' he asked. 'Not that it's any of my business, but I know how little you've been talking to them since we've met. Don't get me wrong. I'm glad you are. It's important. It's just that, well, it seems like you're ringing every five minutes now.'

'Look Paul, I was going to talk to you about this today. I told them about what we're involved in over here. I've explained everything to them. There's an old guy lives on our street. His daughter worked in the Irish Embassy in Sydney for a long time. She's working in the Australian Embassy in Dublin now and has been there for few years. They've been to see to her, to see if there's anything she can do to help. She's looking into it as we speak. That's why I've been making the extra calls. To see what she's come up with. She thinks we need to involve the Gardai back home. I'd rather not say anything to Anuia just yet. We agreed not to involve the law so I don't want her to think I'm going behind her back.'

'I won't say anything either,' Paul said, 'but we should before it gets too far.'

'I agree. I'll keep in touch with home and see what they say.'

We were back at the hostel but I stopped before walking up the drive.

'Paul, we were lucky you spotted us today. I thought we were gonners. I was scared shitless,' I admitted, 'I still am.'

'Thank Dave,' he replied, 'he saw you. And I don't blame you for being scared. It's not a game anymore.'

'Thanks anyway though. We wouldn't have made it much further. Let's see have the guys got some beds sorted out. I wonder if Kai and Stefan are here yet.'

They had booked a six bed dorm and were talking to Tim, the owner, in reception. He seemed like a pretty cool guy, telling them about different stuff to do around the city.

'We've a big night out planned for this evening,' he said, as he showed us the common area and kitchen, introducing us to people as we went.

'Kai and Stefan,' I mouthed wordlessly, when I caught Anuia's eye.

'Not yet,' she whispered.

Tim finished showing us around and we brought our gear up to the dorm.

'No sign of the lads yet,' I asked again, when we were all alone. 'I hope they're okay.'

'What about Lee?' Anuia asked, 'I wonder what happened to him.'

'Don't worry about Lee,' I said, 'that guy is well able to look after himself. Let's wait and see did the two boys see anything after we ran. I'm going to head down to the common area and wait for them.'

I needed some time on my own, to get my head around what had happened today. I was anxious about Kai and Stefan. I didn't want to show it, but the way Kai froze worried me.

'I'm going to try and get some sleep,' Anuia said, 'I'm exhausted. I think we all should.'

'I know,' I replied, 'but I'm too on edge after this morning.'

Paul and Dave said they'd try and get some sleep too.

I went to explore the place while I waited for the lads. The older part of the hostel to the front, and where we had our room, is like one of the old colonial buildings synonymous with Queensland. A beautiful, white, timber clad, multi storey building with balconies all the way around each floor, doors leading from every room and ideal for a hostel where people can hang out and get to know each other.

I met Tim and he introduced me to a couple of guys in the common room. Brad, a Canadian, and Scott, an American. They were the entertainment organisers and asked if I would like to join them out back by the pool. There were a few people there, most of whom knew

183

each other. They talked and laughed as they discussed what would be happening that night. I watched, taking in what they were saying. They seemed like a pretty good bunch and I thought to myself how cool a place it was to be, wishing that we were all here under different circumstances. For the first time since we had left Sydney I wished that things were different, that I hadn't got involved in this. On the other hand, I was asking questions of myself that I don't believe I would have, travelling under normal circumstance. I was discovering things about myself that I had forgotten or that I had never known.

"You okay?' Brad asked, 'you're very quiet.'

'Sorry dude,' I replied, 'I'm just a bit tired and have a few things on my mind. We travelled overnight. I should really get some sleep.'

'You'd better,' he said, 'there's a party tonight and we're expecting you and your friends to come along. No excuses.'

"Looking forward to it,' I said, smiling.

One by one everyone around the pool started to drift away. Some went for food and others for sleep. Some, like me, needed a bit of time on their own. Left alone, I soon dozed off. The sun had already begun to set by the time I woke and went back to the room. They were all up, still waiting anxiously.

'No sign of them still?' I asked.

'No,' Anuia replied, shaking her head. 'Something must have happened. I'm really worried.'

'I'll ring Lee,' I said, 'he might know something.'

I found a payphone in the old entrance hallway downstairs.

184

'Lee Taylor,' he answered.

'Lee, it's me,' I said, 'are you ok?'

'Jeez mate, it got a bit hairy out there this morning. Are you guys okay? How did you know they were there?' he asked. 'How did you recognise them?'

I told him about Kai and Stefan and how I recognised the man from Byron Bay.

'We're worried Lee. The two lads haven't showed up yet. I think something might have happened.'

'Listen,' he said, 'try to stay calm. I'll see what I can find out. I've been speaking to some of our people in Melbourne since this morning and we're looking into who could be involved. We have some ideas but can't move on this until we are one hundred percent certain. My boss in Melbourne is talking to the police. To someone he can trust. Anuia will have to come in eventually.'

'I know that Lee, and she will, but only when the time is right. If she's going to talk to the police and be a witness, she'll need some guarantees for her safety and that of her family. She'll be looking for a deal. They've nothing to go back to.'

'I understand,' he said, 'just keep in touch. I'll have some more answers for you when we talk again. Stay safe.'

'We will,' I said, hanging up.

'Are you ok?'

Startled, I turned to see Tim mopping a floor close by. I didn't see him when I made the call to Lee and hadn't noticed him pottering around. I wondered how much of my conversation he had overheard.

'Yeah Tim, I'm grand. I'm just a bit tired at the moment.'

'You look tired,' he replied, 'if you don't mind me saying so.'

'No, no, not at all. We've covered a fair bit of ground over the past few days. It..... it hasn't been easy. I've to make a few more calls,' I said, hoping for some privacy.

'Here, why don't you come into my office,' he asked, 'let's have a chat.'

I didn't want to but he didn't give the impression that he was going to leave it. I really wasn't in the mood for talking, but I did sense genuine concern in his voice and on any other day I would have appreciated the friendly gesture. Reluctantly, I followed him to his office in the old building.

'Grab a stool,' he said, pointing towards a battered old chair.

I looked around his office and wondered how he managed to keep the place going. It was all clutter. Shelves of books and files, pieces of paper stuck everywhere around the walls, a desk piled high with a million other things.

'Don't worry,' he said, 'I know where everything is. It's an organised mess.'

He handed me a beer from a small fridge, hidden by post-its and bits of notes stuck to its door. I thanked him and couldn't help liking the guy. If there is such a thing as a typical Aussie bloke, then this was it. T-shirt, shorts and a pair of flip flops. Tanned weather beaten skin, shoulder length blonde shaggy hair bleached by the sun and eyebrows to match. He looked as if he had been here longer than the old building he owned.

'How long have you been here?' I asked.

'Oh about twenty-two years in one way or another,' he replied, though he didn't offer an explanation as to what he meant.

'I'd say you've seen a lot of people, a lot of change in your time?' I asked.

'I sure have. So many people, so many faces and so many stories. I don't remember them all anymore. I couldn't if I tried. That's why I got into the business in the first place though. I travelled a bit when I was younger and when I came home, it's all I ever wanted to do. It's a great way to meet people from all over the world. Learn about them and where they come from. It's great to be able to offer people a decent place to stay on their travels, an oasis, something to remember. It's nice and relaxed here.'

'I can see that,' I said. 'Not really the big party place like some of the other ones I've read about?'

'No not so much. We have our fair share though. It just seems we attract people who want to relax a bit as well. It might sound stupid, but a lot of the people we get here seem to come to spend some time on their own. That said, it's a great bunch and everyone gets on together. We've a night out planned if you're interested. We do a deal with one of the pubs in the city. We'll have a few games and they'll supply a few free beers as prizes. That type of thing.'

'Thanks,' I said, 'I don't think Brad and Scott are giving us a choice. We're looking forward to it.'

187

'How long have you guys been travelling together?' he asked.

'We've known each other a while,' I said, 'but only started travelling up the coast recently enough. Why do you ask?'

'Oh no reason really, just curious,' he replied.

He pointed behind me and I turned to see a wall littered with photographs, letters and postcards, different currencies, and many other things.

'See that,' he said. 'There's a thousand different stories pinned to that wall. I've seen them all. These are stories of people who came here looking for something. A good time, answers, themselves, but all searching for something. Every so often though, some come looking for help.

'People keep in touch. They write and send postcards and photographs from all over the world. When they arrive here they make friends for life. Sure, in most cases, I'll never see them again or they'll never see other people they met again, but they can still take something away that will stay with them forever. Memories, friendships, answers. And every so often they'll send back a little part of their journey. To say thanks or to to let us know that they've started another part of their journey. It changes a lot of course. I keep them up for a while but clear it down every now and again to make way for new ones. There are some stories up there that I'll never take down.'

I looked for the ones he was talking about but all I could see were happy smiling faces looking back at me. A world of discovery pinned to a wall. And I wondered if there was a place there for us.

'What I'm saying,' he continued, 'is that no matter what you're looking for, we're here to help you find it. I'm sure you've heard the rumours about the people wanted by the police that are supposed to be travelling the coast? I heard about a bit of a commotion in the mall this morning.'

I didn't answer.

'From what I hear, it seems to me that people in this situation would be the kind of people that would need our help?'

I paused for a moment, deciding how much I could to tell him.

'Yeah, I've heard some rumours too,' I replied. 'If it was me in that situation, I'd appreciate all the help I could get. I think travelling the back packer route would be the best place to get it.'

'I think so too,' he said, and smiled. 'Well, I've got a few things to do so I'll be heading out for a while. Why don't you relax and drink you're beer. There's a phone there if you want to make any more calls. It's a bit more private in here so feel free to stay for as long as you need. When you're done, just pull the door after you.'

'Thanks,' I replied.

'Take as long as you need,' he said, walking to the door. 'If there's anything else, anything at all, just ask. I won't be too far away.'

'Tim,' I said, before he closed the door. 'Seriously man, thanks a million. I really appreciate it.'

It was late evening and I needed to ring home again. It'd be very early in the morning but they were expecting my call. I doubted they'd be sleeping much anyway.

'Hi Dad,' I said, when he answered, 'sorry for ringing so early. I had hoped to ring before now but we've had an eventful day.'

I told him what had happened since I last spoke to them, leaving out the part about the guns.

'It's good to hear from you son,' he said. 'We have some news. We've talked to Leslie Foley.'

Leslie was the daughter of my old neighbour back home. She had talked to her superiors in the Australian Embassy, dad explained, and they had already contacted the Irish Consulate in Sydney.

'They're arranging a call for later today,' he continued, 'and they want you to be part of it. It'll be her, some of the people she works with, the consulate in Sydney, and the Gardai.'

'What's it all about?' I asked, 'what can they do?'

'Look son,' he said, 'you'd be better off talking to them yourself. Can you call home later? It'll be at four our time.'

That was about one o'clock tomorrow morning, Queensland time.

'Sure Dad,' I said. 'I'll make it no bother.'

No fun and games for me tonight, but I hadn't really planned to anyway. I wouldn't tell the guys about this just yet. Let them have what little bit of peace there was to be found here. I wanted something more concrete before I told Anuia anyway.

'Look after yourself son,' he said, as we finished the call.

It was good to hear Dad's voice, always familiar and always reassuring. I was finally calming down after the mornings events. I had one more call to make before I went for a bit of a lie down. I rang the Glebe Village back in Sydney.

'How can I help you today?' a girl asked.

An unfamiliar voice, someone new maybe but that happened regularly enough.

'Hi,' I said, 'I'm looking for Maja. Is she working today?'

'No,' she replied, 'Maja is not working here now. Is there anyone else you would like to speak to?'

Maja not working there anymore?

'What about Luke?' I asked, 'is he there?'

'Yes,' she said, 'I'll put him on.'

'Hello, Luke here, who's this?'

'Hi Luke, it's me. How've you been?'

'Hey dude, it's great to hear from you. How the hell are ya? Where are you now? Do you know how famous you guys are? Everyone that comes in here has heard or met or seen you somewhere along the way. Everyone knows someone who knows you.'

'We're good Luke,' I said, 'I heard you had a bit of trouble since we last spoke. Maja was telling me. Where is she by the way?'

'She's gone dude. A few friends of hers turned up and she thought it was just her time to get out there travelling again. She said if you called to let you know that she hopes your paths cross again, that if they were meant to, they would. She thought an awful lot of you, you know that?'

'I realised it eventually Luke,' I said. 'Did she say where she was going?

'No man, they didn't really have a plan. I'm really sorry.'

'Don't worry about it,' I said, 'if she gets in touch, can you…, can you just let her know that I called. Keep the rumours going. Tell someone you heard we left for China. It won't take long to get around.'

'We will,' he said, 'take care.'

I was gutted. I knew Maja would go travelling again sometime, but I had hoped that something could have happened between us. I had let it go for so long, afraid to let her know because of how much Paul had liked her. And now, when I was finally at a place where I could, the opportunity was gone. I should have told her the other day when we spoke. Was that why she had gone away now, because she had wanted me to say something? Had she sensed it and been disappointed when I didn't or was I wanting to believe that this was the case? Did I have the right to think this? Did it really matter anymore? She was gone and, as Tim had said, in most cases we're only left with memories. With Maja, I had hoped for so much more. I sat for a while thinking about what might have been. I could have stayed all night but I needed to get some sleep. Dragging myself from the chair, I shut the office door and went back to our room. I lay down on the bed, facing the wall.

'Are you ok?' Anuia asked.

'Yes,' I said, more abruptly than I intended, 'any sign of Kai or Stefan?'

'No,' she said, 'I'm sorry.'

'It's me who should be sorry,' I said, 'I didn't mean to snap.'

192

'It's okay,' she replied, 'it's been a rough day. We're going to head downstairs. Try and get some rest.'

When they left I lay there thinking. I couldn't understand why I was so upset that Maja had gone. Nothing had happened between us after all. Sure we got on, and we seemed to click in some way, but still nothing had happened. There was a knock on the door.

'Can I come in?' Paul asked.

'Sure,' I replied, 'what's up?'

'I could ask you the same question,' he said, 'has something happened?'

I told him about ringing Lee, then ringing home and what they had said.

'I rang Glebe,' I said. 'Maja is gone. She finally moved on. I knew she would, I just wish.......'

'You wish you could have seen her before she left,' Paul said, finishing my sentence for me. 'I know dude. I know what she meant to you. I've always known.'

'I don't understand,' I said.

'Sure you do. We all know what you thought of her. Why did you never take a chance with her?'

'Because Paul...., because I know how much you liked her. You told me one of the first times we met. I wouldn't have been much of a friend if I had got in your way.

'Look,' he said, 'it was never going to happen. I would have liked if it did, but there was a spark between you two from the first moment you set eyes on her. I got on really well with her, but there was never any of that electricity there was when the two of you were together. And another thing.'

'What?' I asked.

'You are a great friend. You always will be. There aren't many guys out there who would have stood back the way you did. Especially where women are concerned,' he smiled.

'I'm sorry,' I said, 'I didn't really want to have feelings for her. It's too late now anyway.'

Paul was silent for a minute.

'We'll stick together until we see this through,' he replied. 'That's what friends do. My mum used to say that's it's better to have loved and lost than never to have loved. Not much comfort I know but maybe, if it's meant to be, you'll get a chance to see her again.'

He was right. It was better to have loved. Lost though I wasn't so sure about, but at least I had moved on from where I had been. I fell asleep wondering if I would ever meet her again, but that was a silly thought.

'Are you sure you won't come?' Paul asked when I woke.

I had decided to give the party a miss. Kai and Stefan had still not arrived and someone should be here when they did. I couldn't relax until I knew they were safe. Besides, I wanted to make sure I was around for the call home later on.

'No, honestly,' I replied, 'you go. The three of you need a break.'

I watched from the balcony as they all left, then sat with a beer looking down on the silent, lamp-lit street below. A book sat untouched on the table beside me. At one o'clock, I rang home as planned.

Mam and Dad were there, Leslie, two Garda detectives, and some people from the Australian embassy in Dublin. They explained how Victoria Police internal affairs had been investigating some of their members in Melbourne connected specifically to an illegal immigration racket. They were also investigating a number of leading business men and a politician they alleged were involved. They had no solid evidence. This was the breakthrough they had been waiting for, their first real witness. I went through Anuia's version of events from the morning the men were killed.

'This could be it guys,' one of them exclaimed excitedly, 'finally something solid to go on. We need to get her in.'

Internal affairs would send two men from Melbourne north via Sydney. They would meet with some representatives from the Irish Consulate and arrive in Brisbane tomorrow. I told them what we expected for Anuia. All she wanted to bargain for was the safety of her family. If she co-operated, they would stay for good, bypassing any red tape. They said to leave it with them and to sit tight.

I took my place back on the balcony and sipped on a warm beer. Everything was quiet, and I found the solitude comforting. Soon I heard voices coming down the street. Maybe it was Kai and Stefan I thought, but Dave and Anuia turned up the drive.

'You're back early,' I said, startling them. 'Where's Paul?'

''Didn't see you there,' Dave replied, in a hushed tone. 'He's on his way,' he said, pointing back up the street.

I could hear Paul make his way slowly down the road. He wasn't alone and turned up the driveway, hand in hand with a very pretty looking girl. They stopped and kissed.

'Busted,' I said, as I stood.

'Any sign of the lads?' Paul asked. He couldn't help smiling.

I shook my head.

'And who might this be?' I asked.

'I'm Áine,' she replied, 'it's nice to meet you.'

She was tall and thin, brown hair and blue eyes. They were giggling like a pair of school children.

'I'll see you kids in the morning,' I joked, and they went on in.

I resumed my vigil, the silence only broken by the occasional sound of muffled laughter coming from somewhere out back. When I woke, it was still dark. Someone had covered my legs with a blanket. The empty beer bottle on the table was gone. I massaged the crick in my neck, slowly twisting my head from side to side. Sensing I wasn't alone, I sat bolt upright. I looked about but the balcony was empty. Peering between the old wooden balustrades, I saw him standing at the bottom of the drive.

'Stefan,' I whispered, and I knew something was wrong.

The blanket dropped to the floor as I ran back down the hallway, then down the stairs. He stood motionless, hands by his sides.

'I'm really sorry,' he said. 'I'm really sorry.'

'Why? I asked, 'what's happened. Where's Kai?'

'I tried to stop him,' he replied, visibly distraught, 'but he just wouldn't listen.'

'What is it Stefan? What has he done?'

'This morning,' he said, 'after you ran. Kai froze. I had to drag him away. We ran to the top of the mall but he kept saying 'they saw us, they saw us'.'

'Did anything happen?' I asked uneasily.

'Two men tried to block our escape. One grabbed Kai, the other tried to grab me. I shouted for help. People were stopping, staring, calling for the police, so they let us go.'

I stood, motionless, afraid of what he might say next.

'He's gone to the police,' he said.

'When?' I asked.

'He's probably there now,' he replied. 'I tried to talk him out of it, to stall him as much as possible. You have to go.'

I ran back to the dorm.

'Get everything together as quickly as you can,' I said, as they woke.

'What? What is it?' Anuia asked wearily.

'It's Kai,' I said, 'he's gone to the police. I'll get the van.'

I knew it had never sat right with Kai. He had stayed with us because of Stefan. I thought he might have just went his own way but after what had happened to him this morning, what had happened to us, I could understand. When I got back with the van, they were waiting. Tim was there too.

'I don't sleep much,' he said, with a wry smile.

'There are people coming to meet us here tomorrow,' I told him, as we piled everything into the van. 'Police. Internal affairs. People from the Irish consulate.'

'Don't worry about that,' he replied. 'I'll let them know what's happened and that you had to go.'

'Thanks Tim. I'm sorry we brought this to your door.'

'Just keep the girl safe,' he said. 'Where will you go?'

'North,' I replied, 'I'll ring you as soon as I can.'

'You did what you could Stefan,' I said, as I shook his hand, 'thanks.'

'Thank you,' Anuia said.

She hugged him and then we were gone.

Chapter Twenty-Six

We left in silence, driving across town through Stafford and Kedron, picking up the Bruce Highway north of the city. Travelling by night again, my optimism for a resolution to our problem disappearing bit-by-bit with every mile we travelled, leaving Brisbane behind. It took two hours to get to Noosa, bypassing the Sunshine Coast. I spent the entire journey checking my rear view mirror, unable to escape the feeling of uneasiness, no longer wondering who might be following, but when. Tim had rang ahead to book a dorm at the Koala Beach Resort. It was just before six in the morning when Chris, a friend of Tim, showed us to our room. He didn't ask any questions. We chose a bunk and said goodnight. It was the least we had talked amongst ourselves since leaving Sydney. It was unusual, discomforting too. There were still four of us but we felt more alone than we had at any time before.

Two hours of fitful sleep later, I got up and took a drive. I parked the van at Little Cove and walked the two or three kilometre trail out to Noosa head. I wanted some time on my own, to think about things and what we should do. I'd ring Lee and let him know we were on the move. I had to ring home and let them know we were no longer in Brisbane. We wouldn't be there when they arrived. I walked barefoot in the water, thinking about Kai and Stefan, about Lee Taylor and all the other people this adventure had affected. Lee would have to have someone who could help us by now. If not, I'd tell him about my other plan. He could still have his story, but I wouldn't give him any guarantees.

I knew I could trust the people travelling from Sydney, but I wasn't sure I could rely on them to deliver on the assurances we had asked for. They would take her in as soon as they caught up with us. I wanted concrete confirmation, in writing, that Anuias family would be able to stay and that Anuia herself would not be implicated in any way for getting involved in the first place. I'd give Lee one more shot before deciding.

Then my mind, as it had done so often over the last few days, drifted back to Maja. Was it because of me that she had finally left? Scared of taking a chance in life anymore, of being hurt, of being honest with myself. I thought about what might have been.

When I got back, I found Anuia in the kitchen drinking coffee and picking at a cold slice of toast.

'How did you sleep?' I asked.

'Just okay,' she replied. 'I woke a lot. I can't stop thinking about how things have been going. It's like every time something positive happens, we have to start running again. It has to end.'

'I know Anuia,' I said. 'Don't worry, it will soon.'

'No. I don't think you understand,' she replied. 'It needs to stop. I have been running and hiding for far too long. When it was just me it was lonely and unbearable. Now that you guys are involved it's like I am doing something wrong, involving you in something that you should not be part of. It just isn't fair. With Kai and Stefan gone, it feels like everything is starting to unravel.'

I realised what she was trying to say but before I could respond she started talking again.

'I want it to end, and I want it to end today. I appreciate everything you have done for me but it's time to turn myself in. I will always love you for how you have supported me, but I need it to stop.'

'What are you saying?' I asked.

'Can you ring Lee today to see what he has arranged and who they are talking to? I'm ready to meet them and take my chances that they are people I can trust.'

I remained silent.

'Can you understand why I want this?' she asked. 'It isn't just about you guys. In some ways, yes, it is. You deserve to be out there travelling and discovering. This is your time. You can't look back years from now and wonder what you might have missed. But it's for me too. I've been away from my family for too long. I worry about them every minute of every day. I need to know that they are safe. With Lee's support, at least people will know who we are and what our story is. There is no other way.'

'But what if there is another way?' I asked, then told her about Lesley and the people coming from Sydney. 'I shouldn't have gone behind your back. I'm sorry.'

'That's okay,' she replied, 'I know you only want to do what's best for me.'

'Anuia,' I said, lifting her chin so that I could look directly into her eyes. 'I love you. We all do and what happens to you now is all that we care about. We chose this, all of us, and we can leave whenever we want. Right now I don't want to. I won't give up until I know that you'll be safe. Believe me, Paul and Dave feel exactly the same way. Everything has changed since I met you. I may not have seen all the places I wanted to, but I can see them again. I have discovered so much about myself. Things I needed to know. I believe I need to keep doing this, and that everything I am depends on how this turns out. Can you please do one thing for me?'

'What?' she asked.

'Just think about it,' I said, 'just for one more day. I'll ring Lee, then ring home and tell them where we're going. I'll ring Tim and let him know too. Let's just take one last look at our options.'

'One last look,' she replied, hesitantly. 'That's all I can promise.'

She smiled her brilliant smile and I wondered how she could hide all the sadness she was feeling.

On the way back to the room, I heard a commotion by the pool. Laughing, shouting, splashing, and what was undoubtedly a Dublin accent. I hadn't heard many since arriving in Oz and found it strangely comforting. I smiled as I put on board shorts and grabbed my towel. It would be nice to talk to someone from my own neck of the woods.

There were eight or nine people messing around in the water. More than one Dublin accent I could now tell. Always familiar but I couldn't help thinking that these were more familiar than most. I looked again and didn't recognise any of the faces. A couple of shaggy blonde heads faced the other way. One of them turned and, in his best Dublin accent, shouted.

'Are ye gettin' in?'

We recognised each other instantly.

'I don't bleeding' believe it. Al,' he said, slapping the other shaggy blonde dude on the shoulder, 'look who it is.'

'No bleedin' way,' Alan shouted.

It was Troy and Alan, my two travelling companions for the briefest time when I first left home. I last saw them climbing into a battered old taxi in Bangkok as they set off for Kho Samui.

I hurried to their side of the pool while they climbed out to meet me. Alan threw his arms around me. I wasn't used to hugging half naked wet men, but I went with the moment and hugged him back, then did the same with Troy. Hugging, hand shaking, back slapping, and high fiving as the rest of their friends observed, grinning as they tried to figure out what was going on.

'Guys,' I said, 'I can't believe you're here. You look great. What's up with all the blonde hair?'

'Ah, you know how it is,' Alan replied, 'we were much too boring at home so we said we'd get into this Aussie thing as much as possible.'

'We did it for a bet really,' Troy laughed, 'but it kind of stuck. We look much better as surfers than Irish mullahs. Ya know yerself.'

'Yeah,' Alan continued, 'and it's much easier pullin' women as shaggy blonde Aussies than it is as half bald Paddies.'

It felt like I had only been with them yesterday, sitting in a bar on the Kho San Road, sipping cold beers, talking rubbish and generally resolving to cure all world problems. They had change so much since we last spoke, no longer the quiet boys I met as they left home those short few months ago, now matured, experienced travellers. There was so much I wanted to ask, but the questions would have to wait as they enthusiastically introduced me to all their friends, and so quickly, I could barely keep up with the names. Lucy and Robert, a couple from Kent in England. Robbie, a girl, and the first Scouser I had met on my travels. Sam and Toni, Yorkshire lasses, with accents that made me smile. And Marcus and Jasper from Amsterdam.

'Who are you travelling with?' Alan asked, when things had settled.

'I'll tell you what,' I said, 'let me just go and find them. There's a couple of lads from Ireland and a girl from Thailand.'

'Let me get this straight,' Troy joked, 'three lads and one girl? I don't like the odds.'

'What happened to the two nice quiet lads I met leaving Ireland?' I asked, laughing loudly. 'When did your priorities change so much? I thought you were all about travelling and seeing new places.'

'We are, we are,' Alan yelled. 'But we've done some of that and now we're trying to experience the finer things in life.'

I hurried back to our room, excitedly laughing to myself as I went. I found the others tidying clothes and belongings into rucksacks, preparing to go.

'What are you so happy about?' Paul asked.

'You're never going to believe this,' I said, ''remember I told you about the two guys I met leaving Dublin? I spent some time with them in Bangkok. They're here, staying in this hostel.'

'No way,' Dave replied, 'what are the chances?'

'I know,' I said. 'They were wondering who I was travelling with so I said I'd come and get you.'

I brought them out to meet Troy, Alan and their friends. We sat and talked, told stories of where we had been and who we had met.

They had arrived in Australia via Melbourne and had been travelling the south and east coasts for nearly two months. Their group had grown as they went, arriving in Noosa only a couple of days earlier. An incredible coincidence it seemed, but as I spent more time travelling, I realised that it wasn't such a great coincidence after all – people sharing a common goal, travelling the same routes. When we got the chance, Paul and I pulled Troy and Alan to one side.

'Jeez guys, I still can't believe you're here,' I said.

'The lads looked after me in Thailand,' I said, turning to Paul. 'We spent a few crazy days in Bangkok before I left.'

'Where are you headed for?' I asked.

'We're not really sure,' Alan replied, 'what I mean is, we're not in a hurry to get anywhere in particular. We were hoping to hang out here for a couple of days. Troy fancies himself as a bit of a surfer so wants to try and get a few lessons in. He's turned into a real jungle bunny.'

'I'm just trying to broaden my horizons,' he interjected, with mock indignation.

'Here's a question for you guys,' I said. 'Have you heard the rumours going around about a girl who is wanted by the police in Melbourne in connection with a double murder?'

'Sure,' Troy said, 'everyone has. We've heard people going north say she's going south, and people going south say she's gone north. Everyone has met someone who knows someone who knows her. It's just like the old rumour mill back home.'

'Exactly,' I agreed. 'But what if it wasn't a rumour and they came asking you for help? What would you do?'

'I'm not sure I'm with you,' Alan replied, 'I mean, if she's involved in a double murder, what kind of help is there to give?'

'What if someone told you that she was just an innocent bystander trying to do the best for her family? Everything got out of hand and now she's on the run and a witness to two murders. She can't go to the police because she knows they are involved so she's basically hiding out with the help of some friends until they can figure out what to do.'

'No,' Alan replied, 'still not with you. What has it got to do with us anyway?'

The bleach he had used for his hair had clearly numbed his brain cells. Troy on the other hand was quicker on the uptake, realising what I was trying to say.

'No way,' he exclaimed, 'you mean....'

'No way what?' Alan asked.

'Guys, I want you to meet someone,' I replied, asking Anuia to join us.

'Lads, this is Anuia as you already know. What you don't know is that Anuia is the person that the police and everyone else are looking for. She's been with us for some time now and we're being chased by some very bad people. Every time we think we have some breathing space they find us again. We had to leave Brisbane in a hurry last night.'

The guys were silent, which was unusual for them.

'Anuia has told us everything that has happened, the whole thing right from the start. We believe everything she has told us and, unfortunately for her, we're the people she has helping her.'

I smiled at her as I said it then recounted the story one more time, Anuia or Paul filling in parts that I had missed, right up until we arrived in Noosa.

'How do they keep tracking you?' Alan asked.

'We don't know,' I replied, 'I suppose they just have some kind of contacts everywhere they go. It's the only thing we can think of. What we do know for certain is that we were blessed to escape them once, and had a couple of very close shaves. We're hoping to end it fairly soon though. I've to ring this reporter again today. He's been talking to the police in Melbourne and Anuia wants to hand herself in.'

'How can we help?' they asked.

'We're going to go north again, maybe to Hervey Bay,' I replied. ''Try and put some proper distance between us and them. Then we'll just sit it out until the cavalry arrive, whatever way they arrive.'

'We'll come with you so,' Alan said, and Troy agreed. 'We have our car and the guys have a couple of cars too. It'll help to have some extra transport if we need it. We saw the yellow van out front this morning all right. Pretty cool but no offence and all, it stands out like a sore thumb. I'll let the gang know that we're leaving. Why don't you call this reporter guy and let him know that's where we're heading? Anuia, come with me and I'll introduce you to all the guys properly. They're not going to believe this.'

I found the payphone in reception and rang Lee as planned.

'They found us again,' I said. 'We've had to stay on the move. We're in Noosa but leaving again today. Do you have any news for us?'

'I do,' he replied, 'the cop my boss knows is personally heading up his own team on this. We know we can trust them. They're already on their way. She'll have to go in with them but she'll be safe until they find out who's behind all this.'

'Great news,' I replied, 'Anuia has had enough. All she wants is to be with her family again. Did you talk to them about doing a deal to keep her family here?'

'Yes. We talked about it but she can talk to them again when they meet. It's the right thing to do. You know that.'

I did know it, but I didn't tell him about the people who were on their way to Brisbane from Sydney. I needed that extra guarantee for her safety.

'Thanks,' I said, 'let them know we'll be in Hervey Bay. I'll let you know where.'

Then I rang Tim in the hostel in Brisbane.

'Hi Tim, it's me. Any news?.'

'Hey man, the police showed up shortly after you left,' he said, 'but as far as we were concerned we never saw or heard of you. How are you guys?'

'We're okay,' I replied. 'Any sign of the people from Sydney yet?'

'No, not yet, but it's still early. If they were flying up today I'd guess they should be arriving soon.'

'Let them know we're heading for Hervey Bay,' I said. 'Anuia's ready to go in.'

'Take care mate,' he said, as I ended the call and dialled home.

'Hi Dad,' I said, when he answered, 'we had to leave Brisbane in a hurry. Can you let Leslie know? We've decided to meet the police and get this over with. It's what Anuia wants.'

I told him where we'd be and then chatted briefly before ending the call. I never realised how much, but I was missing Mum and Dad more than I ever thought possible.

Everything was packed and ready to go. The four of us, Alan, Troy, and all their friends.

'Wow,' I said, 'no-one will mess with us now. We'll be meeting the people Lee knows in Hervey. They'll know what to do.'

With that we were back on the road. This time, thankfully, it wasn't by night.

Chapter Twenty-Seven

We drove the ten or fifteen kilometres from Noosa back to the Bruce highway and turned north towards Gympie, then on to Maryborough, leaving the highway there for the coast and Hervey Bay. The journey took about three hours, allowing for a stop off in Maryborough for supplies and the essential few beers for later in the day. We were all back talking again the way we should have been, the end now in sight. We had started out as friends and I was glad that we would come out the other end as friends. Troy and Alan followed in a beat up jalopy they had bought cheap off a backpacker in Melbourne. It had withstood the many miles they had clocked up since, and was still going strong. Jasper and Marcus piled in their back seat with the rest of their gear. Lucy and Robert had their own car too. They bought it in the car park in Kings Cross in Sydney from a German couple who were going home. It was an old red Datsun Sedan with about four million miles on the clock. It still had a few more in the tank. Robbie travelled with them. Sam and Toni travelled in the van with us and it was nice to have new faces on board. Our own little convoy and some perceived safety in numbers.

I thumbed through the book, looking for a good place to stay. Because this whole mess would be sorted out in the next day or two, we decided that those of us who were left would do Fraser. It was part of the trip I had looked forward to most while planning to leave Sydney but I hadn't thought about it much until now. Koalas was the only one offering self-drive excursions to the island. I rang ahead and booked two self-contained apartments.

'I'll ring Lee and let him know where we are when we get there,' I told Anuia. 'Are you still sure it's what you want to do?'

'As sure as I will ever be,' she replied.

We arrived in Hervey at about four in the afternoon. We checked in, cars parked out back, and grabbed whatever space we would call a bed for the next few nights. There were thirteen of us on board now, eight lads and five girls. The girls got first choice on the beds. We drew straws to see who would get any that were left. All settled in, an executive decision was made, and everyone adjourned to the hostel bar in the gardens out back. I made my way, as usual, to find a telephone. Paul came with me.

Lee answered within seconds.

'Where are you guys?' he asked, and I sensed some agitation in his voice.

'Calm down Lee,' I replied. 'We're in Hervey Bay and booked in at the Koala hostel. It's on the main drag across from the beach.'

'Great, great,' he said, 'that's good. The team my boss is talking to are flying up to Brisbane later tonight. They should be with you some time in the morning – two detectives and two more from immigration. They're organising some local backup.'

'Thanks,' I said, 'as long as Anuia comes out of this okay we're happy.'

'No worries. I'm going to be coming up with them too so at least you'll see a familiar face. I'll just ask for you at the hostel.'

'Sounds like a plan Lee. I'll talk to you then.'

'What do you think?' I asked Paul, as I hung up.

'I think you should ring home,' he replied. 'Talk to your dad. Talk to Leslie and let her know what's going on. I think it's important we get her advice and see where her people are. They should be in Brisbane by now.'

'I agree,' I said. 'If they all arrive together then that's all the better. Lee will still get his story. Maybe not the in manner he would have liked it, but we won't lose any sleep over that.'

'Not even a little bit,' he replied, as I dialled home.

Leslie had been waiting to hear from me. Dad had her number.

'Leslie, how are you doing? Dad gave me your number,' I said, when she answered. 'It's hard to believe I've seen you at your father's house so many times over the years and we're only now speaking under these circumstances.'

'It sure is,' she said. 'Where are you now?'

'We're in a place called Hervey Bay a few hours north of Brisbane.'

'I know it well. I visited Fraser Island a long time ago. That's where I fell in love with Australia and why I decided to go back and work there.'

'Hopefully if things work out I'll get to go myself,' I said. 'Anuia wants to hand herself in. She's been running long enough and wants to be back with her family. Is there anything you can do for them? They can't go back to Thailand now. There's nothing there for them.'

'Believe me,' Leslie replied, 'they won't be going back.'

That was the news I had been waiting to hear. I told her all about Lee and our planned meeting with the team from Melbourne the following morning.

'I'm not sure you should trust anyone,' she said. 'This has pretty far reaching implications. A lot of heads are going to roll when this is through. Anuia is the key to it all. They've been trying to nail these people for some time and this is the first clear shot they've got at it.'

'Leslie,' I asked, 'can you tell your people to get here as soon as they can? Between the two groups, I'm sure we can get it sorted out once and for all.'

'Yes,' she replied. 'I'll give you a number for a man called John Gerrard. He's with internal investigations in the Victoria police force. If anything happens, any change of plan, can you call him and let him know? It's a cell number and he'll answer it anytime.'

'I will Leslie. Thanks for all your help. We really appreciate it.'

'We?' she asked, 'how many of you are there?'

'As of today,' I replied, 'there are thirteen of us in our little group. How many have helped along the way? I'm not sure, but I'd say it's thousands in one way or another. I'll explain it to you someday.'

I looked at Paul as I hung up.

'Look,' he said, and shrugged, 'one way or another it'll all be done tomorrow. Let's go and spend some time with Anuia. I don't think we'll be seeing her again for a while.'

'Yes,' I agreed, 'let's do that.'

We found them sitting around a big table out back. Thirteen in all, and a few more who had come to say hello.

Anuia sat amongst them, her usual quiet smiling self. I sensed some sadness in her demeanour, particularly when she looked at one of our own special little group. It was going to be her last night with us. Come tomorrow she would be gone and we couldn't tell when we would meet again.

I was, as usual, up earliest the next morning. I wanted to enjoy the relative quiet of the garden before the day kicked into life. The sun crept slowly into the blue sky promising another beautiful day. The smell of summer flowers intertwined with the aroma of hot coffee as I sipped slowly from the mug now sitting on my lap. I thought about the day and how events might unfold. I smiled a smile that only a morning in paradise could afford.

I wasn't the only one who was up. Alan left earlier to walk the long stretch of beach out front, a similar thought of a moment's solitude on his mind. We had talked a lot about their travels. Where they had been, who they had met, and the things they had done. He told me about his favourite parts and the memories he would keep with him forever. Inevitably our talk turned to home. What it had been like for us before we left. What it would be like when we went back. Would it be different or would we be different? I thought back to when we first met on the plane leaving Dublin. He was so young, naïve and anxious like myself. I looked at him now, grown into a man in such a short space of time, the pallid skin of a wet Irish summer replaced by the tan of a hot Australian one. Uncertainty replaced by confidence. Life for him would never be the same again. The places might, the people might, but he had changed. And I knew that I had changed too. I smiled again.

I made another cup of coffee, deciding to sit for a little while longer. Alan arrived back through reception. He looked worriedly around. Before he even saw me, I knew there was something wrong.

'What is it Al?' I asked, resting my coffee on the table.

'You'd better come with me,' he replied urgently, 'there's something you should see.'

'What is it? What's wrong?' I asked, preparing to set off in the direction from which he had just returned.

'No,' he said, leading me past the bar toward the back of the hostel, 'this way.'

We left the hostel grounds through the big double gate at the back of the property and turned left. At the corner of the turn onto Fraser Street, he stopped, placing his hand on my chest. He held a finger to his lips and whispered.

'Take a look. The black car parked on the left half way down.'

I stepped in front of him, shoulder tight to the fence and looked to where he had said. I saw a black car with four men sitting in it. Waiting.

'What do you think?' he whispered.

'I'm not sure,' I whispered uncertainly, but I knew.

'Come with me,' he said, 'there's something else.'

We passed back by the hostel gates to the corner of Denman Camp Road. He turned to me as he stopped.

'Take a look down the street,' he said, 'the other side of the road.'

I saw what he was talking about. A black car similar to the other and what appeared to be another four men, sitting and waiting.

'What do you make of it?' he asked.

'This is not good,' I replied, 'we need to get back and warn the others.'

Anuia, Lucy, Robbie, Sam and Toni had used the two bedrooms in my apartment. Paul, Dave and I had slept in the sitting room on the floor. They were all up.

'We've got a problem' I said, closing the door behind me.

The apartments were part of the original building to the front of the hostel grounds. From here we could see anyone who came and went. Dave kept watch as I told them what Alan had discovered. Robbie watched the back.

'Do we have a plan?' Paul asked.

'You know me Paul. We always have a plan,' I replied, as one began to form in my head.

The cavalry would arrive this morning but could we take the chance that they would get here in time? Why had they not made their move? Was it because there were too many people around, but that hadn't deterred them before. Or were they waiting for more men to arrive, though we didn't necessarily believe they needed backup. It didn't make sense.

It was eleven thirty when the van pulled out through the back entrance of our hostel. The exact time at which nine four wheel drives left for Fraser Island, the idea being that there may be some cover to be had with so many leaving together, or safety in numbers. It was a hopeful thought but we needed to gain any advantage possible. Koalas arranged self-drive trips to the island attracting a lot of backpackers trying to avoid the organised guided trips, looking for that extra bit of

216

freedom. Robert and Lucy drove close behind the van. If it was followed, they would attempt to slow the pursuing cars in whatever way they could. Troy and Alan were in the van too, their eagerness to help worrying on the one hand, and I hoped they didn't underestimate the magnitude of what they were involved in, but reassuring on the other as we needed all the help we could muster.

Any hope of an advantage would be short lived, the two black cars taking up pursuit as soon as we broke from our convoy and left Hervey Bay. They stayed a suitable distance behind, watching and waiting for what we could only assume was the right moment to make their move.

North from Hervey Bay towards Buxtonville agonising over the quiet nature of what were only back roads, and willing the van on in the hope that we could make it as far as a place called Howard and back onto the Bruce Highway. Northwards to Bundaberg, then Gladstone, then god knows where. The futility of the plan was all too apparent. They were in no hurry. They had us cornered, waiting on the perfect opportunity to make their move should they decide to, or easily tracking our progress if that was all they had planned. All we could do was keep going for as long and as far as possible.

At around one o'clock, on the road into Childers, Alan suggested taking the turn to Bundaberg, to get to a hostel and the relative safety of being among a larger group of people. It made sense but it gave the gang the opportunity they had been waiting for. The road from the highway to Bundaberg was practically deserted and quiet enough for the chance to force a van to the side of the road without attracting any unwanted attention.

Troy watched from the back as the two black cars picked up speed. They would catch Robert and Lucy's car within seconds so

Alan put his foot to the floor and the van lurched forward. Robert swerved his car from side to side trying to slow their pursuit, but it was no match for their powerful engines and they gunned passed him with relative ease. Sensing an opportunity, the lead black car flew past, pulling in front of the van and decelerating. There was no alternative but to bring it to a halt at the side of the road. Four men emerged from the lead car and three from the second which had stopped about fifty yards behind. Two of them stood facing the road, a warning to Robert to keep his distance. They were all Asian. Two of the men in front produced hand guns from shoulder holsters and walked towards the van. They didn't point them directly, but they did enough to ensure that everyone understood the threat. They ordered Alan to step from the driver side and for Troy, riding shotgun, to join him. A third man walked back, opened the side door, and looked inside. He saw Sam, Toni and Robbie. No-one else. He turned to his associates and began shouting. He didn't speak English but it was easy to recognise the anger in his voice. One of them pushed Alan backwards against the van.

'You're friend,' he shouted, waving his gun in the air, 'where are they?'

'Hey, take it easy man,' Alan replied, 'we don't want any trouble. Who are you talking about? There are only us and the guys in the car back there.'

By this time the two men to the back had covered the distance to Robert's car, checked the occupants, and were also shouting.

'What's the story man?' Troy exclaimed, 'what's this all about? You can't be stopping us like this in the middle of nowhere. We're just backpackers doing a bit of travelling. We're not looking for any trouble.'

Whether this was wise or not, it did little to curb their anger.

'There is Asian girl,' he said, 'we know she travel in this van. Where is she?'

'Listen bud, what's this all about? We've had a lot of people travelling in this van since we left Sydney. Can you be more specific?'

It seemed almost comical when Troy, Alan and the rest recounted the story the next time we saw them.

Chapter Twenty-Eight

The ferry from River Heads, just south of Hervey Bay, docked at Fraser Island at one o'clock, roughly the same time that the guys were stopped on the way to Bundaberg. Our four wheel drive was the first to disembark at the sandy dock. Paul, Dave and I jumped from the jeep to let the required amount of air to allow us drive the sandy tracks of Fraser out of the tyres. Moments later we were gone, disappearing into the thick vegetation on a track leaving Kingfisher Bay, heading for Lake McKenzie.

When we had all gathered in the hostel apartment that morning we devised our plan. Paul, Anuia, Marcus and I had talked to the manager of the hostel, explaining our situation and once again looking for the help we knew he would give. We weren't let down.

There was a 4WD drive excursion due to leave later in the morning. Paul, Dave, Anuia and I were booked on one of them. Travelling with five people we hadn't met before. Five people who, once our situation was explained, were eager to go along with the plan. Max, the hostel owner and manager, booked us under different names, bending strict booking rules for obtaining permits for our Fraser Island stay. When the men returned to look for us, which they inevitably would, there would be no record of us. Jasper and Marcus were due to leave a while later, taking Troy and Alan's car and traveling south. Max would suggest that these were the only people to have left that morning and it was possible Anuia could have travelled with them. After acting as a decoy, they would return to Hervey Bay two days from now, the same day we would return from the island, pick us up, then travel north again to Airlie Beach to catch up with the rest of the gang. By that stage our tracks would be well and truly lost to our pursuers.

We had gone over and over how the men could know we were in Hervey Bay. It was impossible to tell but we decided we couldn't trust anyone anymore. I had tried to ring Leslie before we left, to explain that we wouldn't be in Hervey as promised and to explain what had occurred since we last spoke. I couldn't get an answer so left a brief message to say that we just wouldn't be there and that I'd be in touch as soon as I could. With that, we climbed into our jeep, Anuia and I hiding on the floor as the van and the 4WDs left the hostel and our plan kicked into action.

We arrived at Lake McKenzie later that afternoon, our progress slowed by the fact that it had started to rain and every now and again we would encounter huge floods blocking our path. We were advised before leaving not to drive through any of the big pools without first checking their depth. For that, we needed a volunteer.

Jamie, a big, tall, brash Canadian hockey player, duly stepped forward. He had saved for his trip to Australia by shovelling snow from neighbour's drives. During a pit-stop for food on the way to the ferry, he suggested that all we needed was beer and wine. 'If we were hungry,' he said, 'we could eat Witchety Grubs.' He would, for the length of our stay, be the depth-checker as we would call him, dutifully climbing from the front seat to wade, fully clothed, into each pool before we would chance driving through. A role he increasingly revelled in for every can of beer he consumed, but which became progressively more difficult as the rain continued to fall.

Our group included two English girls, Clare and Sarah, a Swedish couple named Anneli and Gunar, and Jamie. We couldn't have picked a better bunch. Clare and Sarah were two good looking girls from Kent, south east of London. They had just finished college and were taking time out to travel before starting work. Anneli and

Gunar were far more seasoned travellers having left Sweden almost two years before. They backpacked extensively in Europe and throughout Asia before finally arriving in Australia about eight months ago. They worked when they needed to, saving money for the next leg of their trip, and never worrying where their next meal might come from. A trait I found enviable and for which I admired them so much.

Arriving at the campsite at Lake McKenzie we made the most of a brief respite in the almost incessant rain to get our tents set up, a campfire going, and tarpaulins strung between trees, covering our small area and giving us some shelter. Then we cooked dinner over a smoking log fire, drank beer and wine, talked and shared our journey with our new friends. We huddled closer together as the rain came down again, and added more wood to the fire.

By late evening we were joined by a number of other groups around the campsite. We watched them struggle to get their tents pitched and fires going in the incessant rain. I got up and made my way to one such group who tussled as much with the tent itself as with the weather. I could see they didn't have much experience camping. As the rain continued to pour, Dave and Paul joined me, helping some of the other groups with theirs. Then Anuia, then Jamie and our whole gang joined in. Everyone now helped as tents were slowly pitched, tarps were strung from tree to tree, and fires lit. At last, everyone was set up and had shelter and warmth for the night, all working together to share the experience and share the moment.

When we settled in again we were no longer alone as a group. And we didn't sit alone as a group. People wandered between different fires, meeting, talking, laughing and occasionally singing. I met people whose name I forgot two minutes later, and I met people whose names I knew I would never forget. I had bought a small tape player in a pawn shop back in Hervey, thinking that a few people might have brought some music with them, but soon realising that I had only one tape, borrowed from Alan that morning. A meagre collection of songs to be played non-stop over the next two days. Man on the Moon and Sidewinder Sleeps by REM, and Night Swimming, a song for which circumstances could not have been more apt.

Sometime before midnight the rain finally stopped, the cloud broke, and the island was lit by brilliant moonlight. Anneli and Gunnar had disappeared some time earlier to walk to the lake. Hurrying back, giddy and excited, they said they were going for a swim. Unfortunately for them, everyone agreed on what a good idea it was. Grabbing what we needed, we made our way the short distance to Lake McKenzie, its beach now lit by dozens of torch lights sitting on rocks or wedged between the branches of trees, casting their light over the still black water of the lake. We spent the next two hours running, swimming and jumping in the water. We shouted and we laughed. We fell on the sand to catch our breath and when we were ready we did it all again, remembering what it was like to be five or six years old. Remembering what it had been like before the world changed and before we changed. Remembering what it was like just to be ourselves.

When we got back to camp, we all drank and talked some more, one by one drifting off to tents, sleeping bags, and sleep. As the firelight dimmed, I sat alone reflecting again on where our trip had taken us. I realised that this journey was more than where Anuias problem had brought us. This journey was about each and every one of us and how we had arrived here. Though starting in so many different parts of the world, I thought that maybe, even though we didn't know it, we were destined to be here at the same time. To help Anuia of course, but, more importantly, to help us to be the people we had once been. As I lay in the tent, a million other thoughts raced through my mind until eventually, I fell asleep.

I was first to wake, rekindling the campfire and throwing on a few extra logs. It was just before dawn so I made my way to the lake once more. I didn't want to be alone but I was glad I had the place to myself. I stepped down onto the beautiful white sand, appreciating for the first time how pristine, clean and unspoilt it was. A million stars twinkled in the night sky as the moon reflected on the lake surface. I stood, ankle deep in the clear water, waiting for the dawn now appearing on the skyline above the dunes and understood why they called it the window lake.

I watched day break on the horizon. I felt the clear white sand between my toes. In that instant I understood that every single thing I had done in my life had lead me here to this one moment, that everything I had accomplished or achieved had lead me to this one place. To share this one perfect moment with nature, in the most beautiful place in the world. To realise that finally all my doubts about where I had been, or where I was going, were suddenly gone, sinking to the bottom of the clear blue lake I was now standing in. I was no longer afraid of what the future might hold, no longer afraid to go on. This was my moment.

I heard a noise and turned. A dingo passed slowly by half way up the beach. I hadn't been alone after all. Dave and Anuia sat on a fallen tree a bit further down. I raised my hand to say hello but didn't speak. They waved back. I looked around and saw Anneli and Gunnar sitting together. Further along the beach I recognised faces from the camps around our own. I wanted to tell them all about the significance of this perfect moment, in this perfect place, but I'm sure they already knew.

I gazed back out across the mirror smooth surface of the lake, the dark night turning a deep purple, then to dark blue. A beautiful clear blue sky followed, morning once again. I don't know how long I stood there, and didn't notice Dave and Anuia as they came and stood beside me.

'It's something else,' Dave said, putting his arm around my shoulder.

'It sure is,' I said, as Anuia linked my arm.

The three of us turned and walked back up the beach. We had our whole life in front of us.

It started raining again around mid-morning. Just long enough for us to have breakfast but not long enough to get the tents and tarps down and packed away. We bundled everything into the jeep as best we could and left Lake McKenzie. I knew I would never be back.

Driving eastwards, we came to the beach. There we drove north along the Fraser Highway's mile after mile of unspoilt sand, the mighty swell of the ocean to our right, the island to our left. At times it rained so hard we could hardly make out where the beach met the sea, and when it didn't we sped along as if we were the only people on the island. It felt like we almost were.

We were aiming for Indian Head towards the north of the island, planning to stop at Eli Creek along the way. Further on we explored the Maheno Wreck, a liner which ran aground there years before. Then we passed Cathedral Beach with its coloured cliffs, eventually arriving at Waddy Point where we planned to spend the night.

We were first there and pitched our tents in the rain. We strung the tarps between the trees and got the camp fire going. Bit-by-bit other groups trickled in. They hung their tarps between the trees around our own, slowly extending the area outwards, pitching their tents, and settling in around our fire. I spent the day exploring the forests and beaches around Waddy Point, sometimes joined by a few of the lads and sometimes alone, but happy either way. Later I spent a few hours sitting on the beach with one of the English girls. We talked about everything and nothing, amazed at how diverse our lives could be but how similar our ideas on life itself were. It never stopped raining but even that didn't matter. I found Anuia sitting alone by the fire.

'It's great isn't it?' I asked her.

'It is,' she replied, 'I have almost forgotten the problems I will have to face. Being here has been a wonderful experience, so many lovely people in such a beautiful place. I know it has to end, but I will remember this forever.'

'Me too,' I said, 'it's hard to believe that life can be this simple when there are so many bad things in the world. I know we have to go back tomorrow but I promise we'll stick with you to the end. One way or another we'll figure out what's best for you and your family.'

'I know you will,' she replied, and for the first time I really believed that we would figure a way out of this. With so many great people ready and willing to help us, even though they knew so little about us, we couldn't fail.

Morning came. Bright and blue, but dark clouds further out to sea told us that rain would soon follow. Considering the last few days, it would have been strange to have it any other way. Packing tents and camping gear as quickly as we could we left for Indian Head, hoping to get there before the rain came. When we arrived we climbed to the top and looked out at the vast ocean in front of us, seventy five mile beach to our right, the champagne pools further off to our left, and the beautiful green and gold of Fraser Island behind us. From our vantage point, we could make out the darkly silhouetted, ominous shape of five or six tiger sharks as they patrolled the area searching for their next meal. We had been warned not to swim in the sea, and while we knew they lurked somewhere beneath the surface, it was truly amazing to be able to see them. We stayed for a while until the sky darkened and the first light drizzle fell. By the time we got back to the jeep it was raining hard once again.

'Man,' Jamie said, 'I thought we were going to have a nice day there for a while. Now that'd just ruin the trip altogether.'

We all laughed but for some reason, it seemed he was right. Already wet through, we drove the short distance to the champagne pools and jumped in, fully clothed. We stayed for as long as we could but soon it was time to go. Driving back down Seventy Five Mile beach I was quiet, listening as the gang talked and laughed. I wanted to remember this feeling for the rest of my life, to implant it somewhere in the recesses of my mind, able to call on it whenever I needed to be reassured that no matter how bad life may seem from time to time, there would always, always be something good. There was one last stop to make before we took the ferry back to the mainland.

We parked and made our way to Lake Wabby. Most of us ran. On the bank of a vast sand dune, we sat and marvelled at the beauty of the lake hidden at the bottom. Then it really was time to go. As the ferry made its way back to the mainland we came across a school of dolphins that stayed with us for a few minutes, leading our way.

Chapter Twenty-Nine

When we arrived at the hostel, Jasper was waiting for us as agreed. Alan was there too.

'I didn't expect to see you here Alan,' I said.

'Jasper and Marcus caught up with us yesterday in Bundaberg,' he replied. 'We thought you might need more than one car considering there are four of you and all your gear.'

'Cool,' I said, 'I hadn't thought of that.'

'Yes,' Jasper added, 'Marcus and I drove south as planned two days ago and stayed overnight in Noosa. There was no-one following so we drove on to Bundaberg yesterday and met the guys in the hostel.'

'Where's everyone now?' I asked.

They had gone on to Rockhampton in the van and would wait at a hostel they had picked out.

'Any sign of them?' I asked, 'did they follow you the other day?'

'Oh yes,' Alan replied, 'they most certainly did. I'll fill you in as we go. Are you ready to hit the road?'

'Pretty much,' I answered.

I asked Max had anyone came looking for us.

'Yep,' he replied. 'A few guys turned up in a black car the evening you left. 'Said they were looking for someone who had stayed here. I showed them the registration books for here and the island. Your names aren't on either so they left. 'No sign since.'

'It's a good bet they have no idea where we are just now,' I said. 'The sooner we get moving the better.'

'I don't think you'll be going anywhere until tomorrow,' Max added. 'There's been so much rain over the past few days that Hervey has flooded. No-one's getting in and no-one's getting out. You can try, but I doubt you'll get far.'

'What about phones?' I asked.

'Sorry mate,' Max replied, 'they've been down since yesterday.'

'Balls,' I said, 'I need to get in touch with Lee and Leslie. This is the last thing we need.'

It rained incessantly late into the evening. Max was right. The streets around Hervey were under water. We wouldn't have made it far. Paul and I sat in the darkness of the apartment sitting room, keeping watch on the black street outside. The power had gone out shortly after midnight and everyone else had gone to bed.

'Why don't you get some sleep?' he asked.

'I can't,' I replied, 'I know I won't be able to.'

Suddenly the distant night sky was lit up by a flash of lightning. I could see the island silhouetted on the horizon. The rain had stopped but the air was still heavy with moisture. Sweat trickled down my back as I anticipated the next burst.

'I wish the phones would come back on,' I said.

'Yeah,' he replied, the tension evident in his voice. 'No-one has any idea where we are. We're totally blind.'

'How do these guys keep finding us?' I then asked, 'why didn't they make their move the other day.'

'I don't know,' Paul said. 'What will we do?'

'I need to contact Leslie. She's the only one we should trust.'

'What about Lee?'

'We still need him,' I replied, 'it's still important that people know Anuia's story. She'll need all the help she can get.'

'She will,' he whispered, 'I'm going to try and get some sleep.'

I kept watch, silently.

'Can I sit with you for a while?' Anuia asked, when she joined me some time later.

'Sure,' I replied, 'are you okay?'

'I can't sleep. I could hear you and Paul talking. If you think it is best to trust your friend at home, I think that is what we should do.'

She paused.

'Do you mind if I say something?' she asked. 'Over the last few days I think we have started to see the real you.'

'Thanks,' I said.

I knew what she meant.

'It's the closest to the real me I have felt for some time,' I said, 'I think I've rediscovered who I am. It's why I came here in the first place.'

'There's a lot more about you I would like to know,' she smiled, 'maybe you can tell me.....'

'Sssh!!,' I whispered, startled.

I heard a noise from down below.

'Get back,' I said, 'there's someone coming up the stairs.'

I backed away from the window into the blackness of the room. Anuia crouched behind me. The muffled sound of footsteps stopped outside the door. They tried the handle, but the door was locked.

'Guys, guys,' he whispered, knocking lightly, 'it's me, Max.'

'Shit Max,' I said, unlocking the door, 'you frightened the life out of us. What is it?'

'The phones are back on.'

Chapter Thirty

'Hi Mum,' I said, when she answered.

'Where have you been?' she asked, 'we've been worried sick. Are you okay?'

'I'm fine mum,' I replied, 'we're all okay. I'm sorry I haven't been in touch. Things got a bit mad a few days ago and we needed to get off the radar for a while.'

'Leslie said you left a message,' she said, 'have you spoken to her yet? Oh God, I'm so relieved. We didn't know what to think.'

'I'll ring her right away,' I promised. 'Is Dad there? Stick him on for a minute.'

'Hey kid. How are you doing?' he asked. 'There are a lot of people looking for you. Leslie's people are waiting to hear from you.'

'I know Dad,' I said, 'I...., I just wanted to hear your voice.'

'Listen son,' he said, 'ring Leslie. Get this business sorted out as soon as you can and get yourself home here where you belong.'

'I will Dad,' I said, 'I'll be home soon.'

Then I rang Leslie.

'Before you say anything,' I said, 'I'm really sorry that I haven't been in touch. The men were back. We had to leave in a hurry.'

'Don't worry about that,' she replied, 'I'm just glad you're all okay. What's important now is Anuia. John Gerard is waiting to hear from you. He has a group of people ready to move in an instant. He needs to know where and when.'

'Will Anuia be okay Leslie?' I asked sadly. 'I mean...., when it's all done.'

'I'll be honest with you,' she replied, 'they'll need Anuia's testimony against these people. Until that happens she'll be placed in police protection. It's a lot to ask from her but once it's all over they'll have a pretty normal life.'

'She'll be okay,' I said, 'she's strong.'

'She'll need to be,' Leslie replied. 'Get in touch with John. Where are you?'

'We're still in Hervey Bay,' I said. 'We had a bit of help with our plan a few days ago. The men chasing us thought we went north and have since thought we went south.'

'Fraser?' she asked.

'Yes,' I replied, 'we had no choice.'

'I had a feeling you might have gone there,' she said.

'You did?' I asked, 'why didn't you send anyone looking for us?'

'It doesn't really matter,' she replied. 'Get in touch with John. Where are you planning on going now? They'll be watching for you everywhere.'

'I'll ring him right away,' I said. 'We're leaving for Rockhampton first thing. We'll keep on the move and aim for Airlie Beach.'

'There's something else,' she added. 'I don't think you should talk to anyone else. Look, I know this reporter friend of yours has people waiting to talk to you, but we don't have enough information on them. They ran a story about Anuia. He seems to have lead on it but it doesn't necessarily read well from her point of view.'

'How do you mean?' I asked.

'It says she's connected to the double homicide in Melbourne. That she's on the run and being helped by various people in the backpack community – people who have no reason to be involved in this. It has excerpts from an interview, advising her to hand herself in, but that she won't. I'm not sure what the angle is, but none of it is helping public perception.'

I was furious. After all Lees promises to be on Anuia's side, to help her in any way he could. It seemed he had done anything but.

I found John's number, scribbled with so many others on the now tattered pages of my part diary, part phone book, Lonely Planet.

'John Gerrard,' he answered instantly, as if he had anticipated this very call.

I told him who I was, my connection to Leslie, and my connection to Anuia. It was only when I spoke to him that I began to realise how big this thing really was and how big a break for their investigation this could be. He told me about some of the high profile individuals they suspected were involved and the incriminations against leading businessmen, politicians, and police.

'We want you to keep moving,' he said. 'If you stay in the one place for too long, it increases their chances of tracking you down.'

'We're leaving for Rockhampton today,' I said. 'We're meeting with some friends of ours. There are rumours going around the hostels about us. We're heading north, south, east and west.'

'That all helps,' he replied. 'I've got some people ready to move on my command. We need to talk to Anuia now.'

'I can get us to Airlie Beach by tomorrow,' I offered. 'Who can we expect to see? Will you be there yourself?'

'Yes. We'll fly to Airlie Beach today and be waiting for you. We have pictures of suspects in this case. We'd like Anuia to look at them, to see if she recognises anyone. We have some other important information that we need to discuss but I would prefer to do it in person.'

'Like what?' I asked.

'I think it better we talk in person,' was all he replied.

'What about our other contact, the journalist that has been helping us?' I asked.

'Don't talk to anyone before we talk to Anuia. This is vitally important. Let me know when you arrive in Airlie and we'll meet.'

'Okay,' I said as I hung up, many more questions now going around in my head.

When I got back to the apartment they were already up. I filled them in on my conversations with Leslie and John.

'What does he mean 'discuss it in person'?' Paul asked.

'I'm not sure,' I replied. 'He just said it's vitally important that we don't talk to anyone before we meet them. We need to get to Airlie beach. I told him we'd be there tomorrow but I think we could make it today. I reckon it's about a fourteen hour drive, plus we'll have to stop in Rockhampton.'

'I agree,' Paul said, 'it might be better to arrive there before anyone expects us. Organise somewhere to stay and have a look around.'

I could see the first glimpse of daylight as we packed our bags and prepared to go. Clare, Sarah, Anneli and Gunnar wanted more than anything to come with us, to help in any way they could, but agreed reluctantly that it wasn't the best idea when I explained how many of us were already involved. Anelli and Gunnar were heading south to Sydney to look for work. Clare and Sarah were staying in Hervey for another day or two before catching the Oz bus to Cairns. I promised we would meet them there, by which time it would all be over. Jamie was coming with us.

'What about Lee?' Anuia asked, as we carried our gear down to the van.

'I'm sorry,' I replied, 'but it seems he was only in it for himself. If there's any way we can use him later, then that's what we'll do.'

'Don't be sorry,' she said, 'I believed him too.'

It was eight o'clock. Already later leaving than I had hoped considering the distance we needed to cover to get to Airlie Beach today.

Then we were off. Paul, Dave, Anuia, and myself in one car, inseparable as always. Marcus, Alan and Jamie in the other. Anneli, Gunnar, Clare, Sarah and Max waved as we sped away from the hostel.

Chapter Thirty-One

It's a five hour drive from Hervey Bay to Rockhampton. Three hundred and ninety seven kilometres and I counted every one. Wondering what was around every corner, or who could be waiting at every turn. We just needed to get there, pick up the rest of the guys and make the mad dash for Airlie. To what should be the end to this nightmare and safety for Anuia. I couldn't help being apprehensive, thinking of John Gerrard's words. Don't talk to anyone else. It's vitally important. What, I thought, could be so vitally important and why couldn't he just tell me over the phone? I thought about Lee's story. If he had been driving it, I expected it to be more favourable to Anuia and her plight. Maybe he wasn't in control of it anymore. Maybe he never had been and the help he promised was never there to be had, thinking only of how he could benefit from it.

'We're all very quiet today guys,' Paul said, as he drove. 'Don't worry, we just need to get to Airlie and this can all end.'

'That's true,' I replied, not fully convinced.

We drove on in silence, our progress slower than expected as flooding hadn't fully subsided. It was already late afternoon by the time we found the Rockhampton Youth Hostel. Troy and Robbie were waiting.

'It's great to see you guys,' Troy said as we walked in. 'I thought you'd be here yesterday.'

'It was the weather,' I said. 'We got flooded in at Hervey and couldn't leave until this morning. Where's everyone? Are you ready to roll?'

'We most certainly are,' Troy replied, hurrying off. 'I'll get the gang together.'

'I kind of thought you knew Alan and Troy before you left Ireland?' Robbie asked, when he had gone.

'No,' I replied, and explained how we'd met. 'I didn't expect that we'd ever meet up again on this side of the world.'

'It is a small world,' she said. 'Do you have a plan?'

'I do,' I said. 'We're going to Airlie Beach. We're going to meet some people there and this is all going to be over. Anuia and her family will be safe.'

'I think it's great what you're doing for her,' she said. 'Don't you wonder how things would have turned out for her if she had never met you? Do you think that she was meant to find you? And that you were meant to find the two guys and that your paths would cross again when you needed them most?'

What I was thinking was that this girl spent too much time smoking some strange weed. She was right of course. I had thought about all of this. It's just that when she said it, the words were coming from her mouth, but the thoughts seemed to be coming from a place somewhere in space.

Troy was back, Robert, Lucy, Sam, Toni and Jasper in tow. While we packed everything into cars and vans, he whispered in my ear.

'What do you think of Robbie?' he asked.

I sensed there was something more than just friendship going on so decided on as politically correct an answer as I could.

'She's nice,' I said. 'Good looking, cool. I like her.'

'Me too,' he replied, a satisfied grin on his face suggesting that he had needed or I had given my approval in some way.

'She's a bit wacko though,' I said, keeping as straight a face as I could. 'Too much time on the happy tobacco?'

He stopped, turning to face me.

'Oh yeah,' he said, 'totally wacko.'

We burst out laughing.

'Okay,' Paul asked, 'what's so funny?'

'Nothing really,' I replied, 'I'll fill you in later.'

'It's getting late,' he said. 'Do you think it's a good idea to keep going for Airlie tonight? It's got to be a six or seven hour drive at best. We won't get there until well into the morning.'

'I know,' I said, 'but I think we should. We'll be travelling by night and much harder to spot. Plus I think it best we get there and get somewhere to stay sorted out. Get settled in and have a look around before we meet John Gerrard in the morning.'

'Case the joint you mean?' he said, eyebrow raised.

'Something like that,' I said, smiling at the surrealism of it all.

I was starting to relax, knowing it was nearly over. One more long drive, one more night and we'd be done. While I still worried about Anuia and if they would look after her, my biggest fear now was when I would get to see her again.

'We'll need somewhere to stay in Airlie,' he said.

'I think I might have just the place,' I replied. 'Anneli and Gunnar told me about a good hostel called Club Thirteen. They said it's on a hill overlooking the whole town.'

'Sounds like a plan. Will we ring ahead?' he asked.

'No,' I replied, 'I'd rather we didn't announce our arrival in any way. I'm probably being paranoid, but isn't it possible someone might be watching these places?'

'Maybe not totally paranoid dude,' he said.

'Besides,' I said, smiling. 'Anneli and Gunnar said it's run by an Irish guy. Let's see what Irish hospitality is like at three in the morning. Let's get going.'

We were on the road again. Probably the last time we would all be together though I was thinking mainly of Anuia, Dave, Paul, and myself. It had been a whirlwind ride. I'd miss her. We stayed together in the car, just the four of us. Troy, Alan, Robbie, Marcus, Jamie and Jasper took the van and Robert, Lucy, Sam and Toni took the other car leaving about fifteen minutes apart.

The last leg, another five hundred kilometres, and I counted every one again. I suppose it was inevitable that I would – so close to our goal and so close to safety. These men were out there somewhere and I was pretty sure they'd be doing everything possible to find us. I saw every sign for every turn-off, to towns that I would never see, longing to explore them all. Parkhurst, Yaamba and Marlborough, Clairview and Carmilla, then West Hill and Sarina.

We were fifty kilometres from Mackay, one of the bigger towns along the coast. Again, progress had been slower than expected and it was already eleven o'clock when we pulled in at the side of the road just outside the town. It wasn't long until the van caught us up, then Robert in his car.

'I could do with some food,' I said, and they all agreed.

'The Great Barrier Reef is out there somewhere,' Dave said. 'Maybe when this is all done we could go and see it together?'

'I'd be up for that' I replied, but I knew it would never happen.

'Me too,' Paul added, 'a diving course and then a sailing trip around the Whitsundays and the Barrier Reef.'

Anuia was quiet.

'I don't think I'll be going with you guys,' she said. 'I think we all know that. I would love to more than anything in the world but I'll have to go back to Melbourne. This will be our last journey together.'

'Let's see what happens,' Dave said. 'You just never know what life will throw at you.'

I wanted to tell her that it didn't have to end that way, that we would get the chance to do it together some day. But I didn't know if it was true or not. None of us knew what path we would be taking after tomorrow.

'Dave's right,' I said, 'life can be funny. Let's just hope that it's not the end. We'll find each other again.'

'Thanks guys,' she said, smiling. 'We made a great team.'

'What about that place?' Paul asked, spotting Billy Baxter's Café.

'Here it is,' I said, checking the book. ''Seems like a pretty good place to eat according to this.'

Paul pulled up outside. It was late but there was still a few people knocking around. I went on in as the other's got out and followed.

'How are you doing?' I asked the guy behind the counter. 'Are you Billy?

'Not me mate,' he said, smiling. 'What can I do ya for?'

'I know it's late and all,' I replied, 'but could you rustle something together for a gang. We've been on the road all day and we're trying to get to Airlie Beach tonight.'

'Sure,' he said, but his eyes widened as the rest of them filtered through the door and he realised just how many of us there were.

'Grab some seats,' he said, with a wry smile.

'Cheers mate,' I said, 'thanks a million for this.'

We pushed a few tables together and sat, everyone in a relaxed mood except for Dave. While he didn't really show it, I could tell he just wasn't himself, keeping as close to Anuia as he possibly could, something she didn't seem to mind. I talked to the guy behind the counter.

'Where are you all from?' he asked.

'I'm from Ireland. So are the two boys there,' I said, pointing at Paul and Dave. We've got English, Dutch, Canadian, and even Thai. Do you get many backpackers coming through Mackay?'

'Oh yeah mate,' he replied 'there's always a few backpackers knocking around at any time of the year, always coming in here when the bars shut.'

The Oz accent becomes more pronounced the further north you go and the further you are from the major cities. Not a whole lot different to back home I thought.

'What about all this rumour of some people on the run along the east coast?' he asked. 'It seems to be the big story with travellers these days.'

'We've all heard it,' I smiled, unconsciously glancing towards Anuia, then realising what I had done.

He glanced quickly in her direction. I hoped I hadn't given anything away.

'Anyway,' he said, 'maybe you could help me out a bit and ask your lot what they're going to have.'

'Sure,' I said, 'no problem at all. Thanks again. I know it's late.'

'Don't worry mate, there'll be a few in long after you're gone. Some of these backpackers never know when to go home.'

I went around the tables asking what everyone was going to have. Burgers, chips, curry sauce and dips.

'Healthy food all round,' I said, relaying the order to Chris, as he introduced himself, and he set about deep frying and chopping like his life depended on it.

Back at the table, I told Paul what Chris had said about the rumours going around.

'Don't worry,' he said, 'there's no way he could know. It'll be okay.'

I watched as he prepared our food. He looked Anuia's way more than once, a hint of recognition in his expression.

I helped bringing out the orders and Chris was genuinely glad to have the extra pair of hands. By this time, a few other people had filtered in. Backpackers mostly, and he lost interest in Anuia, even if he had had an interest in the first place.

We ate and talked amongst ourselves, no longer in that much of a hurry. We already knew how late it would be when we got to Airlie and an extra hour or two on the journey wasn't going to make a difference now. It was well past midnight when we finished and prepared to go. I collected money from the gang and went to pay as everyone moved out the doorway, thanking him as they went.

'All done?' Chris asked. 'Hope it'll fill the gap for you.'

'It sure will,' I replied. 'Thanks again for looking after us this late on. How much do we owe you?'

'Here, take a look at this,' he said, handing me a newspaper over the counter. 'Recognise anyone?'

Sure enough, there on the front page was a picture of Anuia. Not a recent one but, to me, instantly recognisable.

'Maybe they're not rumours after all?' he asked.

'Maybe not,' I replied, scanning quickly through the story.

Leslie had been right. It didn't do much to help Anuia's cause or dispel public perception of her involvement. It said she was being helped by a group of Irish men. We were famous at last.

I looked at Chris, trying to find something appropriate to say. But what could you do in the circumstances except hope for one last person to understand, to be on your side, and to help.

'Don't worry about it mate,' he said, before I could reply. 'You were never here.'

Relieved, I thanked him, once again reassured.

'How much do we owe you for the food?' I asked.

'It's on the house mate. If you ever make it back this way, I'm good for a few schooners. Look after the girl.'

'I will,' I said, offering him my hand.

The guys were waiting when I came out.

'What was that all about?' Dave asked, as we pulled away from the curb.

'He knows who Anuia is,' I replied. 'He recognised her from the paper. If he recognised her so easily, anyone could. Let's get moving.'

I took the wheel for this leg of the journey and we drove in silence. The guys may have drifted off to sleep but I didn't know. Alone in the darkness, I watched signposts pass. Kuttabi, Mount Ossa, Calen. One after another, eventually coming to Prosperine and taking a right turn for Airlie Beach. It was close to three o'clock as I rounded the bend coming down into the town. Taking the next right to Waterson Road and up to Begley Street, I looked for Club 13, the hostel where we planned to stay. Anneli was right. It rested high up on the hill on the west side, the town below lit up but showing little sign of life. Even for a backpacker stop. Lights sparkled on the water, boats and yachts moored just off the coast. The view would have to wait. Tired and weary, we needed sleep.

The office door was locked, a note on the bell saying to ring for assistance. So I did. For about ten minutes non-stop until some lights came on and we heard movement inside. A sleepy, dishevelled head peered through a window before opening the door.

'What?' he asked angrily, 'do you know what time it is?'

An unmistakable, distinctly Irish accent.

'Sure it's early yet,' I replied, over pronouncing my own, 'any chance of a bed for the night.'

'Dubs everywhere,' he said. 'I came all the way to Australia to get away from them and they still find me.'

His tone softened.

'How many of you are there?' he asked, looking over my shoulder. 'Throw your bags down there and come on in 'til we get you settled for the night.'

We piled in behind him. All fourteen of us and, one by one, he checked us in, giving directions to each room.

Club 13 was a hotel at some stage in the past but was now being used as a hostel. The rooms were spread out in different sections, over different levels, plain enough with two or three bunk beds in each. Anuia, the two lads and I shared as usual and Sam and Toni occupied the beds in the other bunk. Now that we were here, I

246

didn't feel as tired. I walked back to pool we had passed on the way down. Grabbing a white plastic lounger, I pulled the zipper up tight on my hoodie and sat back, hands tucked into my pockets. I wasn't alone for long.

'So this is it?' Paul asked, pulling up a lounger beside me.

'It's been a bit of an adventure all right,' I replied, 'more than we came looking for anyway.'

'We'll miss her when she's gone.'

'I know Paul. He'll miss her more though,' I said, as Dave joined us.

'That I will,' he agreed, settling in beside us.

Anuia wasn't too far behind, Sam and Toni in tow. And it wasn't long before most of the other guys were gathered round, trying to hold onto this adventure just a little while longer. We sat together talking until dawn broke on the horizon, moving to the topmost terrace as the sun rose. The sea sparkled beneath a beautiful blue sky and we watched Airlie Beach slowly come to life.

'Are you okay Anuia?' I asked, noticing how quiet she had become.

'I'm just very sad,' she replied. 'I hope you know how much you all mean to me. I'll never be able to thank you for standing by me and believing in me. You didn't even know me.'

'But look around you,' I said, 'how many of these people know you or know us. That's why all these people are here. That's what makes them different and makes them stand out from the crowd. Look at all the people who have helped us along the way. You've given them something too. That belief that they have done something different, that they have done the right thing. Something that will stay with them and they can say 'yeah, we were there.'

'I'm just worried,' she paused. 'I'm just worried that I won't get to see you guys again.'

'Anuia,' I said, 'whatever it takes, I promise you we will.'

'All for one and one for all,' Paul added, smiling. 'Let's make the call.'

I found a payphone and dialled John Gerrard's number.

'John, it's me. Where can we meet?'

'G'day mate,' he replied. 'There's a place called the Sidewalk Cafe on Airlie Esplanade. Who's with you?'

'Anuia, myself, and two friends. We'll be there as soon as we can.'

Anuia had her bags packed when I got back to the terrace.

'Time to go?' she asked.

'Time to go,' I replied sadly, as she said goodbye to them all.

Chapter Thirty-Two

Dave carried her bag as we walked down the hill and into town. We knew exactly where the café was. Down Shute Harbour, veering left along the beach front. My eyes scanned the area, alerted to every movement, worried about who could be here watching and waiting. I examined every face, looking for any indication of recognition but thankfully there was none. We walked apprehensively into the café, empty except for six people in suits talking and drinking coffee. Their conversation paused as we walked towards them.

'John Gerrard?' I asked, aiming my question at them all.

A tall, worried looking man in a grey suit stood and offered his hand.

'That's me,' he said, as I shook it.

'Anuia?' he asked, turning towards her.

She shook his hand confidently. Not overawed in any way by the sight of these men that had been searching for her for so long.

'Yes,' she replied, 'I'm pleased to meet you.'

'We're pleased to meet you too,' John replied, 'we've been looking for you for quite some time. Let me introduce you to some of my colleagues.'

He went through the names one-by-one, outlining their role and why they were there. Two men from the Victoria police force, one a detective like John Gerrard himself and one from their Internal Investigations department. The latter present, as John explained, because the investigation not only centred around criminals and high ranking government officials, but also on members of their own force.

He then introduced a middle aged woman who shook Anuia's hand, explaining that she was representing Australian Immigration and including a few quick words on her family's welfare. She would outline the options available to Anuia's family when the time was right. He then introduced a man named Paul Sheehan from the Irish consulate in Sydney. He was there because of Paul, Dave and me. I didn't know if I should be worried or happy and hadn't, up until now, considered the implication of our involvement and how we had helped Anuia. I'd worry about that later. Somehow, Leslie had managed to pull all the right people together.

'You probably didn't notice,' John continued, 'but you passed two unmarked police cars on your way down. Some additional resources from the Victoria force. Plus, Queensland police are providing all the necessary backup. We have all the bases covered.'

He was right. We hadn't noticed anything.

'If you'd like to take a seat Anuia, we have some things to discuss,' he said, showing her to their table.

Paul, Dave and I remained standing.

'Here's where we're at Anuia,' John started. 'I'm not sure how much information Leslie has been able to give you over the last few days but this is a lot bigger than you might think. This investigation has been going on for some time but admittedly without much success. We just haven't been able to get the break. We're hoping that what you know and witnessed will be the game changer. We believe there are certain prominent business men and government officials involved. We also believe, unfortunately, that there are some members of our own police force involved, making the process particularly difficult. We have had to be extremely careful when asking questions and at whom we point the finger, as I'm sure you can all understand.'

I had given Leslie the shortened version of events from the morning of the shootings. She believed, as did John, that this pointed directly to police involvement verifying all that Anuia had told us originally. I was glad I had never doubted her.

'So,' Anuia asked, 'what is it you want me to do?'

'Okay,' John continued, 'this is where things get a little more difficult than you may have been expecting. I'd like you to take a look at some photographs. See who you can recognise. Then I'll explain who they all are and where they fit in.'

Over the next ten minutes John and his colleagues produced a number of photographs, presenting each to Anuia and asking if she recognised anyone. Some contained a number of people which she studied intently before moving on to the next. Others contained pictures of individuals. Again she studied them closely before nodding her head to move on. When John finished showing the photos he looked at her and asked.

'You recognised some faces?

'Yes,' Anuia replied, taking some of photos from the pile and examining each one again.

'This man,' she said, on the fourth. 'This is the man who arrived in the black car that morning. I am absolutely sure of it.'

John looked at his colleagues, obviously pleased. His day had just got so much better.

'I also recognise this man,' she said, pointing to a different photo. 'He was there too. He is the man who fired the first shots.'

He was Asian. I thought I recognised him from the morning we had the trouble in Brisbane but couldn't be sure.

'He chased us the morning we arrived in Brisbane,' she said, re-affirming my thoughts.

John took the photographs back, removing one in particular from the pile. The picture of the man in the black car.

'This man,' John said, 'is the key to everything. He is the link here in Australia and runs, among other things, an illegal immigration racket worth millions of dollars every year. We know it's him but we haven't been able to tie him to anything so far. He has covered his tracks and his involvement extremely well – mainly by buying off all the right people, local businessmen, politicians and the police. He is very successful and is well respected among the elite in Melbourne. It makes him very hard to touch. This is the first mistake he has made but then I don't believe he expected things to go so badly wrong.'

'This man,' he said to Anuia, 'is the one who is after you. Everything he has, and is, now depends on finding you and taking you out of the picture. He will do anything to make this happen. If we can bring him down, we can bring them all down.'

'So what's the problem?' I asked.

I had an uneasy feeling. They had their witness. Anuia was there, ready and willing to tie him directly to what had happened that morning, placing him right at the scene. So what was wrong?

'The problem is,' John answered, 'that it'll be his word against hers. There are a thousand people who will gladly give him an alibi for the morning of the shootings.'

'So why bother with Anuia at all?'

'He won't take the chance,' John continued. 'Why take the chance when he can eliminate the possibility for good. We believe he's done it before.'

Anuia had been quiet during the little exchange between John and me.

'Something tells me this isn't as clear cut as we thought,' she said.

'Unfortunately no,' John replied, 'it's not. When it comes down to it, believe me, we won't win. We need to put you both in the same place at the same time. Leave no doubt.'

'You want Anuia to be the bait?' I asked, realising where this was going.

'Yes,' he replied, turning again to Anuia, 'we need to you to be the bait. It's a huge thing to ask and the risks are high but it's the best chance we'll ever get to bring down his organisation. To stop the exploitation of families just like yours all over Asia. You must understand that for most of these families, it doesn't stop when they get here. More often than not these families borrow the money from the same people who smuggle them, ending up indebted to them. Working and slaving to pay back money on loans that will never be cleared. A thousand times worse off than they had been before they left home to promises of a good life, finding themselves in a nightmare that will never end – wives, children working inhumanly long hours, or daughters being taken and put to work in brothels. For these people, it will never end and this is our chance to put a stop to this small empire, to make some of this right.'

Everything he had worked for now hung in the balance. Everything depended on the next few minutes.

'We,' he promised, 'will take all the steps necessary to keep you safe.'

'What do I have to do?' Anuia asked.

'Anuia,' I said, 'don't you think you should think about this first?'

'I don't need to,' she said, looking towards me. 'If this is something that I can help stop, I'll do it. I hope you can understand that.'

'Yes, I do,' I said, 'and you won't be alone. We'll be there with you all the way.'

Paul and Dave nodded in agreement.

'How can this happen?' I asked, addressing the group of people sitting around the table. 'It's not like we can just ring him up and ask him to come all the way from Melbourne for a chat.'

'That's true,' John replied, 'but he is already in Queensland. It appears he has taken a particular interest in this problem and has decided he needs to be here to sort it out himself. We're not sure where he is at the moment but I'd say he's just waiting for word that Anuia has been found.'

'Still,' I said, 'how do we make the link to him?'

John pushed the pile of photos he had towards me.

'Take another look.'

I joined them at the table, taking the pile of photos. I went slowly through them, one at a time.

'Damn,' I said, banging my fist on the table. 'Damn, damn, damn.'

'What?' the others asked.

'I told you on the phone,' John said, before I answered, 'that there was something I needed to talk to you about but preferred if we could do it face to face. Can you see the connection?'

I went through the photos again and took out four of them, pushing the rest back across the table. I laid them beside each other and turned to Anuia.

'Do you recognise anyone else?' I asked.

She studied intently for about thirty seconds.

'I do,' she said, pointing at each. 'There, there, there and there.'

'Guys,' I said, turning to Paul and Dave and pointing at a face in one of the photos, 'this is Lee Taylor.'

Everything clicked into place. How else could they have tracked us so easily? All the way along the coast? We had put it down to many things but betrayal was not one of them.

'What's the connection?' I asked, incredulous.

John's colleague who up until now hadn't said very much took over. He had introduced himself as Daniel Alden when we first came in.

'Let me ask you this,' he began, 'where did you come up with Lee Taylor's name?'

'Newcastle University,' I replied, 'in newspaper archives from some of the Melbourne dailies. Then we did some research on the Internet. Lee Taylor's name was the one that came up most. I thought that with his profile, and previous writing on the subject, that he might be able to help.'

I paused.

'It was my idea,' I said, apologetically.

'Don't be too hard on yourself,' Daniel said, 'it was a very reasonable assessment of things in the circumstances and not knowing who to trust.'

'He's right,' Anuia added, 'it's not your fault. It was a great idea. Our only idea.'

Daniel told us more about him.

'Lee Taylor is the up and coming crime writer in Melbourne. He's broken some major stories over the last two years – a real go-getter. He's cracked investigations that the police couldn't get a break through on, more than once. When the police couldn't dig up anything that could possibly make a case, Lee Taylor has been able to bust it wide open. We tried to approach him, requesting help and the use of his sources but he refused. He was making a name, winning awards, and making some serious money. When this didn't work we went down the route of trying to force him to reveal his sources, but as with all things journalistic, this is easier said than done. The journalist always protects....well you know the rest I'm sure.'

A concept we were all familiar with. If a journalist can't provide confidentiality then he won't have a source.

'Here's the thing. When he cracks a major story on criminal gangs, corruption, or whatever it may be, he has been giving the police the big breaks they were looking for. We have made some major arrests over the last two or three years based almost solely on Lee Taylor's evidence. A good thing you might think and, in reality, it is. We all look good and there's one other bad guy off the streets, one more criminal gang out of business. But there's always someone waiting to take their place. Lee Taylor has been writing about some major criminals but the big one, this man here, he still hasn't given anything that might indict him or his gang.

'Sure he's written about him on more than one occasion but always with the opposite slant, pointing out all the good things this man has done in Melbourne over the years – business, employment, charity. Manipulative to make this guy look good. Just like the stories they wrote about Anuia – subtle persuasion of public opinion. Not saying Anuia is the bad guy, but also not saying that she's the victim.'

I thought of the article I had read last night in the café in Mackay. It was true. It didn't make her look bad, but it hadn't made her look good either.

'What's this man's name?' Anuia asked quietly.

'Matt Brereton,' Dan replied.

'So this guy, Lee Taylor, you think he's connected to this Brereton guy?' I asked. 'He writes some good stuff, keeping popular opinion on Brereton's side and in return gets the inside track on other criminal gangs. He gets the big story, gives the police the break they are looking for and they get the bad guys. Lee Taylor wins journalist of the year, Brereton looks good, there's one less gang, and Brereton is right there to step in and take over. Everyone's a winner.'

'You nailed it,' Dan replied, 'and it's been going on for the last few years. It's not only illegal immigration. We're talking about drugs, protection, corruption and bribery. You name it and he's doing it. Brereton's doing it well and he's getting a lot of help.'

'Lee Taylor seemed like a genuine guy,' Anuia said.

'He did,' I replied, 'I mean, I had my doubts about his motives, but I thought that once he got his story he'd be doing the right thing.'

'What now?' Anuia asked. 'He told us that he had people from the Melbourne police force available to meet us.'

'He was setting you up,' Dan replied. 'Who knows what might have been waiting had you met them. You were walking into a trap.'

'Which is what you want us to do now?' she said.

Anuia looked at us with resolute determination in her eyes. I had known since I met her how kind and loyal a friend she could be but this was something way beyond that. To put herself on the line for the good of so many more people, made us love her that much more.

'If we don't do this now,' she continued, 'it will never end for me and my family. I will always be a threat to them.'

She looked at Dave, then Paul, and finally me.

'It's something I have to do.'

The decision was made and John began to outline what he wanted from us.

'We need you to talk to Lee Taylor again, tell him that you had to lie low for a while. Let him know that you have read some of the stories they have published and that you aren't too happy with the way they read. Let him think that you're not that interested in any help he can provide and that you plan to work it out yourselves. Reverse psychology.'

'Okay,' I said, 'if he thinks we're breaking off contact with him, he'll do his best to convince us that he is still best placed to help. Play hard to get. Agree, reluctantly, to meet him. Let him think he's still in control.'

I looked at Anuia, Paul, and Dave.

'What do you think?'

'Yeah, I can see how it would work,' Paul replied, 'but this is real life with real people and real guns. From what they've just told us, this guy will do whatever it takes to keep himself in the clear. I know John and Dan are saying they'll provide all the protection they can, but what if something goes wrong? Are you all prepared to take the risk?'

He was right. The most sensible head amongst us as usual. He wanted to make sure we all understood the gravity of this situation. These men killed people, no questions asked. Dave was first to respond.

'I'm prepared to do whatever it takes. For Anuia.'

'Paul?' I asked.

'Well....we've come this far together. Count me in.'

'Me too,' I replied, 'but the decision is down to Anuia.'

'What about you?' I asked her.

She looked at us as she thought for a moment then turned to face John, Dan, and the rest of them.

'Yes,' she said, unhesitant.

Suddenly, we were no closer to the end than we had been yesterday, all hustle and bustle, people on phones asking questions, barking orders, and mobilising the troops. I tried to read the guys faces. Dave looked determined, steeled, wanting to show a brave face. For himself, but more so for Anuia. Paul looked around, calculating, listening to everything that was going on, weighing everything up so that nothing was missed, no chances would be taken. Anuia looked, as ever, dignified and brave.

I don't know how my face looked but, essentially, I was bricking it.

Chapter Thirty-Three

Much of the next four hours was spent going over all that had happened, as Anuia recounted everything leading up to and since that morning in Melbourne. John and his team listened intently, recording every last detail. Eventually, a lot of talk and coffee later, he turned his attention back to me.

'Are you ready to make the call?' he asked.

'I am,' I replied, 'but I have to tell you, I've never been much of an actor.'

'You'll do okay,' he said confidently, sensing my apprehension and trying his best to put me at ease.

'There's a pay phone over here,' I said, 'I'll ring from that. Can you give me a bit of space? I'm not sure I can pull it off if everyone here is watching me.'

When I was ready I picked up the receiver. Johns team attached a number of wires to it, presumably to record what was said, then retreated an appropriate distance as I had asked. I took a minute to gather my thoughts before dialling his number.

'Lee Taylor.' The brash, confident reply I had been accustomed to.

'Lee,' I said, 'it's me.'

'Streuth mate,' he said, 'where the hell have you been.'

Without giving me the opportunity to reply, he went off on a rant about how everyone was looking for us, the time they had spent on getting help together, and the time they had so far invested in the story. I zoned out, thinking this guy had some neck. It reminded me of what a two faced crook he was and of the crooks he worked for. I wasn't afraid anymore.

'Look Lee,' I said, 'hold on there just a minute. What do you think we've been doing for the last few days? Enjoying the sun and having a few beers? Relaxing? Just shut up for a minute and listen. Everywhere we've gone they've been able to find us. How we don't know? And that raises questions over who we can trust. Including you.'

It was a risky thing to say but if I wanted this to be believable, it was a chance I had to take. John gave me the thumbs up.

'Listen mate,' he said, trying to calm himself, 'I'm on your side. Believe me.'

'We've had to lay low for a few days,' I continued. 'Where doesn't really matter, but we wanted a few days with no-one chasing us, to get our heads around this and decide just who we can trust. We've read some of the newspaper stories your paper has written. To be honest, they haven't really done her any favours. She is the victim in all of this whether you believe it or not. I thought that's what we had agreed, so it's got us thinking what your motive is.'

'But that's the way papers work,' he said. 'I can't just come out and say that she's innocent without being able to prove it. You've got to let people form their own opinion when they read the story. And I think most people will see it and understand that Anuia is the victim. When the time is right and we have the proof we'll tell the whole story.'

'Look,' I said, 'we're thinking that the best thing to do here is just hand ourselves in to the Queensland police. We'll take our chances. It's been going on too long and we're getting nowhere.'

There was a pause on the other end of the line. He was thinking fast. He knew it was getting away from him.

'Hang on, hang on,' he pleaded.

I wondered what exactly he had at stake here. A man of Brereton's stature wouldn't take kindly to assurances not being delivered upon.

'I've got people here from the Victoria police force, immigration, and representatives from the Queensland police. Talk to them. I know they can help you. Talk to them, tell them what they want, and Anuia and her family will be safe.'

'How can we trust you Lee?' I asked.

'It's a fair question mate,' he answered, 'you have no reason to. I know you think this is just a story to me, and I'll be honest, it is. But there's right and wrong involved here and I want to do what's right.'

'Bullshit,' I thought.

'Talk to these people. Believe me. They'll do the right thing,' he added, laying his last cards on the table.

I said nothing for a few moments. For effect.

'Lee,' I said, 'we'll be in Cairns the day after tomorrow. If you're people aren't there we're going directly to the police. No questions asked. I'll ring you when we arrive.'

'Excellent mate,' he replied, and I sensed utter relief in his voice.

Maybe I was a better actor than I had thought. All systems were go as the cogs started to turn and the plan was put in motion.

We got back to the hostel later that evening. They weren't keen to let Anuia go but they agreed, reluctantly, when she convinced them that she wasn't running anymore. Even if we couldn't see them, we knew they'd be watching us very closely.

'Anuia,' Jamie cried, seeing us walk out on the upper terrace, 'what are you doing here? What happened guys?'

They were genuinely happy to see her back, even those who knew her least. It was a testament to the kind of person she was. Personally, I was glad that we'd get to spend a bit more time together. We went over all that had happened since morning. There were exclamations when we told them about Lee Taylor and his involvement, and more than a few reservations when we told them the plan.

'Don't worry Anuia,' Alan said, 'we'll be there to look after you. I know Paul and Dave are with you, but you'll need a bit of serious muscle with you in case things go wrong.'

We couldn't help but laugh. A hungry dog had more meat on them than the mad lads from Dublin. But everyone agreed that they would all be there to help.

'Let's see how it goes,' I said, 'I'm sure John and Dan won't want hundreds of us turning up, but at least you'll be close by.'

They were hard to convince but in the end we all agreed that we would do whatever was asked of us. For today at least, we had more time to spend together. More time to spend with our friend. I couldn't help worrying, but I had to believe that things were going to work out okay.

'Let's enjoy this evening,' I said, as we sat talking, admiring the beautiful sunset over Airlie Beach.

'We'll get on the road in plenty of time tomorrow morning and get to Cairns as early as we can.'

'Maybe it would be better to arrive in Cairns the day after tomorrow,' Paul suggested. 'They could be watching for us, expecting us to arrive.'

'It's a fair point Paul,' I said. 'John is calling up later. We can ask him.'

John did call up. He spoke to Anuia, Paul, Dave and I. He would be leaving for Cairns first thing the next morning. Some of his people were staying and would be close by and always in touch should we need them. We had picked a hostel in Cairns, deciding to stick to our routine as closely as possible so as not to arouse suspicion. As long as they could look after us in it, he said, they were happy.

'We were wondering if we should arrive in Cairns tomorrow,' I said, 'or if we could spend tomorrow night somewhere else along the way.'

'Have you anywhere in mind?' he asked.

'Not really,' I replied, turning to the others guys and asking, 'what about Townsville. Magnetic Island is just off the coast. We'd be out of the way.'

'Let's see how it goes,' John decided. 'We need to get to Cairns. It might make sense to keep you out of sight in the meantime.'

'I'm glad you didn't have to leave us today Anuia,' I said, after John had left.

'Me too,' she replied. 'You guys are like family to me now.'

'Thanks,' I said, 'you mean the world to us too.'

Chapter Thirty-Four

They say that when you want a trip to be over the last part is always the longest and this was certainly the case in point. The end was in sight and it couldn't come quickly enough.

We left Airlie Beach the next day, bidding farewell to Club 13, Begley Street. Our little convoy made the short trip back to the Bruce Highway at Prosperine, but there was no longer any real need to stay together. We had picked accommodation in Cairns. Anuia, Paul, Dave, and I were booked into Hostel 89, one of the smaller hostels on the Esplanade but we wouldn't be arriving tonight. Everyone else was booked into places very close by, John advising it would better if we didn't have too many people in the firing line when it came to the crunch.

We drove north through Bowen and Ayr to Townsville where we stopped for food. Then we said goodbye to them all. We were getting a ferry to Magnetic Island, much to Alan and Troy's dismay.

'Let us come with you,' Alan pleaded, when we told him of our change in plan.

'Al,' I said, 'we need to do this, just the four of us together. Get the rest of the gang to Cairns. Get yourselves sorted out and we'll see you there tomorrow. Watch for us at the hostel. That's where we'll need you most.'

Reluctantly, though they all understood, they left to make their way to Cairns. John had booked our tickets on the ferry to the island after we agreed to allow some of his team to accompany us at every step. We knew, finally, that this time it would be our last night together. The adventure would be over.

We arrived back from Magnetic Island just before lunchtime the next day and got back on the road. Townsville to Ingham, on to Innisfail and finally to Cairns. Kilometres or hours wouldn't matter today. What did matter was that we were together and we always would be, no matter what conclusion it would bring.

We made our way to Hostel 89 and found Alan waiting for us. Himself and Troy had spent much of the day taking turns watching for our arrival, wanting to be there for us, to help in any way that they could. John and Dan arrived soon after we had checked in.

'We've picked up Lee Taylor and some associates of Brereton,' Dan told us. 'They're staying in one of the big hotels further down the Esplanade. There's no sign of Brereton himself.'

'Maybe he won't come?' I asked.

'He'll be here,' John said. 'He's got to be,' he added, as an after-thought.

'Will I ring Taylor now?' I asked.

This was it.

'Lee, it's me,' I said, when he answered. 'We made it.'

'Great mate,' he replied, 'all our people are here waiting to talk to you.'

'Good,' I said, 'where do you want to meet? Can we make it somewhere informal where there are plenty of people about?'

'Sure. Have you anywhere in mind? Where are you staying?'

'There's a place called the Woolshed,' I replied, ignoring the second part of his question, 'it's a bar on Shields Street.'

Alan and Troy had done a bit of recon, as they called it, after they arrived the previous day. The Woolshed was a popular backpacker haunt, selling cheap beer, playing loud music, and always guaranteed to have plenty of people hanging around. We had discussed this with John and his team and he agreed that we should steer them towards it. They already had teams setting up surveillance in the vicinity and believed they could cover all eventualities. If things got hairy, they could move in seconds. But there was no 'ifs'. This time it was for real.

'Sounds good,' Lee replied.

He sounded confident, really believing that they were in control of this situation. I thought, or hoped, that this would all go smoothly. They'd get the bad guys. Anuia could go home to her family, and we would be the heroes.

'What time?' he asked, 'my people are eager to talk to you.'

'Us too,' I said, looking at my watch. 'How about...?'

John held up nine fingers.

'How about nine o'clock?' I asked.

It was already seven thirty.

'Nine o'clock it is mate,' he replied, 'I'll let them know.'

My heart was racing but I thought I came over well enough.

'One other thing,' he said before hanging up. 'This is gonna make a great story. You've no idea what this will do for me.'

'Sure,' I replied, 'anytime.'

I always thought I was a decent judge of character, good or bad. My initial instinct had been to dislike him and it had been right. I wondered where in his life he had decided to take the wrong road. I didn't feel sorry for him, wanting more than anything to look him in the eye as he got everything he deserved.

'Good job mate,' Dan said, 'let's get you ready.'

We decided that Anuia and I would be the only ones to go. Dave and Paul weren't happy about it but the argument was that Lee Taylor knew both of us. New faces at this late stage might worry them and they could back off. Logic they couldn't argue with.

John, Dan and their team of people briefed us on how things might pan out. They wanted us to understand exactly the type of people we were dealing with, to remember that these people had killed that particular morning in Melbourne and wouldn't hesitate in doing whatever it took to solve their problem. All this they told us as their team fitted compact wireless transmitters, concealed beneath our clothes.

'If we're going to get them,' John said, 'we need to make this case as watertight as possible. The wire is the key and our insurance. Get them on this and they're ours.'

My hand shook nervously. I looked at Anuia, so calm and collected, for reassurance. She knew just how much was at stake.

'It'll be okay,' she said, 'we'll get through this.'

'Don't worry mate,' Dan said, sensing how I was feeling. 'It'll be all done before you know it.'

I couldn't help thinking 'what if it wasn't all done?' What if something went wrong? That happened in the movies too. I looked at

Anuia's face again and she smiled, giving me the strength and courage I was going to need to get through it.

'Anuia,' John said, 'if Brereton shows, we need to make the connection to the morning in Melbourne. We need to get an admission that he was there. You'll need to get him to talk about it. Do you think it's something you can do?'

'I'll try my best,' she replied, and we knew she would.

It was near time to go. Alan, Troy, Jamie, and the rest of our gang, left earlier and had arranged a night in the Woolshed. It hadn't exactly been in the plan and we weren't completely honest with John and his team about it, but it was reassuring to know that they'd be there. Close by should we need them.

Five minutes to nine. The Woolshed wasn't far away. Down the Esplanade and turn right onto Shields Street. I shook hands with Paul and Dave.

'Good luck,' Paul said, 'be safe. No risks okay?'

'No risks,' I promised.

Anuia hugged Paul, then Dave.

'Are you ready?' I asked.

'As I ever will be,' she replied, and we hugged too before leaving.

Chapter Thirty-Five

We turned the corner onto Shields Street to be met by a huge group of people gathered around a pub called Johno's Blues Bar. They were coming from all directions and spilling out onto the street.

'What's going on?' Anuia asked, straining to be heard over the crowd.

'Free beer,' someone cheered, hearing her.

'How come?' I shouted.

'No idea mate,' he shouted back, 'but who cares.'

It bothered me how easily I had was distracted. I had told myself to look out for anything out of the ordinary. All we needed to do was get from the hostel to the Woolshed, and I cocked it up completely.

In the confusion, Lee Taylor appeared in front of us.

'Guys,' he shouted, 'sorry about this, but there's a change of plan. It's a bit manic around here. Is it okay if we go somewhere else? I've a car ready.'

I took Anuia by the hand.

'Why Lee?' I asked, 'this isn't what we had agreed.'

We had a choice to make. If we refused now and turned to leave, what was the message we'd send out. If we backed out now, he'd know something was wrong.

'Too many people around here mate. The bad guys could be here anywhere.'

'I'm not sure Lee,' I replied, tightening my grip on Anuia's hand.

A car pulled up beside us. Lee opened the rear passenger door.

'Get in,' he shouted, as the crowd was getting louder.

Hesitantly, we got in and he closed the door. He sat in front.

'Where are we going?' I asked.

I needed him to tell us, knowing that John and his team were listening. Just let them know, and everything would still be okay. But we were dealing with serious criminals here, away ahead of me and not likely to be caught out by something so trivial.

'Just to a bar down here mate,' he said, 'it isn't far. They're waiting.'

It had all gone wrong. Anuia and I hadn't prepared ourselves for this, naive enough to think that we just had to waltz in there, and we'd get the bad guys. We were relying on John Gerrard and his team to get us out of this, our fate no longer in our own hands, and all we could do was play along and hope they were doing their job. We were no longer in control.

I thought we'd be whisked away somewhere, but we didn't go that far. They drove further down Esplanade, took a left turn at a sign to Marlin Jetty, then left again at Pierpoint Road. We stopped in front of The Pier Marketplace, a shopping centre, lit up brightly but deserted at this time of the night. I noted every street sign in my head, hoping to get a chance to somehow relay it back to the team.

'Just down here,' Lee said, turning towards us. 'They'll be glad to see you.'

I could see the fear in Anuia's eyes but we had no choice other than to keep going.

We followed him to the corner, turning right down the promenade, away from the main drag towards the far end of the shopping centre. The further we went, the more deserted it appeared to be, much less street noise and the sound of the sea lapping on the rocks. Looking back over my shoulder, I could see our hostel. So close, but just out of reach. I hoped they could see us too.

A gang of men waited as we turned right at the end of the pier. Now completely obscured and out of sight, the deserted shopping centre stood behind us, the wide open ocean in front.

'No,' Anuia whispered, 'it's him.'

I didn't know who 'him' was but we stopped instinctively, moving to turn back the way we came. The driver of the car was blocking our path. He was holding a gun.

'Don't say a word,' Taylor said quietly.

His hand moved behind my back and under my t-shirt, disconnecting the wire from the transmitter. Then he did the same to Anuia. We were on our own.

'What?' I asked, looking at him.

'Just business mate,' he replied, 'just business.'

'You're a fool and a coward Lee,' I said, but I was wasting my breath.

We turned to face them. Some I recognised instantly having almost met that day they chased us in Brisbane. All but two were Asian, guns pointing menacingly in our direction.

'You've led us on quite a chase miss,' one, an Australian, said to Anuia as he stepped forward. 'I believe we have met before.'

Anuia glanced at me and I knew then it was Brereton.

'And you,' he said, turning towards me. 'Irish I believe? To whom do I owe the pleasure?'

I didn't answer and didn't expect the blow to the ribs from the man standing closest to me, surprised and unable to protect myself as he struck. I dropped to my knees, winded, holding my right side. Anuia came to my aid, placing her arm around my shoulders. With her help, I struggled to my feet, every breath already torture. Some bones were broken.

'Oh it doesn't really matter,' Brereton continued, 'but it does appear we have quite a serious problem.'

I was sickened by the irrelevance he portrayed. That only a man with so much power and wealth could show. This was a man who believed he was above everything and everyone, used to getting his way with a simple click of his fingers.

'What problem?' I asked. 'Leave us alone and there's no problem.'

He looked at the man who had hit me. Before I could move to defend myself, I was hit again but on the other side. I dropped to my knees, coughing, spluttering, and gasping for breath.

'Stop,' Anuia pleaded. 'What do you want?'

'Oh I think that's already perfectly clear,' he replied.

'Not to me it's not,' I said, between breaths. 'Who is this man Anuia?'

Blood splattered on the ground when I coughed.

'You mean you don't know?' he asked.

He sounded genuinely surprised.

'Mmmm,' he said, 'Miss Anuia and I have met briefly before it seems. Have you not told him?'

'Told me what Anuia?' I asked.

I was stalling, trying my best to draw him out.

'This is him,' she said. 'This is the man who was in the car park the morning I went to meet my family. This is the man who has been after me since then.'

He seemed pleased, full of his own self-importance.

'This is your operation?' I asked. 'These are your men? What do you want from us? What are you going to do?'

'My dear friend,' he began, 'I think we both know how this is going to end. We can safely assume that your young friend here will be coming with us. She has some information that we cannot allow her to share with anyone. Ever!'

'No,' I spluttered, 'no she's not.'

I was still on my knees when I was kicked. My right ribs again, pain searing through me.

'Listen to the man,' Lee Taylor said, and I actually believe there was some concern in his voice.

'Get away from us Taylor,' I spluttered.

'Miss Anuia here,' Brereton continued, 'is not your concern anymore. She's nobody's concern and will be going on a trip that she won't be coming back from. You on the other hand have a choice.'

For all his power, all his money, and all his arrogance, he had just made his first fatal mistake.

'What do you want from me?' I asked.

'You can be on a plane out of Australia within the next two hours,' he replied. 'I have friends who will see that you never come back here again. A week from now and this will all be a distant memory.'

'It's not that simple,' I replied through gritted teeth, every word compounding my agony, 'what's to stop me from going to the police. I don't have to be here to do that.'

'Don't be stupid,' Lee said, 'you're talking to one of the most influential businessmen in Australia. Who'll believe you?'

'What's the alternative?' I asked.

Brereton hunkered down beside me and spoke in a low, menacing tone.

'You'll be going in the same hole in the ground as you're little friend here. People like you are like an itch. I only have to scratch and it's gone. Don't underestimate me kid, I've done it before.'

It wasn't loud enough for anyone else present to hear, but it was loud enough for the second wire that I had had fitted. Taped to the inside of my right leg, the miniature microphone barely visible above the front of my shorts.

'What's it going to be?' he asked, getting back to his feet.

I paused for a moment, probably longer than I needed to, but just long enough for him to think that I would even consider it.

'Not a chance in hell,' I replied.

This time he kicked me himself. Like a man with no respect for life in any way would kick a puppy and feel no remorse.

I felt the click of more bone breaking and cried out in agony.

'What?' he said.

'No,' someone answered, but it wasn't me. 'He said No!'

I was in a bad way, barely conscious. Anuia was by my side. I struggled to see who had said it.

Alan and Troy stepped from the shadow at an entrance to the shopping centre. How they had got there I didn't know. How they knew where we were, I didn't know either. Brereton's men spun, agitated, guns raised.

'This is not your concern kid,' Brereton's Australian colleague shouted. 'Get out of here.'

'Not without our two friends.'

It was Jamie this time.

'We're not going anywhere without them.'

Brereton's men backed towards us. Brereton himself, for the first time, looked uneasy. I sensed that this could spiral out of control very easily. Did the guys know just how dangerous it was?

'Wrong kid,' Brereton shouted, 'they're coming with us.'

'Didn't you hear him?' someone else shouted, the voice coming from a different direction.

I turned my head slightly. It was Marcus and Jasper, then other faces coming from all sides. Robert, Lucy, Clare, Sarah, Toni, and others too. People I had never seen before, moving slowly towards us, standing together. And somehow, right there among them, I saw Maja. She looked right at me, wanting to help. And I believed I was dreaming, my mind playing tricks as I struggled to maintain consciousness.

'Leave them alone,' someone cried.

The crowd took on a voice of its own.

'Leave them alone.'

It was here that Brereton made his second fatal mistake. He took a gun from one of the Asian men, grabbed Anuia by the hair, and pulled her away from me. I lost my grip on her hand.

After all this, I thought, after all we'd been through there was nothing I could do now to help her. The situation was out of control and was going to end in the worst possible way. All the promises we had made to her, the promises to keep her safe, to stay with her until the end would mean nothing. As my breathing became more difficult and I struggled to stay focused, I thought of John Gerrard. Where were they? Don't the good guys always come just in the nick of time?

The crowd moved closer. The Asian men were shouting, pointing their guns. Brereton had Anuia and was backing quickly towards the pier.

'A boat,' I thought, hearing an engine roar to life. That's how he had got here without Gerrards team knowing.

They came suddenly and from everywhere. Spotlights, guns, police uniforms.

'Drop your weapons,' a voice screamed through a loudhailer.

'It's over. Drop your guns. You're surrounded.'

I could see Brereton's face. Panicked, scared. The stand-off ended quickly. Brereton smiled, slowly dropping the gun to the ground. He released his grip on Anuia and she moved away from him. Brereton's men followed suit, dropping their guns, and raising their hands in the air. The police moved in quickly.

Even after all this, Brereton still had the audacity to believe that he was untouchable, that he was powerful enough to get out of this.

That was his third, his last, and his most fatal mistake.

I blacked out.

When I came to, Anuia was already gone.

Chapter Thirty-Six

Paramedics treated me at the pier. Maja was with me and held my hand through it all.

'How?' I asked, 'When?' I couldn't understand.

'I decided to come and look for you,' she said, smiling.

'I thought you were gone,' I told her. 'I never thought I'd see you again.'

'I couldn't let that happen,' she replied. 'I couldn't let it go without seeing just what might happen. Without seeing how you might feel about me. Or without telling you how I feel about you.'

'How did you find us?' I asked.

'Well,' she said, 'I knew you had come north. It was easy enough after that. You've left quite a trail. Everyone knows someone.......'

'...who knows someone,' I said, finishing the sentence for her.

Just like it was between us in Sydney. I hadn't realised how much I had missed her until that moment.

She was right. What would it be like to never know? That slim chance, the tiniest possibility that this could be something really special.

'Time to go,' one of the medics said.

'He'll be at the hospital. It's on Esplanade,' he told Maja.

I was rushed to hospital and admitted straight into surgery. My injuries were inflicted by someone who knew how to cause maximum damage, someone who had done this before. Pumped full of painkillers, I was soon out for the count. I awoke late the following day, surrounded by all my friends. Maja, Dave, Paul, Alan and Troy of course, and all the gang.

'How're ye feeling'?' Troy asked, when my eyes opened.

'Better than last night. What's the verdict?'

'Broken ribs each side,' Alan replied, 'they managed to do some pretty serious damage so you'll be taking it easy for a bit.'

'I would have knocked them out,' Troy added.

'Except for the guns?' I asked.

'Absolutely man, you know yourself. Except for the guns.'

I couldn't help but laugh, pain searing through my sides.

'Anuia?' I asked, turning to Paul and Dave.

'She's safe,' Paul replied, 'she's gone back to Melbourne. We only just got to say goodbye. She told us to tell you thanks.'

There was nothing more she needed to say. We had kept our promise to her after all.

'Fill me in guys,' I said, suddenly remembering how things had gone the night before.

'How did you know where we were?' I asked.

'That's pretty much down to Troy and Alan,' Paul said. 'You know how they were supposed to go to the Woolshed with the rest us?'

'Yeah,' I said, raising an eyebrow. I should have been surprised, but I wasn't.

'Well,' Paul continued, 'they decided to play detective again and followed you the minute you left the hostel. They were the ones who saw you get in the car. They followed on bicycles. Can you believe it? It was just as well you weren't taken too far. When they saw the car turn to the marina, they raced back to the Woolshed.'

'Bicycles?' I asked.

'We didn't have time to wait for a taxi,' Alan replied, grinning.

Hearing me laugh, a nurse came running into the room. When she saw the pain etched on my face, she began to usher everyone out.

'That's it,' she cried, 'he needs rest. You'll all have to leave.'

'Can Maja stay?' I asked, and the nurse agreed reluctantly.

As they piled out of the room, a thought occurred to me.

'Why?' I asked, of no-one in particular.

They all stopped.

'Why what?' Dave asked.

'Someone could have been seriously hurt,' I replied. 'Someone could have been killed. If you hadn't come just then, that was it for us.'

He thought for a moment.

'Look around you,' he said, 'all these guys here, all the guys who have helped us along the way. Every one of them would have done the same thing, every single one of them. Do you know why?'

'Why?' I asked, though I knew the answer.

'Because that's who we are,' he replied. 'We are different. That's what brought us all here. That's why we all met. It can't be just co-incidence. We were meant to be here, to help Anuia, to help each other. To figure out who we are ourselves.'

I was a sceptic. I always had been. Not believing in chance or fate, everything for a reason and all that.

I'm not anymore.

Mum and Dad rang every day as I spent the next two weeks in hospital. I was never short of visitors. If it wasn't my friends or guys I knew, it was John Gerrard and people from his team.

'What happens now?' I asked, the first morning he came to see me.

'We have Brereton bang to rights,' he replied. 'There's no way out for him.'

'Did you get everything you need?' I asked.

'The second wire is always a good idea,' he said. 'We got every word. When we played it back to him he knew he was done and is looking to make a deal. Either way, he's going to prison for a very long time and taking a lot of people with him. He's named two politicians, councillors, businessmen, and, unfortunately for us, a number of high ranking police. There's going to be a lot of work to clean this up but it's a great result all round.'

'What about Anuia?' I asked.

'Anuia will be well looked after. She's with her family now, being kept somewhere safe until Brereton and others go to trial. After that I think she can expect to lead a normal life here in Australia.'

I remained quiet.

'I'm sorry mate,' John said, sensing why. 'You know we can't tell you where she is. I can get a message to her.'

'Just tell her thanks,' I said, 'and tell her not to forget Magnetic Island.'

'Sure,' he replied, with a puzzled look, 'I'll make sure she knows.'

'Thanks John. You left it pretty late the other night. I thought that was it.'

'It's a decision I had to make,' he said. 'I had to make sure we had him. I don't expect you to understand but this is the end of a small empire. We just had to make sure.'

But I did understand. Right or wrong, he had his job to do. This time it had worked out.

'Lee Taylor?' I asked.

'Just a stupid kid,' he replied, 'he wanted too much too fast. He'll be spending a long time behind bars.'

I didn't feel sorry for him. We can all choose.

When I was on my own, I thought a lot about Anuia. I was glad she was safe and hoped more than anything that she would be lucky in life. She deserved it.

Chapter Thirty-Seven

Paul Sheehan kept us informed and looked after Paul, Dave and I. He said that we were free to stay in Australia and to travel a bit more if we wanted, but I wouldn't be here for very much longer.

'I came to Australia for a year,' he told us, 'I had some adventures, but nothing like this.'

Before I got out of hospital a lot of the guys had already left, their own stories to finish. They all came to say goodbye. Paul, Dave, Troy, Alan, and Jamie stayed. And Maja of course. They were there when I booked back into Hostel 89 where I spent a further week recovering. Clare and Sarah were there too, leaving the following day but not before an appropriate send off. They were flying back to Sydney and then back home to England.

I spent as much time as I could with Maja. We were so at ease with each other, so much in common, so many thoughts and ideals that we wanted to share. Something I had never had before. Understanding. Belief.

As we spent those extra few days there, Paul and Dave decided it was time for them to leave. They were heading back to Ireland fairly soon but had an important stop to make before they did. Paul had been in touch with the hostel in Glebe. Áine had arrived there as she said she would and was waiting around to try and get some work. We all knew that she was waiting for Paul.

'Guys,' I said, as we stood on the sidewalk outside Hostel 89, 'it's been a great pleasure.'

'For us too dude,' Paul replied, as we hugged and shook hands.

'Dave,' I said, 'careful with this guy. Don't let him fall in love too quickly. He'll be married and have kids before you know it.'

'Tell me about it,' Dave said, 'he never shuts up about her.'

'You know how it is,' Paul said, nodding in Maja's direction.

'I do Paul. I'll miss you guys.'

'Just do what you have to do,' he said. 'We'll catch up with you again back in Ireland. I don't need to tell you that that'll be the first thing we do when we're all home.'

He was right, I did know and it was something I'd look forward to. For now, we all had some things that we needed to take care of.

When they were ready to go, we helped load their gear in the back of the van. The Yellow Submarine, the big yellow bus with the big wheels and the big bull bar. We'd put a fair few miles on it since we left Sydney. The lads were bringing it back to sell for whatever they could. They'd deposit what I was owed in my bank account. They pulled off, waving from both sides. They blew the horn all the way down the street and until they turned out of sight.

'See you soon guys,' I thought.

I should have been sad and I suppose, in a way, I was. But Maja was here with me. We were heading north to spend a few days at Cape Tribulation, taking Troy and Alan's car and some of the camping gear from the van. It was packed and ready to go and they were here to see us off. Jamie too.

'Guys,' I said, 'we'll see you in a few days.'

'Take your time,' Alan said, 'no hurry with the car or anything.'

'Don't do anything I wouldn't do,' Troy quipped.

'Look after these two jokers Jamie. Don't let them get into any trouble.'

'I won't dude,' he promised, shaking my hand.

We were all laughing as Maja and I pulled away from the kerb. That's the way it had been since this whole thing started. There had never been a moment, even when bad things were happening, that we hadn't been able to laugh together.

We left Cairns, heading north once again. That night we stopped in Port Douglas, checking into the Port o' Call Lodge hostel, the only backpackers in town, splashing out on a double. The following day we drove further north to Cape Tribulation. We checked into PK's Jungle Village hostel where we stayed for about ten days. We would have stayed longer but alas, finally, our money had begun to run out.

We spent the days walking on beaches and in the Daintree rainforest. We went on organised tours and we trekked by ourselves. White water rafting, sea kayaking, always the two of us together. The Port is a great place for parties and nightlife. More than once they organised a bonfire on the beach and, when the party would finally end for the night, we would sit and talk for hours on end. Talk about love, about life, about hopes and aspirations. And when it suited we would sit in silence and it would never be awkward, each happy with each other's company, the only sound being the wind and the sea.

When we got back to Cairns, Alan, Troy and Jamie were ready to go. They were all partied out and eager to explore some more of this vast country. They were planning to drive north to Darwin, then down through central Australia to Alice Springs and Ayer's rock. Uluru as it is now, rightfully, known. To say goodbye to them was nearly the hardest

288

of all. They were the last of our little group. The group that had made a promise to Anuia and who had came through. But things have to move on. That's the way life is.

They asked us to go with them and, while I was tempted, I was eager to go home. Part of my adventure still lay there, eager to see my family and my friends and show them that the person they had known and loved was still here. He had just lost his way for a while.

'Lads,' I said, before they left, 'I'll see ye for a few pints back in Dublin.'

'You sure will,' Troy said, 'you sure will.'

'Jamie,' I added, 'thanks for your help. Look after these two. And look after yourself. It's been a great pleasure.'

'It sure has man,' he replied, as we hugged.

I would never see him again.

That left just me and Maja. Back in Hostel 89, our last few days together.

'Do you think we'll get to see each other again?' Maja asked, as we shared dinner in a restaurant on Esplanade a few nights later.

'I hope so Maja,' I answered, 'I really do.'

'Me too,' she replied, looking out towards the sea, lost in thought.

No matter what happened for either of us in our lives, the time we spent together over those few weeks was something that few people get to share during the course of a lifetime. Was it sometimes too much to dream and hope that something like this could last forever? Who knows? But it would always be there in our hearts.

I caught a flight from Brisbane. Maja was there to see me off. She cried as we hugged, her face buried in my chest. She knew it would be the last time we ever embraced. Deep down, I think I knew it too.

Singapore Airlines to Singapore, a ten hour stopover, then on to London. The last leg of the journey, as ever, took the longest. Four hours in Heathrow waiting on my flight back home, finishing my journey as I had started.

I got a taxi from the airport. They knew I would be arriving but I didn't tell them exactly when. It dropped me off at Mum and Dad's. A beautiful Spring evening, my favourite time of the year and my favourite time of the day. I stood outside looking at our house, the house in which so much of my life had passed. So much happiness, so much laughter, and sometimes, even sadness. It felt like I was looking at it for the very first time and, in some ways, that's exactly what it was. I wasn't the same person who left here what seemed like a lifetime ago.

There's a great line in a book that says 'every story starts with a door, you just have to walk through it'. Every story ends with a door too.

I picked up my rucksack and walked up the driveway. I rang the doorbell and waited for someone to answer.

'Hi Mum, hi Dad.'

I was home.

Chapter Thirty-Eight

It took me a while to get used to being back but not too long. All my family around me all the time, so many questions to ask, so many to answer.

I came back to Ireland, came back to the same life I had before, the same mundane existence. But it wasn't the same life, it wasn't the same people, and it wasn't the same mundane existence. It never had been.

Could everything have changed so much in the time I was away? Of course not. I had learned to live, learned to understand that every single thing we do has meaning. We just have to know where to look for it. I had discovered how to believe in myself and to believe in life and all the wonderful experiences it has to offer.

People travel for many different reasons. For some, it's the desire to see new places, to experience new cultures and ways of life. For others, like me, it can be the voyage to self-discovery that comes with all that. But, what I have always found most fascinating is the people you meet, and it is the memories of these people that I like to take with me when my voyage has ended. When the time has long past and I sit and think, sure I remember the places, the beauty, but what I remember most is the people who were there and who made those experiences possible.

We promise and we hope that these friendships can last forever. But inevitably, most of them don't. That night on Magnetic Island, Paul, Dave, Anuia and I made a promise that our friendship wouldn't fall by the wayside. A promise that even as time passed and we started to grow older, forgetting much of what we did, that we would always find each other and always share the happy or sad stories that our lives would bring.

We all move on, but for that brief moment in time, that split second, we were more than just friends. We were people who shared the same aspirations, the same dreams. We were family.

In September 1997, three years after I had set off on that wonderful adventure, Leslie called around. We had become friends after I came home. It was hard to believe we had passed each other so many times on my street and it took what happened for my family to come to know her. She only called to see her father every now and again, but she would always call in. Just to say hello.

'Hi Leslie, how's it going?' I said, as I answered the door.

'I'm good,' she replied, taking a white envelope from her pocket and handing it to me. 'I have a bit of news for you.'

'What is it?' I asked.

I opened it, unfolding a letter that I had been waiting a long time for. It was from Anuia, short, and explaining briefly why it had taken so long to write. This I understood. I had followed the case as much as possible when I came home, always looking for little details about her. It dragged on for some time until, eventually, it was no longer headline news and my own interest started to wane.

She enquired about the other guys and how they were, and included a number to ring, as she put it, if I still remembered her. At the bottom she scribbled the small note.

P.S. I never forgot Magnetic Island. And I will never forget what you did for me.

'Thanks Leslie, how are they all doing now?' I asked.

'Anuia and her family are all well and living in Melbourne. She has helped to give her family the life that she had promised.'

'Leslie, why did you never tell them that we were on Fraser Island?'

'I don't know,' she replied. 'I can only say that when I went there I thought it was one of the most special places in the world. What if you never get the chance to go back?'

'Thank you,' I said, 'thank you for everything.'

I was still in touch with Paul, Dave, Troy, Alan, and of course, now Áine as well. I rang to let them know.

Then I rang Anuia.

'Hi Anuia,' I said, when she answered the phone. 'It's me.'

We talked for hours.

Chapter Thirty-Nine

And now, for the second time in my life, I find myself sitting here in Bangkok on the Kho San Road, having a beer and watching the world go by.

I came with Paul and Áine, gate crashing their honey moon. They got married about two months ago. Dave was best man and I, for some reason that I didn't fully deserve, was groomsman. It just goes to show you though. Sometimes it's not too much to dream and hope for the happy ending. Sometimes dreams do come true.

I was waiting for Anuia. She had travelled to Bangkok and arrived here this morning. We had stayed in touch and spoken many times over the last few months. She had long been planning to come back, to visit the village from which she had originally came. She asked was it something that we might be interested in and we jumped at the chance. Paul and Áine would be here in a few minutes. Dave was going to be a few days late and would follow us.

Anuia and her family came from a small, rural, and very poor village around four hundred kilometres from Bangkok. I was looking forward to seeing it.

It's fitting that I write the last lines of this story here. In many ways you could say that this is where it started. I gaze out the window at the hustle and bustle on the street. The tuk-tuk drivers whiz by and I wonder how much it has changed.

I'm thinking about Maja, Wildwind, Jamie, and as many of the others as I can. I remember Byron Bay and that morning on Fraser Island. I remember how much it meant to me. I carved my initials on a tree near Lake McKenzie. If I never get the chance to go back, I know a part of me will remain there forever.

Someone taps me on the shoulder and I turn.

'Anuia,' I shout, jumping from my seat, grabbing her and lifting her in a huge bear hug.

She looks beautiful, older and more mature than I remember.

'It's great to see you,' I exclaim.

'It's great to see you too,' she replies, and we hug again.

The simple beauty of true friendship. It was like we had only left each other yesterday.

'Are you ready to go?' she asked.

'Yes,' I replied. 'Yes I am.'

With Special Thanks to:

My Family – the single most important thing in my life

John Malone & Glenn Grimes – thanks for reading and your encouraging words

Troy & Alan – for the great laugh, I still remember it well

The Big Smoke Writing Factory, Dublin, Ireland

Brandi Doane McCann - ebook-coverdesigns.com

To the travellers, the dreamers, the searchers, the believers. You can achieve anything

Printed in Poland
by Amazon Fulfillment
Poland Sp. z o.o., Wrocław